A CALCULATED BETROTHAL

SCOUTS OF THE GEORGIA FRONTIER
BOOK FIVE

DENISE WEIMER

WILD HEART
BOOKS

Cover design by Evelyne Labelle at Carpe Librum Book Design. www.carpelibrumbookdesign.com

ISBN-13:

CHAPTER ONE

T he morning after her husband's funeral, Lady Tabitha
Gage opened her eyes to bright winter sunlight and
shuddered—with relief.

She was free.

But a lady no longer.

Terror crowded out the relief. Free, yes, but also alone on a
thousand-acre South Georgia rice plantation. Across the
Altamaha River, Creek and Seminole Indians, allied to the
British who held East Florida, roamed the no-man's land of
tangled swamps and bogs. Lord Riley's allegiance to the Crown
had not kept his cattle from being raided. Should an invasion
come, her late husband's loyalty would not protect this plantation, either—especially now he was gone. After Henry's name
appeared on the St. Andrews Parochial Committee's list of
twenty-nine suspected Tories last autumn, River's Bend was
equally susceptible to Patriot retribution.

And yet it was to River's Bend Tabitha had returned—fled,
more like—the day after she'd seen Henry laid to rest in the

Christ Church burying ground following his extended bout with lung sickness. Keeping up appearances in Savannah had required more fortitude—and fortune—than she possessed now. Not to mention that her twin, Temperance, was too apt to see past Tabitha's façade. And their father, too apt to pull her back under his control.

Tabitha sat up but clutched the covers beneath her chin, not yet ready to relinquish their warmth for the chill of the January morning. Maybe she could stay here all day.

When she'd first set eyes on her new husband's country house, she'd cried with dismay. The white frame home with its two tiers of piazzas and saltbox-style extension in the rear set among the live oaks and palms appeared so parochial compared to his elegant brick Savannah residence.

What a little fool she'd been to think that if not love, luxury at least would reward her sacrifice for her sister.

Her upstairs room, with its twelve-foot ceilings, walnut furniture, and tapestry curtains and counterpane, had since become her refuge. Lord Riley had sought her out here less and less frequently as his hope for an heir dwindled over the eleven years of their marriage.

Now, the burden of that expectation was gone, along with the silent judgment of the man who'd imposed it. She knew not whether to stretch her shoulders with the relinquishment or continue to cringe under the accusation she'd come to expect. Her own head supplied it in the absence of Henry's voice. What kind of wife was she to not mourn her husband?

Tabitha released a shaky breath and rubbed the sleep from her eyes.

The strips of light slanting through the cracks of the shutters promised a warm midday, and flames crackling on the hearth reminded her she was not alone. Dulcie had already been in to light a fire. The daughter of the white overseer and the enslaved cook, Dulcie had every right to spend the winter as she normally did with her husband across the river. She was free, as was her husband, Cyrus. But she was here instead. For Tabitha.

A brief knock sounded on the door.

Pushing her dark braid back, Tabitha called a "come in."

As if summoned by Tabitha's thoughts, Dulcie entered bearing a breakfast tray. "Good mornin', Miss Tabitha. How are you?" Sliding the tray onto the foot of the goose-down mattress, the golden-skinned woman peered at her. Looking for signs of grief?

Dulcie had served as housekeeper and lady's maid to Tabitha long enough to know better. And that silent sensitivity of hers meant she'd long ago discerned the way of things with Lord Riley. Tabitha had glimpsed Dulcie's firmed lips and tightly clasped hands on plenty of occasions when Tabitha had stumbled into another of Henry's verbal ambushes.

She might as well be honest with the servant now. "Terrified."

Dulcie poured steaming coffee from a pewter pitcher into a cream-ware mug, picked up a tiny silver spoon, and stirred the brew. "I put chocolate in your coffee," she said, as if this were the answer to all her problems.

Tabitha stifled a laugh. The sound so surprised her that her hand flew to her mouth. She choked on a tangle of emotions that rose into her throat and promptly started crying—something she never used to do. She instantly hated herself for it. But nearly a dozen years with a man who despised her had eroded her spirit until she'd become an emotional weakling. "What am I to do, Dulcie? How am I to manage on my own?"

Dulcie touched the hem of Tabitha's linen nightgown. "You aren't alone, Miss Tabitha. Pa and I will help you."

Dulcie spoke like a white woman, thanks to the tutor her father had hired when she was a child. Henry had permitted it, he'd told Tabitha, not because he approved of educating a woman, especially a mulatto, but because Marcus Long was the best overseer in St. Andrew's Parish and he wasn't willing to risk losing the man over something so trivial.

Tabitha had shared her husband's views about slavery when they'd first wed. But now she knew what it felt like to have a master. And Dulcie's discretion and wisdom had helped Tabitha avoid many a misstep over the years, even when Tabitha had not condescended to acknowledge her.

"I know not where to begin."

"You have time." Dulcie handed her the mug. "Planting's not until March. But Pa says you should meet with him. Talk about clearing another section."

Tabitha sipped her favorite combination of coffee and chocolate. The warm liquid soothed her empty stomach. "That would be a good idea." She should learn just how bad of financial shape they were in while she was at it. "I shall meet with him this afternoon."

"There's no hurry, Miss Tabitha. If you need a few days—"

"No." Tabitha lowered her cup to the tray. "The sooner the field gets cleared, the sooner we can plant more rice and hopefully get us out of the mess Lord Riley's brother-in-law got us into." Henry had sent more and more money over the last few years to his sister, whose wastrel husband continued to indebt their ancestral estate back in England—though he'd gone to great pains to conceal their genteel poverty from Tabitha's family.

Dulcie uncovered Tabitha's porridge and sprinkled some cinnamon on top. "'Tis all over now. You have a new start. A chance to change things. At least..." She glanced up from under her dark lashes. "The lawyer in Savannah said Lord Riley left everything to you, did he not?"

Tabitha had made sure of it before leaving the city. "The house in town, River's Bend, and even his grazing lands across the river." Where Cyrus tended to Lord Riley's pinewoods cattle herd. When she'd expressed amazement at the cattle ranging free south of the Altamaha, he'd told her they were *criollo*, cows born in America but descended from European herds—Spanish, to be exact. The animals browsed the wiregrass and bluestems in warm months and the switchcane at the edges of the savannahs and streams in cooler months, often retreating to the thick stands of great cane in the winter. Herders like Cyrus moved or secured them with a series of wilderness cattle pens.

Dulcie's eyes sparkled. "That makes you one wealthy woman."

"Once we can get things turned around now that we no longer must send funds every few months to England, perhaps." Tabitha reached for her spoon and tasted her porridge. Delicious, as always. Dulcie's mother, Annabelle, was an excellent cook. "I expect it shan't be long before all the toothless widowers in the parish are tapping their bejeweled canes on my door."

But she could ignore them all once she got on her feet. A sliver of something warm and precious slid through her—independence. With it, hope stirred. Her appetite sharpening, she dipped her spoon back in for another bite.

"Speakin' of that ..."

Tabitha's gaze snapped up. She cared not for Dulcie's uneasy tone.

"You already have a caller. Two, actually."

Her chest tightened. "Who?"

"Hugh and Julian Jackson. They be waitin' in the parlor."

"At this hour?" How dare they? When she had yet to set her foot out of bed the day after returning from her husband's funeral?

"Said they missed catching you at the townhouse and wanted to pay their respects. But I suspect ..."

Tabitha's stomach bottomed out. "They have something else in mind." The Jacksons owned the vast plantation adjoining theirs just southeast, closer to Darien, the town settled by the Scottish folk on the coast. The reputations of both father and son with the ladies and the ruthless manner in which they drove their slaves made Julian Jackson the last man she'd allow to call. Or to purchase her land.

A flicker of the spirit Henry's disapproval somehow hadn't managed to snuff out had her throwing back her covers. "Help me get dressed, Dulcie, for I shall have no avaricious men sniffing around River's Bend."

~

Half an hour later, Tabitha swept into the parlor with her chin held high. The back hem of her rouched black cotton robe à l'anglaise whispered over the Turkish rug. Light from the hallway and a fire on the grate illuminated the room, the shutters of which were closed and tied with black ribbons. Dulcie had also draped the mirrors and paintings with black cloth—no doubt in anticipation of the guests who would call more than heartfelt grief over the master.

The two men who rose from their chairs and cups of coffee by the hearth also wore black, their single-breasted frock coats tapering back to reveal embroidered waistcoats and riding boots that reached their knee breeches. Both bowed as she entered.

Silver-haired Hugh Jackson stepped forward, his hawk-like features sharpened by his somber expression. "Lady Riley, may we convey our deepest condolences?"

"Mrs. Gage is fine now, Mr. Jackson." If she had her druthers, she'd go back to being Tabitha Scott, and she'd never have sacrificed herself on her sister's altar. Look where her one dramatic noble act had gotten her. "Please, sit." She indicated their chairs as she settled on the golden settee. "May I ask what brings you out so early on the morning of my return?"

For such impertinence to one of his peers, Henry's ghost would probably haunt her tonight. But her irritation at her neighbors' presumption trumped the subservience her husband had trained into her.

The corner of Julian Jackson's lips twitched.

Tabitha avoided meeting his thick-lashed dark eyes. She sensed that he might find a challenge attractive. He would prey upon her vulnerability, that one. He'd not consider her a potential mate. After all, he could be no more than twenty-five to her three score and two.

"Our apologies, Mrs. Gage." Perched on the edge of his seat, Hugh dipped his head. "We attempted to call before you left Savannah, but you had already quit the city."

"Thank you for attending the funeral. I noted your presence."

"Naturally, we would not miss it. There are few enough of us Englishmen on the Altamaha. With all the Scots about, your husband and I always agreed 'twas a necessity to stick together."

Tabitha inclined her head. In these times, Hugh Jackson had been far more concerned about Patriots than Scots.

Julian at least seemed to pick up on the implication that their presence at the burial had sufficiently paid their respects. His brows drew into a gentle furrow. "'Tis understandable you would haste to the comforts of your home. But it is in the spirit of the camaraderie my father mentioned that we come so quickly. 'Tis our desire to relieve any fears you may have about the future."

Tabitha straightened her back. Why did these men assume it was their place to relieve her of anything? "Thank you. I do have a daunting task before me, but with the help of Mr. Long, I'm confident I shall find my way forward." Perhaps they had come to offer their assistance with business matters or agricultural advice.

But Hugh and Julian exchanged a glance, both frowning, and something in that look unsettled the breakfast in her stomach.

Hugh cleared his throat. "What way forward is that, Mrs. Gage?"

"Why, to continue as my husband conducted affairs, Mr. Jackson. Indeed, to expand. I shall be meeting with my overseer this very day to discuss clearing more ground." She lifted her chin. She would not show these men that she possessed even less confidence than they did that she could take the helm of a rice plantation. She had no other choice. She would never go back to her father in Savannah. Never put her fate in the hands of another domineering man again.

Hugh gaped at her. "Can it be...that you have not heard?"

"Heard what, sir?" The needling of insecurity produced a slightly impatient tone. Why had they not left her to her solitude? She wanted nothing more than to right her world, and their manner threatened to further upend it.

Julian leaned forward. "Did you not meet with your lawyer in Savannah?"

"Of course, I did. Now, what is this about?" Tabitha sprang to her feet, ready to show them out.

The men stood too. Hugh rubbed a hand over his clean-shaven jaw. "Mrs. Gage, before your husband passed, he called me to his bedside. Do you recall that visit?"

"Yes." Her heart began to thud. "I assumed it had to do with some loan or gambling debt."

"Not a loan, but a sale. A bill of sale, to be exact." Hugh reached into the pocket of his waistcoat and pulled out a folded paper. His ruby ring winked in the firelight. "I filed a copy with the property clerk in Savannah, but apparently, your lawyer had not yet been notified...which puts me in a very bad position, I fear."

"What do you mean?" Tabitha's gaze swung between the two men.

"Let her see it, Father." Julian tipped his head in her direction.

Hugh stepped closer to hand her the paper.

Tabitha scanned a document in Hugh's hand. It had been signed by both her neighbor and her husband. Her vision narrowed on the looping words, and her hand began to shake. "But this says...this says Lord Riley sold River's Bend to you."

"The property, house, furnishings, and slaves. Along with the house in town. Excluding only your personal possessions."

She continued to search the paper for a phrase that would make it not so, but everything she read said it was. "But there's no way. He told me nothing about this. The lawyer said it was all left to me in his will."

"The bill of sale supersedes the will, Mrs. Gage. It will stand up in court."

The gaze she swept up to Hugh caught the way his lips started to turn up before he pressed them into a line of false regret. False humility. Heat swept through her chest. Ten years ago, she would have flown at the man and scratched the smirk from his face. Now, the paper that forfeited her future slipped from her numb fingers to the floor.

Had Henry deposited the money in the bank in Savannah? No. The lawyer would have disclosed that. Any money would have gone where it always did...to England.

The room spun. Tabitha put out her hand but contacted nothing firm to grasp—nothing but Julian Jackson's arm when he leapt forward to steady her.

"Please, Mrs. Gage. Sit down. You have had a terrible shock." He wrangled her gently back onto the settee and bent over her with what appeared to be genuine concern in the lines of his handsome face. "Can I ring for some brandy?"

Tabitha pulled at her tucker, suddenly desperate for air. She turned an accusing gaze on him. "How can you come here and tell me this? You couldn't wait one day to throw me into the street?"

Julian drew back, eyes wide.

"There's no call for theatrics, Mrs. Gage." Hugh's voice had deepened with impatience. "We thought you knew and wanted to spare you the suffering of waiting or the indignity of coming to us. We're hardly ogres. 'Tis the off-season, so there's no need for you to go anywhere until spring—although I will be taking management of River's Bend in hand immediately. 'Tis I who will meet with Mr. Long today, not you."

She hardly heard the last sentence. She blinked at him. "But where will I go?" Not back to Savannah, to be pitied by all and pawned by her father onto another of his cronies. No.

As Julian bent to retrieve the bill of sale from the carpet, Hugh let out a soft breath. "Your husband left you his land south of the river. I believe there is a house there, is there not?"

Tabitha's mouth fell open. "A house? You call that a house?" She'd only seen the dwelling once, and thinking of anyone living in that rude log cabin set among the pines and the snakes and gators had made her cringe. For Cyrus, a free black man, it probably seemed a palace. But for her, a lady of first rank who had danced the minuet in Savannah's finest ballrooms...?

She shot to her feet, snatched the page from Julian's hand, and shoved it against Hugh's chest. "Get out." Henry may not have loved her, but his pride alone would have demanded he not leave her the laughingstock of the coast. If he'd signed that paper, it had been to, in some way, outmaneuver the Jacksons, whom he'd always viewed as his competitors, no matter what he had said to their faces. He would have believed that, upon legal inspection, the bill of sale would be proven powerless.

Hugh's face colored. His eyes darkened. "Due to your shock and grief, I will pardon your untoward reaction."

Tabitha's heart squeezed. *Untoward.* Her father had used that word to describe her more than once. She clenched her teeth.

Hugh continued, his voice a soft growl. "But you force me to remind you, madam, that this is now *my* house."

"Get out!" At Tabitha's screech, Dulcie came running, skidding to a halt in the doorway as Tabitha pointed at Hugh's chest. "Go now and take your lying piece of paper with you."

Hugh's fingers curled around the page, but only to thump it down onto a side table. He locked gazes with her. "I will leave it —because you will need it to ascertain its legitimacy. Once you have—once you are reasonable—you may send a message to Jackson's Bluff, and we will talk. Like civilized adults. *You* may come to *me*."

He stalked to the door, brushing past Dulcie, who stood with her lips parted and her hand upon her chest. The servant hurried to fetch Hugh's hat and coat.

Julian faced Tabitha again. "I am sorry." He searched her face. "My father is a hard man."

Despite her furious blinking, a tear spilled from one of her eyes. Brusquely, Tabitha swiped her hand across her cheek. "I will prove him wrong."

"Mrs. Gage...Tabitha..." He attempted to touch her arm, but she jerked away. Did he think her so dim-witted—or so vulnerable—that his show of compassion would make her forget his reputation as a rake? Still, the pity did not leave his expression. "No, you shan't. I was there the night Father returned from your husband's bedside. What he says is true. Lord Riley needed the money for his family estate."

As she had suspected, but still, the injustice, the betrayal, twisted like a blade in her chest. "And he wanted to make sure his sister got it rather than his widow?"

"He said your father would support you."

Her father? "I can never go back." No, she had to settle this one way or another. She would send a message to the lawyer in Savannah posthaste. There had to be a solution that didn't involve her landing back under her father's roof—and thumb.

"There is another way." Julian's hushed tone made Tabitha's eyes snap up. He pressed his lips together, then reached for her hand. "What Father said about like sticking to like was true. We are neighbors. Englishmen. *Loyalists*." He whispered the last word, and Tabitha widened her eyes, too stunned to withdraw. "We should unite. Father would be amenable to you staying if he thought...well, that there was good cause for you to remain."

Tabitha's breath came fast. "Surely, I misunderstand your meaning." For him to speak thus the week of her husband's funeral flouted all the rules of society and proper behavior. Not to mention...

Why would he want to marry her?

"I would not dare to suggest such a thing so soon except for the dire circumstances you find yourself in."

She shook her head. "I can see no benefit in that for him... or you."

"Then you are not looking closely enough." Julian raised his other hand to her temple, twirling a curl of her dark hair around his finger. Perhaps he meant the gesture to convey tenderness. But the flicker behind his eyes made her stomach shrivel. It was a look she'd seen before—on the faces of suitors who'd wanted only to claim her for their own lascivious purposes. On the face of her husband before he'd tired of her.

Tabitha stepped back. "Please, sir. I must beg that you take your leave."

His gaze dropped to the shallow heaving of her bosom, and a faint smile stole up the corners of his lips again. He cut a quick bow. "And so I shall. Yet I trust you will think about what

I said. I will give you the proper amount of time, of course. But I forsee an outcome beneficial to us all."

As soon as Julian followed his father out the front door, Tabitha's legs gave way, and she collapsed in the middle of the parlor floor. That was where Dulcie found her. The servant took one look at her face and broached a gulf that never would have been crossed if Tabitha's world had not just crumbled. She pulled Tabitha into her arms.

CHAPTER TWO

"Rider from Fort Howe! Open the gate!"

At the cry from outside Fort McIntosh, Sergeant Edmond Lassiter used his ax to knock a rectangle of wood he'd just cut from the blockhouse wall. Light poured through the new loophole, and he put his eye to the horizontal opening. From his elevated position in the center of the hundred-foot-square compound, he'd a view of the messenger riding in.

"Maybe he brings the post." Holding his adz, Private Dougal O'Connor edged up next to Edmond for a look. They both had laid off their hunting tunics and worked in the close quarters in linen shirts and woolen breeches. Judging from the way Dougal's scent overpowered that of freshly cut pine, he could stand a bracing dip in the Satilla River, which ran about eighty yards south of the fort.

Soldiers below converged on the new arrival, eager for news from closer to civilization—if you could call Fort Howe that. 'Twas nearer to Darien and thus to Savannah than this far-flung outpost, true. They had almost finished rebuilding Fort McIntosh, the southernmost Patriot fort in Georgia. And while the confinement grated on Edmond, 'twas from here he was most likely to see action against the British-allied East Florida Rangers and their Indian recruits. And action was what he needed if he was ever to make lieutenant and get posted away from the swamps of South Georgia.

He'd hoped to have achieved that when he'd first been assigned to the frontier with William McIntosh's Georgia Regiment of Horse Rangers. After the enemy had raided cattle and plantations and attacked Fort Howe—then called Fort Barrington—last summer, William and his brother, Lachlan, had led their troops all the way to the St. Mary's River in Florida. Lachlan had become a brigadier general and William a lieutenant colonel, but Edmond was still a sergeant.

They had been in Florida again when an attack came in late December on Beards Bluff, a small defense on the Altamaha River, forty miles above Fort Howe. The fort had fallen under siege, and the underpaid Patriot soldiers deserted. Ever since, the country had been swarming with Loyalist rangers, Creeks, and Seminoles. Their troop of Patriot rangers had just arrived here with orders to reconstruct this outpost when William received news of Beards Bluff and departed, leaving his men under the command of Captain Richard Winn of the Third South Carolina. Edmond had requested a transfer to Fort Howe, but word of his skill at figuring, measuring, and building had already reached Captain Winn.

Edmond palmed the adz handle. When Dougal drew back and glanced at him, he tilted his head toward the gate. "Go on, then. I know you want to see if there's a letter from your sweetheart." The men regularly needled Dougal for his undisguised pining.

A grin split the man's ginger-whiskered face. "Thankee, Sergeant." He wasted no time clambering down the ladder to the floor below.

Edmond rested both tools against the wall and reached for his water flask. He took a swallow and watched the commotion in the yard through the slit. He had no sweetheart. He'd already lost Evangeline when he joined up a year ago, though he had not known it yet.

He capped the flask and stowed it as a jagged lance of pain speared his heart, followed swiftly by the battle he was far more accustomed to than fighting Tories—the one between anger and self-loathing. Edmond clamped down on it and reached for the adz. Planing the wooden opening he'd just created with the curved edge of the blade also helped smooth his emotions.

He needed to return to Fort Howe closer to Darien not for the benefit of a sweetheart, but for his mother. His task now lay in taking care of what his father had been too weak to do. But first, Edmond needed the extra income a promotion would provide.

"Sergeant!" Dougal's head appeared in the opening in the floor. He waved a dirty, folded, wax-sealed paper above it.

"You got one." Edmond did his best to infuse enthusiasm into his tone. If only the man would have savored his missive outside, where Edmond might have avoided hearing all the endearments.

"Not for me." Dougal hoisted himself up and sat on the floor next to the ladder. "For you."

"What?" Edmond dropped the blade of the adz on the floor with a thump. He never got letters. Knowing how Edmond felt about reading, Mother only wrote when something was amiss. He strode forward and snatched the paper from his private's hand. His heart started thudding as soon as his gaze fell on the handwriting. Not Mother's.

"Something wrong?" Dougal got to his feet and came to stand beside Edmond as he unfolded the letter. His tone implied genuine concern rather than nosiness.

Edmond focused on the signature. He had to stare at it a good ten seconds. Stress always made it harder to discern the letters. "'Tis from my uncle."

"The one in Darien?"

"Yes. My mother's brother." After Edmond's father...*died*—Edmond always balked at that word—and Edmond had joined the rangers, his uncle, Ian Grant, had taken Edmond's mother in. Though Uncle Ian still had children at home with his second wife, making for a lean board to set in a crowded home next to his blacksmith shop, they could come up with no other options. It pained Edmond that his mother had been foisted on her Scottish kin rather than being properly taken care of by her only child.

Dougal frowned. "Is that unusual? Ye seem addled."

He was always addled when he had more than a few words to read, especially under pressure. If he stood here much longer staring at the letters as they tangled and reversed, his private would think him an idiot. Not an impression he wanted to portray. Edmond shoved the letter at him. "Read it to me."

"What?" Dougal took it reluctantly. "I thought ye went to university. And ye want me to read for ye?" The hot glance Edmond sent him made the private's lips clamp shut.

"My mother has a weak heart. This cannot be good news, else my uncle would not be writing. Humor me, O'Connor." Edmond took up his ax and turned toward the wall while the private held the paper to the light. Of the two weaknesses, being slow-witted or soft for his mother, Edmond preferred Dougal think him the latter. He scraped the blade with slow precision along the opening, shaving off tendrils of wood.

The private cleared his throat. "Um, it says here that yer mother has been stitchin' ye a new coat, though she wonders if you will get it if she sends it to Fort Howe. And they are worried ye might be needin' supplies since the Continentals in Darien are short of ammunition."

Hardly a concern now that Captain Winn had returned from pursuing the Loyalists with a quantity of arms and ammu-

17

nition. Edmond grunted and glanced over his shoulder. "What else?"

Dougal squinted at the looping script. "Apparently, Colonel McIntosh has been granted leave. People are sayin' he failed to protect the Southern frontier and the settlers who went down to retrieve their stolen cattle."

The blade slipped, and Edmond narrowly missed slicing his finger. "What a clanker!" He need not tell Dougal that William McIntosh was the most able commander he'd ever served under. "The man slogged through the swamps for months when no one else would. He recovered far more goods than Winn, while so sick a lesser man would've fallen off his horse."

Edmond had nothing against Winn personally. He seemed an able enough sort, though at twenty-seven, he was only a year or so older than Edmond. But for a man to succeed, opportunity must couple with ability—an equation that entitled some while others of equal or greater skill and character struggled all their lives. 'Twas the very inequality the Patriots sought to throw off.

Dougal snorted. "'Tis because Button Gwinnett coveted Lachlan's commission for himself, from all I hear."

Indeed, the president of the Georgia Congress could be attempting to discredit his rival. Edmond shot his private a sideways glance. "What of the personal news?"

Dougal consulted the letter again. He glanced up, his mouth drawn flat.

Edmond's chest seemed to cave in. "What?" He put down the adz. Judging by the private's hesitation, Edmond ought not to be holding a sharp object when Dougal rendered the report.

"'Tis yer ma. Yer uncle said she had an episode."

"How bad an episode? Is she well, man?" Edmond grabbed the missive and scanned the last paragraph. *Pain...in...her...chest. Lost...her...hearth.* No. *Breath.* "Weak. It says she is weak."

"Aye, but recovering." Even the Scottish lilt in Dougal's voice failed to make his attempt at encouragement convincing.

"She needs a better doctor." The one in Darien had never done anything to help. Most likely, he'd bestowed the honorific title upon himself after reading a medical book. There had to be some treatment that would help her—maybe in Savannah.

Edmond folded the letter and tucked it into the top of his breeches.

"Yer uncle did ask when ye would be back. If I may speak freely, sir, I'm wonderin' the same thing." No doubt, judging by his wheedling tone, hopefulness wreathed Dougal's round visage.

Edmond ran his finger over the loophole, testing for jagged sections, brushing the sawdust from the edge. Why did his men think he had any power over where they were stationed? Nevertheless, he found himself saying, "I shall speak to Captain Winn. Now that the fort is almost complete, it may be that he will release the Georgia troops." If not all twenty, at least the few Edmond regularly rode with on patrol. With the tall palisade walls and sturdy blockhouse in place, the commander should be able to hold the river crossing with his forty South Carolinians.

Like William McIntosh, Edmond had already sacrificed too much to the frontier. This time, he wouldn't be too late to make a difference where it mattered most.

~

MID-FEBRUARY 1777

Under the watchful gaze of the sentry in the southerly bastion of Fort Howe, Tabitha and Dulcie boarded the Altamaha River ferry. Once they were seated on a bench, the Creek Indian man who would row them across took up the oars.

A shrill whoop made Tabitha clutch the side of the boat. She surveyed the bluff, but 'twas only a wary crane standing in the shallows some twenty yards distant. What did she expect, Indians lying in ambush mere feet from a Patriot fort?

As they pulled away from the northern bank, her heart lurched. The Old Post Road, which ran down to St. Augustine, Florida, split River's Bend's land from Fort Howe's. She was leaving behind everything that had become familiar over the last decade. Had it been only three mornings prior that her life had crumbled?

Tabitha surveyed the two trunks of clothing and supplies weighing down the ferry boat. Even combined with the contents of the saddlebags on their two horses Mr. Long had swum across the river to meet them on the other side, the items contained within offered paltry little substance with which to start a new life. She turned to Dulcie and could not disguise the anxiety in her voice when she asked, "Are we doing the right thing? Should I have stayed at River's Bend until your father heard back from the lawyer?"

The servant conveyed comfort with her eyes that propriety forbade she demonstrate by touching a white woman. Even before Dulcie answered, Tabitha's heart knew the answer. No. Waiting to hear from Savannah would have taken far too much time—time she couldn't bear to spend in a house no longer her own, fearing every visitor might be Hugh or Julian Jackson. But they weren't the visitors now. She was.

Tabitha's hopes that the bill of sale was forged had been dashed when Dulcie's father confirmed it was legitimate.

Still, she needed confirmation. Again. It had been Dulcie who finally pulled Tabitha out of bed two days after she'd taken refuge there following the Jacksons' visit.

"You are doing the right thing, Miss Tabitha." As the cool breeze feathered the curls that sprang free from her linen cap, Dulcie pulled her cloak closed over her striped short gown and woolen petticoats.

"This is just for a time. Until we can make a plan." Tabitha's statements came out like questions. There had to be some way out of this that did not entail the former Lady Riley living in a cabin.

"We'll talk everything over with Cyrus." Dulcie had reminded Tabitha that she and her husband still depended on Tabitha for employment. Even though they were not slaves, positions for freedmen were scarce. "And remember, you shall have your own space in the cabin since Cyrus added the second crib last year. We'll make it comfortable. You shall see."

"But your father will send for us if we can return."

The way Dulcie drew up her lower lip told Tabitha she set no stock by that possibility. Tabitha's fingers tightened on the side of the boat, and she focused on the water slipping past. If she had produced an heir as a decent wife should, she would not be in this predicament. Henry's voice came back to her, curling her ears with its bitterness. *Useless.*

She jerked at a touch to her sleeve.

Dulcie's dark eyes skimmed her face with a fleeting, compassionate smile. She opened her mouth, then closed it again. Finally, she spoke. "Miss Tabitha, there's something I be wanting to say."

"Say it." Nothing that would come out of Dulcie's mouth could spear her as her husband's disdain had.

Dulcie drew her hand back and gave her the courtesy of lowering her gaze as she spoke. "The woman I see before me today is not the one who came to River's Bend more than ten years ago." She looked back up, as if she could not help it. "*That is the woman you need to find again.*"

Tabitha stared at her a moment. How dare this servant advise her? Confusion clouded Tabitha's mind—but out of her indignation rose a recognition of the truth. Once upon a time, she had cowered at nothing. That had been before she learned how cruel life could be, how she could not always wrangle it to her designs. But perhaps even a naïve determination would come in handy now. She gave a single nod, and Dulcie relaxed, facing forward in the boat.

That would be the last reassurance she sought from her servant. It had to be. Somewhere inside, she had to find the Tabitha who had confessed in her sister's stead to writing the Townsman Letters that accused prominent Loyalists of supporting the Stamp Act, the woman who'd eloped with Lord Riley on his schooner to evade punishment. She'd swiftly come to regret that decision, but the fact remained—she'd turned a disaster around once. Could she do so again?

This time, she wouldn't make the mistake of looking to a man for help.

She steeled herself as the boat slowly traversed the hundred yards of the slow-flowing river. The deep greens of switchcane and Dahoon holly provided color alongside the barren hard-woods. A bald eagle nest poked from a high nook in the tallest spruce pine. A river otter slid through a slit in a massive cypress trunk and disappeared downstream.

Across from Fort Howe, they approached Mount Venture, once the fortified home and trading post of another woman who'd also known how to bend fortune to her will—Mary Musgrove. A Creek woman married three times to white men, she'd bartered English guns for deerskins and information that had helped James Oglethorpe establish the Georgia Colony. Now, Marcus Long waited by the ruins of her store with the mounts that would take them to their new home.

As soon as the boat touched the other side, the overseer hurried forward to help them alight. Then he and the ferryman transferred their trunks from the boat to a small cart Mr. Long had attached behind his own draft horse.

After securing the load, he faced her. His salt-and-pepper beard hid most of the pock marks on his cheeks. "Can I help you mount, Miss Tabitha?" He did not smile. Occasion certainly did not warrant it. But behind his gruff manner, she sensed kindness.

"Thank you. I can manage." Tabitha might not be much of an outdoorswoman, but one thing she could do was handle a horse. She slid her foot in the stirrup of her mare, Cora, and hefted herself into the saddle while Mr. Long assisted his daughter onto her mount.

Somehow, the man got astride his own horse—small for a draft horse but still massive in Tabitha's reckoning—and clucked for the stallion to start down the road. The mares followed. He called over to Tabitha, "'Twill be a mile down this road before the turnoff to the cabin. After that, 'tis not far until you come into the clearing where the cattle pens are, and the house sits just beyond."

"On a small creek, if I remember correctly?" Tabitha shot him a glance.

"That is right, Miss Tabitha."

Only Mr. Long and Dulcie had ever called her *Miss Tabitha* instead of *Lady Riley*, the formal address used by slaves and strangers.

Dulcie attempted to trot her horse up next to Tabitha's. Or maybe the mare just got away from her. "Cyrus won't be expectin' us, but it will take us no time to set the place to rights. I can put some soup on to simmer while we—whoa!" As her mount gave an agitated toss of her head and pranced in place, Dulcie pulled back on the reins. "What is she doing?" Anxiety deepened her voice.

Her father chuckled. "I daresay she doesn't care for being caught between the other two. Let her drop back." As Dulcie complied, Mr. Long explained, "You shall find our Dulcie is an excellent housekeeper, whether she be in a fine house or a log cabin. But she is not much experienced around horses."

Tabitha offered a grim smile. "I'm afraid I'm the opposite."

He cast her a sideways look. "Then you will have to take care of each other, Miss Tabitha. And I shall do my best to look out for your interests from across the river."

"And my mother's?" Dulcie's tentative question wended up to them, almost apologetic.

Mr. Long put a hand on his horse's rump and swiveled to meet her gaze. "Rest assured, I will take care of your mother."

Of course. Why had she not thought of it before? Hugh Jackson now owned Annabelle. Tabitha's stomach shriveled at the thought of anyone she loved being at the mercy of such a man. She ventured a quiet question to her former overseer. "Is that why you are staying on at River's Bend?"

He blinked at her a moment, seeming to weigh how honest he could now be. "If what I've heard of Jackson's methods are true, yes, I think 'tis best I stay on for Annabelle...and all the others."

Dulcie drew up next to them as they halted at the turnoff, her brown eyes dark with misgivings. "You can always come over the river, too, Pa. You and Ma."

He nodded. "I almost have enough money to buy her freedom, but I hope it will not come to me having to leave. I need an income, or what will we all do? For now, you and Cyrus take care of Miss Tabitha, and I will look out for your ma. You hear?"

"Yes, Pa."

Tabitha blinked back sudden tears. Could these people actually feel some allegiance to her, some tenderness? How long had it been since someone had truly cared about her welfare?

No. That was her vulnerability talking. She'd trusted Dulcie in the past, but as a servant, not a friend. She'd been raised to believe that servants, even those not enslaved, were unworthy of personal attention. Lord Riley's workers knew their places. And she was still their mistress, for she owned the land south of the river and its herd of cattle. She would continue to pay Cyrus and Dulcie just as Henry had done.

But how? If they sold the cattle, after that...she'd have no income.

The blankness of sheer terror froze Tabitha in place as her companions headed down the pine-needle-strewn trail.

Mr. Long twisted to check on her. "You coming, Miss Tabitha?"

She swallowed hard and got her mount moving. "Y-yes."

They had not ridden far with the pale winter sun playing hide-and-seek through the trees, the cart creaking, and their mounts' legs brushing the saw palmettos when hooves beat the path in front of them. A burly black man with a close-trimmed beard beneath a floppy-brimmed hat rode toward them. He drew up the reins upon sight of them, his eyes going wide. Cyrus.

Tabitha had seen him on some of his trips to River's Bend to report on the cattle. The last time had been shortly before Henry died.

"M-Miss Tabitha!" His astonishment was warranted. The last time he'd seen her on *this* side of the river, she'd been taking her one and only introductory tour eleven years ago. Before he could inquire about her presence, Mr. Long addressed him.

"Cyrus, where are you bound?"

"To see you, Mr. Long...er, or Miss Tabitha, I suppose." He cast her an uncertain glance. So he knew of Lord Riley's passing, likely having been told by Dulcie during Tabitha's absence, but he had yet to hear that same event had also dispossessed her.

Dulcie allowed her horse to nibble at some underbrush. "What's wrong?"

"Cattle rustlers." He swung his arm behind him. "I had ten head rounded up and penned to sell in Darien, and this morning when I came outside, they were gone."

Tabitha gasped. Ten head would bring a substantial sum at market—income they needed now more than ever. "Did you attempt to follow them?"

"I followed 'em south for about a mile." He rubbed his beard. "The tracks of the ponies around them were unshod. Indian, I 'spect. Long gone and too many for me to confront alone. I was comin' to the fort to report the thievin' and then to gather men from River's Bend to ride with me."

Mr. Long stretched his legs out in the stirrups and shook his head. "That you will not be getting."

"Why not?"

"Everyone at River's Bend now belongs to Hugh Jackson. Including me."

Cyrus's gaze swung to her. "But Miss Tabitha—"

"Miss Tabitha is coming to live at your cabin south of the river. *Her* cabin. You and Dulcie now work for her, but I no longer do. Lord Riley sold River's Bend just before he passed."

"Ohh." The breath Cyrus let out more resembled a groan. He removed his hat and smacked it against his leg, the crown caving in. He closed his eyes for a moment, then opened them, beat his headwear back into shape, and resettled it on his head. "Then it be more important than ever to catch them cattle."

At his display of determination, Tabitha's chest squeezed. She still had a few people in her corner. "Yes, Cyrus, it is." And it fell to her to provide direction in this upended world she found herself in. Like it or not, she would make the final decisions about what happened from here on out. "Do as you said and seek help from the fort while Dulcie and I settle in. Mr. Long, I assume you must return to River's Bend?"

He inclined his head. "Just as soon as I see you settled, ma'am. But I fear you shan't get help from the fort either. Given the recent troubles, the rangers stay out scouting. Only those necessary to guard the river crossing remain. You'd have better luck running across a patrol as you head south."

That she had not expected. Panic clawed its way up from Tabitha's chest, almost blocking her ability to breathe. Could things get any worse?

She could hardly send Cyrus to track the rustlers alone. Someone must go with him. As far as the cattle foraged, distinguished from others by only their brands, it would take too long to round up more heads to fill the order. She clung to the memory of the strong walls of Fort Howe. "But surely, we should at least inquire. Is that not what they are here for, after all?"

Mr. Long's pitying gaze said that for all her years on the edge of the frontier, she had yet to truly experience it. She feared the many dangers lurking in this vast and primeval unknown would swallow her whole. "Yes, ma'am, I can do that on my way back, and for certain sure, I shall beg they send whatever men they can. At the very least, they ought to know more cattle have been stolen. 'Tis probably only River's Bend's proximity to the fort that has saved us thus far. But the Loyalists grow ever bolder, Miss Tabitha. If you want to keep your cattle, you're going to have to fight for them."

His words echoed like a clarion call in Tabitha's mind. She'd lost status, wealth, title, home, and respect. Self-respect too. She'd given that up long ago, when she'd chosen to remain with a husband whose contempt eroded her from the inside out until only a shell remained. She was left with two loyal servants, a log cabin, three hundred acres of pinewoods, and two hundred head of cattle. Make that a hundred and ninety.

Well.

Not if she had anything to say about it.

She lifted her chin. "Good thing Lord Riley taught me to shoot."

CHAPTER THREE

The clink of metal and splashing of water alerted Edmond to vacate the narrow game trail that led to a shallow section of the Satilla several miles above Fort McIntosh. Someone was approaching from the south—by the sound of it, many someones.

He and Dougal had dismounted so they could confirm the cattle Captain Winn had them tracking had indeed crossed the river here. When Edmond requested transfer to Fort Howe, the commander bid him complete the last labors on the new stockade. Just as they finished a couple days later, a scout brought back news of several Indians lifting cattle north of the fort. Winn had sent Edmond, Dougal, and Privates Shelton and Bailey to investigate before releasing them. They had split up this afternoon to cover more ground.

Now, there was no way they could mount fast enough to canter north on the narrow trail. Instead, he pivoted to gesture to Dougal, waving him toward the opposite side of the path. They needed to plunge as far into the forest as possible before whomever it was passed. If only it were a month hence, the foliage and underbrush might provide better cover. At least the light was almost spent.

Edmond led his stallion, Maximus, behind a massive red cedar about fifty yards off the trail. He smoothed the horse's brown muzzle with its white stripe, shushing the animal as voices carried from this side of the Satilla. Edmond reached into the saddlebag for a handful of oats and held them under the stallion's nose. Hot horse breath and velvety lips skimmed his palm. Meanwhile, Edmond peered around the trunk.

Through the trees, he had enough of a view to count the number of horsemen slipping through the shadows. The riders wore the same type of hunting shirts, cocked hats, and breeches that the Patriots did, neither side having developed a standard uniform to date, but there was nothing else familiar about the twenty men who rode past. British-allied Florida rangers, then, as he'd suspected since he knew of no Patriot companies dispatched south. And more a larger company than would be required to thieve cattle. A raiding party, bound for plantations on the Altamaha?

"No campfire tonight." The comment from the man at the tail end of the group made to the comrade who traveled before him reached Edmond's ears. Apparently, the ranger felt himself far enough away from any officer to verbalize his thoughts. "I'm starving. How far to the savanna where we bivouac?"

The man ahead of him turned and hissed a warning.

Edmond knew the clearing he spoke of, which was about a half mile farther along the trail. If the soldiers were passing the night so close to Fort McIntosh, it likely meant their plans involved its capture.

Edmond had to find Dougal...and fast.

He waited a good ten minutes after the rangers left to make certain no scout followed them. Then he eased across the path and plunged into the ever-darkening woods on the other side. He expected to find the private hunkered down roughly the same distance from the trail he had, but no one was in sight.

He chanced a loud whisper. "Dougal?"

A whip-poor-will gave its mournful cry.

Edmond rustled through the palmettos as quietly as possible, then followed some trampled underbrush back toward the river. At last, near the bank about twenty yards distant, a flash of Dougal's beige hunting shirt prompted Edmond to let out a soft breath of relief. The man's horse was tied a little distance away, and his back was turned. Was he relieving himself? No. He seemed to be wrestling with something.

A mournful lowing brought Edmond's feet to a halt. A cow?

Yes. A boney brown-and-white steer had its horns stuck in a privet hedge, and Dougal was attempting to free it.

Edmond had just started forward again when a figure in a baggy coat, a floppy hat, and knee breeches stepped out from a pine right behind Dougal. The boy—for boy he must be, given his diminutive size—raised his arm, a pistol extended. Edmond's inhale froze in his throat. He mustn't make a sound. And no shots must be fired, lest they summon the Florida rangers. But Edmond had to gain the advantage, even if he did not plan to shoot. He dropped Maximus's reins and reached for his own dragoon pistol as the boy spoke.

"'Tis my family brand on that steer."

Dougal wheeled around, his hands shooting into the air.

"I will thank you to let him go." The slight tremor in the youth's voice betrayed his bravado.

"I'm only tryin' to get him free. See?" Douglas gestured ever so slightly toward the bovine in question. "Then ye can have him."

"How do I know you are not the one who stole him?"

"I—I'm a Georgia Continental. We do not..." His wide gaze slid to Edmond as Edmond brought his pistol up.

The boy whirled, and Dougal sprang into action, tackling

him before he could train his weapon on Edmond. The boy grunted as Dougal's substantial barrel chest pinned his legs. The pistol flew through the air and skidded past Edmond into the underbrush. He ran for it at the same time their feisty opponent wriggled out from under Dougal and scrambled for his pistol.

"Don't." Edmond cocked his weapon.

The boy looked up at the same time Dougal seized him from behind, jerking him back. The floppy hat fell off, and long, dark hair tumbled down.

"What the...?"

The rush of blood in Edmond's ears nearly drowned out his private's exclamation. A woman? Indeed, for the hair that escaped from the remnants of a bun framed a face far too dainty to belong to even a boy. Pink splotches marked high cheekbones. Thick black lashes studded the edges of wide brown eyes rich as chocolate. It was all Edmond could do to keep his pistol pointed at her as he said with far more firmness than he felt, "Get up. Hands in the air."

She braced herself on the ground with one hand while she did so, the other hand raised. As soon as she stood erect, her chest heaving while little puffs of breath escaped her rosy lips, she lifted the other. She met his eyes. "If you are who you say you are, you will not hold a lady at gunpoint."

"That lady just held us at gunpoint." Edmond stood stock still while Dougal retrieved this...*woman's* weapon. She was beautiful, there was no doubt, but no youthful innocent. Older than he, and despite her homespun masculine clothing, possessing the delicate look of an aristocrat.

His chest tightened. He'd yet to meet a member of the upper class he'd consider a comrade, whatever side they were on. "What are you doing here?"

Her chin lifted a fraction. "I was attempting to retrieve my h —my cattle. Ten head were stolen from our land on the

Altamaha. This is the only one I found." She tipped her head toward the sinewy steer, which had broken free during their confrontation.

As if to punctuate her statement, the beast snapped off a small shoot from a black walnut tree and munched.

"You tracked them all that way by yourself?" Edmond did not even attempt to relieve his tone of its incredulity.

Her lips flattened into a thin line. "No. I had two servants with me, but we got separated in the swamp." She paused and took a quick breath, a flash of emotion narrowing her eyes. Fear? She must've been terrified. "Then I found this game trail. I figured it might lead to water, so I followed it. And saw the prints."

She showed common sense, at least. "Right. Well, the cattle are long gone."

Some of them might've victualed those Loyalist troops right before they crossed the river, though 'twas probably best they did not alarm this woman by saying so. If she was the sort that anything could alarm. What kind of lady took off through the wilderness after cattle with only two servants at hand? A tight-fisted aristocrat, that was who—one determined not to yield even a single steer. Foolish. And brave. Yes. But probably not a threat to him.

Edmond uncocked his weapon and stashed it in his belt. "Dark is fast falling." What was he to do with her?

"Best to take her straightaway to the fort." Dougal's meaningful look revealed that he'd also gotten a gander at the Floridians.

The woman turned on him. "I shan't go to any fort. I must find my servants before dark. If you truly wish to be helpful, you could assist me. If we spread out and call them—"

"No!" Edmond and Dougal said in unison.

She looked between them, the little space between her slender dark brows dimpling. "Why not?"

Edmond rolled his tight shoulders. "Because doing so would also summon the East Florida Rangers, who are now setting camp north of here."

She sucked in a soft breath. As a sibilant whisper of a breeze slid past them, chill with the damp of the river, a visible tremor passed through her. "But then, how are we to get home?"

"You shan't, tonight."

Her gaze narrowed. "With soldiers that close, you had no intention of shooting me." She pivoted to face Dougal and held her hand out. "Give me my gun."

Dougal tucked it against his side, but his eyes sought Edmond's.

"Pardon, ma'am," Edmond said, "but we still have no idea who you are. Methinks it best Private O'Connor holds onto it for now."

Dougal slid the extra pistol into his belt.

"For heaven's sake." She let her arms hit her sides and swiveled back to him. "Does it matter who I am? I am a lady lost in the wilderness with an unknown number of Florida Rangers between me and home. And you will not even return my pistol so I can defend myself? What are you going to do, leave me here alone?"

"No, ma'am." Dougal was right. There was but one thing to do. Edmond spoke over his shoulder as he strode to fetch Max's reins. "We will take you to Fort McIntosh."

"But I cannot leave my servants out here. What if they stumble into the Loyalists' camp?" The thickening of her voice indicated the threat of tears—and compassion that slowed Edmond's steps. "Please, I must warn them."

His heart squeezed, and he turned back to consider her request.

Then she added, "They are all I have."

They were all *she* had? Just as he'd anticipated, she cared more for her own preservation than for that of anyone beneath her. The servants—*slaves*, no doubt—would be better off without her. Maybe they could take the opportunity to flee to Florida themselves, as so many others of their kind had done, finding refuge among the Seminoles.

Edmond spoke through stiff lips. "Then you should pray they hunker down for the night. We head for McIntosh. 'Tis more important the soldiers be warned than your slaves."

"They are not..." The woman raised her knuckles to her lips, stifling a small sob.

"Pray dinna fash yerself, milady." Dougal took a hesitant step in her direction, daring to touch her sleeve. "All will be well. Ye shall see."

She cast him an entreating look. "What of the cow?"

The lanky steer rooted among the cordgrass, tail peacefully swinging. Dougal stifled a little bark of a laugh.

Edmond released a disbelieving huff. "We are not herding that cow to the fort." He caught up Max's reins and led the horse forward.

Her jaw firmed. "And I am not getting on that horse. I do not even know your name, sir."

"Sergeant Edmond Lassiter, Georgia Regiment of Horse Rangers." He wouldn't ask her name. Once he delivered this woman to Fort McIntosh, Captain Winn could contend with her. She was no concern of his. "And no, we shan't be mounting up. We will lead the horses through the woods as quietly as possible." In case they needed to take rapid cover. The inconvenient presence of this foolish female made confronting any patrols ill-advised. But Edmond wouldn't let her prevent him from warning the fort.

The woman sniffed. "I have my own horse. My mare is tied just over the ridge." She tilted her head.

"Then go fetch her." Had Edmond succeeded in keeping the exasperation from his voice?

Judging by the way the lady stalked off, probably not.

Maybe she would mount up and ride away. 'Twould be a relief if she did.

But she returned a moment later leading a pretty bay mare.

Dougal retrieved his horse from the pine where he'd tethered him, and they set off following the river. Their unwanted guest made little sniffling sounds that Edmond had to restrain himself from shushing. What had she expected, striking off into contested land between two armies? A pleasure jaunt through the woods?

Roughly a quarter hour into their trek, a sneeze from ahead froze Edmond in his tracks. He flung out his arm, signaling those following him to halt.

When Dougal edged up next to him, Edmond handed him Max's reins and held up a finger. Then he crept a few feet forward, keeping to the cover of a spreading waxy-leaved magnolia. The land undulated downward to the Old Post Road. Every few feet in the dip before him, a man lay wrapped in his coat, rifle at hand.

They were too late to warn the fort. The enemy already had it surrounded.

CHAPTER FOUR

The only thing worse than being forced to shelter at a Patriot fort in the wilderness would be spending the night in that wilderness with two strange men. Yet that was exactly the prospect Tabitha faced. As soon as the broad-shouldered sergeant with the thick queue of auburn-brown hair had ascertained the Loyalists had surrounded Fort McIntosh, he'd waved them back the way they had come.

As if that weren't bad enough, a light rain had begun to fall.

Finally, Sergeant Lassiter paused, removed his hat, and looked toward the rising moon visible through a break in the cloud cover.

Tabitha dared a whisper. "Where are we going?" Maybe he sought a trail that would lead them north.

"I know a place we can overnight."

"Overnight?" Her question had squeaked out too loudly.

Sergeant Lassiter whirled and clamped his hand over her mouth. "Hush, woman. Do you want to get us killed?" Had a whisper ever held such harshness?

She pushed his arm down. "Do not touch me, sir."

"Then pray, be silent." His forbidding manner stifled further questions as he set out again, leading his horse.

Tabitha stood frozen beside Cora, her middle hollowed out like the gourds that Annabelle had hung around her kitchen garden. Could she trust these men? Even if she could, should anyone learn of the time she'd spent alone in their company, whatever remained of her reputation would be ruined. Good thing she had no intention of marrying again.

The private who'd confiscated her pistol touched her arm. When she looked at him, he gave a small nod. Reassurance? That must be his intention, as it was too dark to read his expression. 'Twas enough encouragement for Tabitha to draw a deep breath and set her feet in motion.

She followed the sergeant through the forest as he avoided patches of palmettos and underbrush that could give away their movement. A chuck-will called from a nearby tree. Tiny rustles all around put Tabitha in mind of creatures that only stirred at night, and she suppressed a shudder. When Sergeant Lassiter led them toward an embankment that curved out over the river, she froze. Did he intend them to cross in the darkness, taking her even farther into the wilderness? He turned and looked back at her.

She shook her head. "I'm not going down there."

"The bluff will provide some shelter." Sergeant Lassiter spoke in a soft voice but not the whisper she'd used. And at least he did not mean for them to ford the water.

"What if there are gators?" In the winter, the deadly beasts sheltered in muddy dens along inlets and banks just like this one. Tabitha had always avoided solitary walks along the Altamaha for just that reason.

"Gators are docile in this weather. They won't even know we're there." Was that humor in his voice?

Tabitha drew back. She wasn't willing to take that chance.

Desperation clenched her chest, and she flung out her hand. "Why are we not riding north? To Fort Howe?"

The man let out a sigh. "Believe me, I'd like nothing more. Not just to deliver you there, but to seek reinforcements for Fort McIntosh."

"Then let's go." Tabitha clutched Cora's reins. Had the sure-footed mount not brought her safely through the swamp Cyrus and Dulcie must have gotten lost in? Her heart squeezed. What if they had been injured in that tangled bog? They might need help as much as the men at the fort. And they were her responsibility, same as the soldiers were this sergeant's.

"Ma'am." The burly private drew her attention. "We cannot chance runnin' across a patrol or a picket in the dark. Sergeant Lassiter is right. We must bed down for the night."

A shuddering breath betrayed Tabitha's anxiety. She laid her face against Cora's, seeking the warmth and reassurance of something—anything—familiar. What nightmare had she gotten herself into?

"Dinna fash." The private stepped closer, his Scottish brogue a comforting murmur. "We will keep ye safe. I will scout the bank before we go down."

Tabitha lifted her head. "Thank you, sir." Her voice quavered.

Before the man could move away, Sergeant Lassiter held up his hand. "I will go." The impatience in his tone made clear his gesture was not a sacrificial one. No, most likely, he simply preferred not to be left alone with her, even for a moment. He measured and snipped off every word he spoke to her like a grumpy tailor cutting a length of cloth. She was an inconvenience, a burden. An impediment to his mission. He handed his stallion's reins to the private. "Tether the horses."

As he disappeared down the bank, the shorter man tipped his head toward Cora. "Best get what ye want from her packs." He pulled a length of rope from his own saddlebag.

Tabitha rooted for the Johnny cakes and salted ham Cyrus had provided them for the journey, slipping the wrapped bundle into the pocket of the oversized frock coat she wore. At first, she'd resisted his suggestion that she and Dulcie don his clothes, but Dulcie had assured her doing so was the wisest choice. Apparently, ladies did not venture south of the Altamaha.

Sitting the horse had been much easier in breeches, but Dulcie's hope that the masculine attire would deceive anyone they came across had proven futile the moment the private knocked the hat from Tabitha's head. Now she was at the mercy of these men...the very thing she had vowed to avoid. While they seemed unlikely to harm her, the private for his kindness and the sergeant for his disinterest, she'd feel a whole lot better if she could get her pistol back. Maybe if she could remember how to charm a man...

"I do not know your name, sir," she said as she untied the blanket from behind Cora's saddle.

He glanced up from securing a loose picket line between two pines. "Private Dougal O'Connor, ma'am."

"'Tis nice to make your acquaintance. I appreciate your kindness."

The man's abashed spluttering was interrupted by the return of his sergeant, his tall form a looming shadow on the bank.

"And what should we call you?" Suspicion laced his dry tone.

Tabitha clutched the blanket in front of her. She couldn't give her wedded name. These men likely assumed they were aiding a fellow Patriot whose cattle had been thieved by Loyalists. If they knew her husband had been an ardent Loyalist himself, who knew what they would do? "My name is Tabitha Scott." That was who she wanted to be again, anyway.

"Scott." Sergeant Lassiter tilted his head, and her breath

hitched in her throat. Did he recognize her family surname? Her father was a well-known judge and a Loyalist to boot, but she'd gambled on the distance from Savannah providing some anonymity. "*Miss* Scott?"

Ah, he simply sought the correct form of address. Tabitha's shoulders relaxed a fraction. "Mrs. I was...I am married."

Again, she'd almost erred. Best he think she had a husband —perhaps serving the Patriot militia or the Continentals like himself—who would not hesitate to address any grievances visited upon her person. The type of protection her sister enjoyed from her husband, Ansel Adams, now a captain of militia in St. George's Parish north of Savannah. If only that had ever been the case for Tabitha. No, she'd sacrificed her chance for that sort of security when she'd surrendered her own hopes of Ansel to her twin. Her perfect twin, who would never have gotten herself into a situation such as this.

Before Sergeant Lassiter could inquire of this mysterious mate of hers, Tabitha straightened to her full height and changed the subject. "Given the presence of an army nearby, might I have my pistol back?" She held out her hand. "Should it come to it, I can shoot."

He hesitated a moment, then gave Private O'Connor a quick nod.

The shorter man drew the weapon from his belt and placed the handle in Tabitha's hand. She tucked it into the waist of her breeches.

Sergeant Lassiter swept his arm toward the river. "Now, then, Mrs. Scott. The bank is clear of gators and other unpleasant creatures. And you are armed should any surprise us in the night."

Was he making fun of her? She clamped down on her query about how well he could have ascertained that in the dark. She knew better than to hope for a torch or a campfire. Not that one would have done much to warm or dry them if the steady rain that had already dampened their clothing continued. Tabitha took two steps and peered down. Except for a shimmer of moonlight on the water below, the darkness yawned like a bottomless pit.

Sergeant Lassiter let out a light breath, and his voice was gentler when he spoke again. "One moment, and I will assist you."

Somehow, the first sign of softening from the man struck fear all through her. Maybe because fighting him forced her to maintain her guard. To dig deeper for a solidity within herself that must surely be buried beneath all the mush.

She waited while he fumbled about his mount's saddle. After a moment, he returned with a bag and an oiled cloth flung over one shoulder. He offered the opposite arm, and with a burning deep in her abdomen, Tabitha accepted. Relying on a man for anything—especially one who would consider her an enemy if he knew the truth—stuck in her craw. With one hand clutching her blanket and the other his elbow, she edged down the approximately eight-foot sandy embankment.

Halfway down, one of her feet slid out from beneath her, and she grasped the hard arm beneath his linen hunting shirt. Muscles flexed beneath her grip, and the strong fingers of the sergeant's other hand encased hers. Then he wrapped his arm around her waist, drawing her up the bank against him. "Careful." His breath stirred the hair on her neck.

When Tabitha turned her face toward him, she inhaled the scent of leather and pine.

"Lean on me."

That was something she most certainly could not risk. She disengaged from him, lowering herself to a crouch and using her hands for leverage as she made her way down the damp bank—something she could never have done in petticoats. Sand skittered away beneath her fingertips, and damp tendrils of what she hoped were plants stuck to her palms, but she reached the bottom with a grunt of triumph.

When Tabitha turned to judge where the sergeant might end his descent, the heel of her boot caught on something. She tipped backward, arms flailing against the unknown. With a thud, she landed on her bottom. Her calves thunked onto what must be a fallen log.

"Are you all right?" The sergeant's question conveyed his alarm...and perhaps even some concern. Maybe he wasn't completely unfeeling, after all.

Tabitha drew her knees under her and shot to her feet, her pride damaged more than her limbs. She couldn't even traverse a riverbank on her own. What a dolt. "I'm fine." But her movement brought her toe to toe with the young officer as he hurried forward to assist her—stepping over the felled tree with no apparent hesitation. Did he possess the vision of an owl? When she raised her head, the front of her hat smacked him in the face. "Sorry."

He made a spitting sound but secured her by the elbows. "If you will allow me to lead you, Mrs. Scott, I found a spot where we might shelter from the rain."

"A cave?" Tabitha stepped back carefully this time, avoiding the tree.

"Nothing quite as nice as that, but there is a slight overhang where a large tree leans out over the river."

"Very well." Her desperation to get out of the rain grew apace with her exhaustion. When had she last spent a full day on horseback? Never.

His fingers laced through hers. In her surprise, Tabitha narrowly resisted hissing in a loud breath. He only meant to avoid further clumsiness on her part. She allowed him to tug her a few feet along the sandy spit of land to where, just as he'd described, a narrow concavity had formed among the roots of a forest giant. She bent and peered inside. "Are you sure there's nothing in there?"

"Not unless it crawled in during the last few minutes."

Was that teasing in his voice? Tabitha couldn't make out his expression in the dim light. The last time a man had teased her, she'd been a good bit younger than the sergeant. And he must be five or six years her junior. "You go first."

He definitely chuckled. He dropped his saddlebag and shook open his oiled cloth. "First, this should help." On his knees now, he spread the square material on the ground inside the overhang. Then he sat, scooted back, and held out his hand to her. "Come."

Tabitha tossed her blanket at him. With his hands thus occupied, she crawled in next to him. The underside protrusion of a root snagged her hat, and when she looked up, dirt crumbled onto her face. She spluttered, settled onto her rear, and wiped her eyes with her sleeves. The gesture only seemed to drive the scratchy particles past her lashes.

"For heaven's sake." Tabitha groaned. "Could things possibly be worse?"

"Here." Sergeant Lassiter pressed a square of cotton fabric into her hand. "And yes, that man might not have sneezed earlier. In which case, we'd be prisoners just now."

Tabitha wiped her eyes until her vision—what remained of it in the inky darkness of the shelter—cleared. But no sooner had she lowered the handkerchief than tears flooded in. She couldn't hold back a small cry of dismay. "But I'm supposed to be back on my land now, with Cyrus and Dulcie...and the cows meant to be sold in Darien."

Sergeant Lassiter's shoulder touched hers. Did she imagine it, or did he lean ever so slightly into her? "Mrs. Scott, I must ask...where is your husband? Why did he allow you to set off into this wilderness in the first place? No man worth his salt would endanger his wife in such a manner."

The ire in his statement carried more than the expected measure of protectiveness. Why did the notion of her abandonment provoke him so? "My husband is gone." Let him think whatever of that he may. Tabitha bolstered her resolve, handing back his handkerchief. "'Tis only myself I have to rely on now."

A beat of silence met her pronouncement. Finally, he said, "Not while Dougal and I are here." Something had changed in the way he viewed her. He spoke with calm determination. "In the morning, we will ride north. Where is your home?"

Home? A dingy cabin she'd barely glimpsed before riding off on this ill-considered venture? She had not allowed herself to think about it then. She mustn't now either. And he mustn't know where she lived until they reached it, for anyone who had bided in these parts for over a month would recognize Lord Riley's land. "I can find my way from the Altamaha ferry."

Sergeant Lassiter let out a puff of incredulity. "I may not be a gentleman born, Mrs. Scott, but I would never leave you alone in this unsettled territory."

And yet that was exactly what her husband had done.

Thankfully, Private O'Connor's arrival saved her from further explanation. He barely fit beneath the overhang, forcing her to scoot closer to Sergeant Lassiter, packing her so tightly between them that she could scarcely dig the parcel of cornbread and ham from her pocket to satisfy her cramping stomach. She ate a few bites off the napkin they were wrapped in, disdaining to touch the food with her filthy fingers. Dry crumbs lodged in her throat, causing her to cough. Moisture filled her eyes.

Tearing off a bite of jerky with his teeth, Sergeant Lassiter passed her his water flask. She'd forgotten hers in her saddlebag. Foolish. Now she had little choice but to unstop it and place her mouth where his had touched. Tabitha grimaced and bolted back a couple of swallows. She handed the canteen back to him, rewrapped the remainder of her supper, and tucked it away.

Every inch of her ached, and the scratchy, damp wool of Cyrus's clothing stuck to her skin. Tabitha wanted nothing more than to curl into a ball and seek the solace of sleep. But how was she to do that with a strange man on each side?

As if reading her mind, Sergeant Lassiter stashed away the rest of his jerky and reached for the cocked hat he'd laid on his lap. "I shall take first watch." He took Tabitha's blanket and spread it over her, tucking it beneath her legs. Then he scooted out from beneath the overhang, but he paused at the opening and looked back. "I will be close by." Half warning, half reassurance.

He wanted her to know she would be safe with O'Connor. Perhaps his brusque manner earlier had caused her to misjudge him. Experience had taught her that a man's actions, not the station assigned at one's birth, determined whether one was a gentleman.

His absence allowed Tabitha to stretch out on her side facing away from the private, who had settled back with his hat over his face and his arms folded. Despite the sergeant's reassurance, she ought not to trust either of them. Certainly not enough to sleep in their presence. She'd thought Lord Riley a man to be led by the nose, and look where that had gotten her. But for the moment, she had little choice. And she had her pistol, which she laid within easy reach.

She would not hesitate to use it. And while she was no longer the Loyalist she'd been when she married Lord Riley, she'd use whatever allegiances worked to her advantage. At least until she could regain some control over her life.

CHAPTER FIVE

E dmond's brief stint of fitful sleep ended when he jerked
awake shortly before dawn. The faint gray light showed
that the rain had stopped, though a low fog hovered over the
river and moisture dripped from the trees. Edmond's long boots
had kept his legs fairly dry where they stuck out from beneath
the hollow in the bluff.

Was Dougal still on guard on the riverbank? A faint movement on the bank confirmed it. Edmond started to sit up, but
something was pressing his shoulder down. A dark head. Mrs.
Scott's.

As he gazed upon the crescents of her dark lashes resting
above her cheeks and her full lips parted in sleep, he failed to
summon even a smidgen of the irritation that had filled him
when first he'd been saddled with her. Despite her bravado, the
reverses of the prior day had allowed glimpses of vulnerability.
Especially when she spoke of her husband. Something wasn't
right. The woman was convinced she had to rely on herself

alone. Even if Edmond had originally rued the position she had placed them in, he admired her grit.

In repose, she looked so soft and sweet that his heart tugged. Whether she acknowledged it or not, she needed him. The weight of that responsibility settled over Edmond with less distaste than it had yesterday.

The situation had its perks. A beautiful woman slumbering on his shoulder next to the Satilla River was the last thing Edmond would have expected.

The unmistakable pop of muskets about a mile distant brought a timely end to his dangerous musings and Mrs. Scott's eyes open with a start.

"What's that?" She sat up and struck her head on the root above. "Ow." Dark hair ran like inky rivulets over her fingers as she rubbed the offending spot.

Edmond propped himself on his elbows. "I reckon the Loyalists have attacked the fort."

Dougal approached the hideout, his rifle in his hand, and crouched before them. "This will give us the chance to flee north, Sergeant." His optimistic statement overlooked the obvious—that they could have prevented the attack had Mrs. Scott and her cow not delayed them.

Edmond tamped down a wave of impatience as he rubbed his eyes. "We will give it a bit to make sure they are well engaged before skirting northwest of the fort."

"'Tis boggy territory." Mrs. Scott paused in her attempt to run her fingers through her hair. "Where I was separated from my servants."

Edmond took a swig from his water flask. "All the less likely the Tories will find us there." He scooted out from beneath the shelter and went to see to the horses.

By the time he returned, Mrs. Scott had braided her hair and sat on a fallen tree beside Dougal. He joined them, and they partook of the leftovers from yesterday's supper. The rattle of musketry continued from the fort, distant enough that morning birdsong flowed around them. Upriver, a mother otter and her two babies emerged from beneath the roots of a tupelo tree and frolicked in the shallows.

Edmond pointed them out, and the delight that transformed Mrs. Scott's face punctured his midsection. How breathtaking she would be clean and dressed as a lady. Regal, no doubt. Not that her waif-like appearance did not hold its own appeal. That smudge beneath one eye, though...she must have acquired it when the dirt fell on her face last night.

He stepped over to the water and dipped his handkerchief in, then returned and handed it to her. At her blank look, he pointed to her cheekbone. "You have, uh...some dirt..."

"Oh." Her face flushed, and she wiped it with the cloth. "Is it gone now?"

He nodded and looked away. When she tried to hand him the handkerchief, he waved her off. She needed it more than he did.

After attending to personal business in the woods and placing their belongings back on their horses, they mounted up and set out. Mrs. Scott was correct. Swamps and tangled bogs riddled the land northwest of Fort McIntosh. They picked their way slowly through sabal palms, evergreen viburnum, and devil's walkingstick. Swamp azaleas were just putting out leaves.

Having met the famed naturalist William Bartram when he visited the McIntoshes before the war, Dougal had taken to studying the local flora and fauna and loved to force his knowledge on everyone else. He occupied himself during slow stints of service by attempting to sketch the plants. Thankfully, today he refrained from regaling Mrs. Scott with a botany lesson.

After riding a quarter of an hour, they came to a stretch where clusters of tupelo trees and massive cypresses, six feet in diameter, emerged from murky greenish-brown water. Mrs.

Scott drew back on her mare's reins and sent Edmond a frowning glance.

"There is no help for it, ma'am. We must go through." Skirting east would bring them to the Old Post Road, a heavily patrolled route they needed to avoid, and going farther west would take too much time. Edmond urged Maximus forward on the most solid ground available.

"Will there be snakes out yet?" The faint-voiced query from Mrs. Scott barely reached his ears.

He turned in the saddle to answer as quietly as possible. "'Tis early yet, but keep an eye out." He wouldn't mention that even in the heart of winter, the reptiles had been known to sunbathe on warmer days in these tropical environs. Facing front, he made a mockery of his own warning when a thin branch thwacked him in the face. Edmond spluttered and shoved it away.

Muffled laughter echoed from behind. 'Twas what he got for coddling a woman.

Minutes later, Edmond ducked to avoid a tattered gray shawl of Spanish moss as he passed beneath a live oak. Only when a commotion behind him ensued did he realize Mrs. Scott had chosen to go around the other side of the tree and ridden into the water. Her horse splashed, and she screamed.

"A snake! A snake!"

Edmond rounded the tree, expecting that the creature had fallen onto her from a branch above. Instead, a harmless green water snake rippled away from the flailing hooves.

"Mrs. Scott, 'tis not poisonous." Dougal's admonition did little to calm the distraught woman, who sawed at her mare's mouth in an attempt to pull her away from the reptile. Instead, her efforts led them deeper into the muck. Mud oozed up to the mount's fetlocks.

"I cannot get her free." Mrs. Scott's flushed face and wide eyes portrayed her panic.

Edmond rode right past the snake to the woman. He leaned out and grasped the mare's reins, bringing her next to Max, who stood stock still like the war horse he was. Edmond ran a soothing hand down the bay's face. The poor beast rolled her eyes and blew air out her nostrils. Calming her rider might prove even more of a challenge. "You're not stuck. We shall just go slowly, and I will lead you out."

He must've spoken coaxingly enough, for Mrs. Scott blinked, met his gaze, and nodded. Leading the mare behind Maximus, Edmond succeeded easily enough in bringing them all back to dry ground. "There now." He'd just turned to behold Mrs. Scott's relieved smile when the hammer of gun clicked back.

An Indian with his face painted red stepped around a tree in front of them, his musket pointed their way.

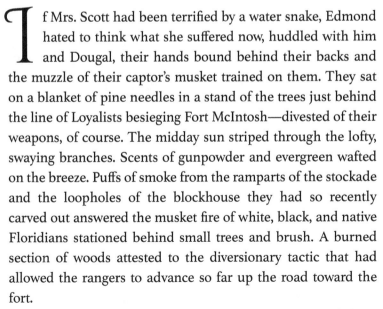

I f Mrs. Scott had been terrified by a water snake, Edmond hated to think what she suffered now, huddled with him and Dougal, their hands bound behind their backs and the muzzle of their captor's musket trained on them. They sat on a blanket of pine needles in a stand of the trees just behind the line of Loyalists besieging Fort McIntosh—divested of their weapons, of course. The midday sun striped through the lofty, swaying branches. Scents of gunpowder and evergreen wafted on the breeze. Puffs of smoke from the ramparts of the stockade and the loopholes of the blockhouse they had so recently carved out answered the musket fire of white, black, and native Floridians stationed behind small trees and brush. A burned section of woods attested to the diversionary tactic that had allowed the rangers to advance so far up the road toward the fort.

They should be grateful the Indian who'd captured them

had not killed them on the spot. But Edmond could see no good way out of this. Even if the Patriots prevailed, he, Dougal, and Mrs. Scott could be bartered with the fort's occupants as hostages or executed in reprisal.

The tremors that shook Mrs. Scott's body showed she was all too aware of the gravity of their predicament. Edmond leaned his shoulder against hers in an attempt to still her trembling. It seemed to work, though a tear tracked down her cheek.

She bowed her head and murmured a familiar Psalm. "'Yea, though I walk through the valley of the shadow of death, I will fear no evil: for thou art with me.'"

Memories of Edmond's boyhood, sitting between his mother and father in the Presbyterian Church in Savannah, washed him with a sudden peace. Back then, he'd believed in God's goodness. His good plan. He could almost smell his mother's sweet lilac scent and hear her lilting voice as she recited the liturgy.

When Mrs. Scott choked on a quavering breath, he nudged her. "Go on."

Her brown eyes darted from the left to the right. "I cannot remember."

And Edmond couldn't recall the last time he'd prayed, either, but he'd never forget the Twenty-third Psalm. "'Thy rod and thy staff...'"

"Yes." She joined him. Together, their voices grew stronger.

"'They comfort me. Thou preparest a table before me—'"

"Silence!" The Indian's musket barrel swooped down, separating them and knocking Edmond's cocked hat from his head.

With a whimper, Mrs. Scott cowered.

Edmond glared at the man and deepened his voice. "'In the presence of mine enemies.'"

The Indian drew back the length of metal and whacked it hard on Edmond's temple. He ducked, but it was Mrs. Scott who cried out. Her protest rang especially loud in the sudden silence that had fallen. What had happened?

As a cold trickle of blood trailed down his forehead, Edmond sucked in his breath, not from the pain. From amazement. A man whose dark frock labeled him an officer had stepped from the tree line sheltering the Loyalists and was approaching the fort, a white cloth in his hand.

With the Indian distracted by the parlay about to take place, Mrs. Scott dared to whisper, "He is not surrendering?"

He shook his head, sending pain through his temple. "No. He'll be *demanding* a surrender."

"Will the commander accept?"

Dougal scooted closer. "Captain Winn will wait for reinforcements from Fort Howe."

A vise tightened on Edmond's chest. Reinforcements that might be on their way had Mrs. Scott not screamed like a banshee over what his private would call a wee green serpent.

No, that was not fair. Chances were, the Indian would have set upon them in the swamp regardless. Whether Creek or Seminole—it was impossible to tell, for both tribes dressed similarly in hunting shirts, leggings, and moccasins—his sharp ears had probably already heard their conversation. And now the man took note of Edmond's hat on the ground a few feet away. He lunged for it and settled it over his half shaven, half roached hair.

Edmond looked away. If his hat was all he lost during this wilderness confrontation, he'd count himself fortunate.

The fort gate opened just enough to allow someone to accept a paper the officer delivered, then closed again. The Loyalist officer limped away, his uneven pace probably due to a previous injury.

"What happens now?" Mrs. Scott asked softly.

"Now we wait." When Edmond said no more, she looked at him, and her brow furrowed.

"I'm sorry about your head. You can wipe it on my—"

Their captor moved closer again. At a scowl from him, they sealed their lips. A moment later, another brave joined him, and they talked in their own language. If only Edmond could understand what they were saying—most likely something about the terms offered.

The man who had delivered the surrender demand had retreated to a live oak where he conferred with two other officers. Mrs. Scott's gaze swung to them. Suddenly, she straightened and raised her voice to address their captors.

"Take me to your leaders." When the men's heads swiveled in her direction, glares returning to their painted, angular features, she cringed, but she tilted her chin toward the white officers. "Take me to them."

Edmond fumbled behind him and managed to grab her wrist. "What are you doing?"

Her body was trembling, but she pulled away and attempted to stand.

The brave who had captured them strode forward and jerked her to her feet, gripping her by the elbow.

"Help!" She raised her voice and called toward the officers. "Help, sir!"

The Indian's hand flashed out and struck her across the face. She cried out as her head snapped back.

With a roar of fury, Edmond reared up and plowed his shoulder into the man's legs. It was enough to break his hold on Mrs. Scott and send him stumbling, but Edmond crashed face first into the ground. When he rolled to one side, he looked up to find two muskets pointed at him.

"Stop!"

The sharp command froze fingers on hammers and Edmond with his head raised. Black riding boots stomped into his vision, the gait of their owner uneven. As the natives lowered their weapons, Edmond struggled into a sitting position.

The officer stopped before him, looking the three of them over with his forehead creased up to his wig—and a scar that gleamed like a fat pink worm just below it. Edmond's insides went hollow. The limp. The mark of a scalping knife. He knew who the man was before the notorious Loyalist demanded Edmond reveal their own identities. He'd just finished giving their names and ranks when Mrs. Scott stepped forward.

The Indian's blow had left a red mark across her cheek, but she held her head high as she addressed the officer. "Sir, you must release me at once." Despite her forceful words, her voice quivered.

Edmond shook his head, but she paid no attention, just stared down the officer, oblivious to the fact that she faced Colonel Thomas "Burntfoot" Brown, the man every Georgia ranger simultaneously feared and aspired to kill or capture.

In the imperious voice of an aristocrat, she dared to continue. "If you knew who my husband was, you would do so immediately."

Brown sneered at her. "What do I care who your husband is, madam, when my scout captured you in the company of two Georgia Continentals from this very fort?"

She sucked in an unsteady breath. She did glance at Edmond then. "I came upon them when I was looking for my stolen cattle. I know them not. My maiden name was Scott. My married name is Tabitha Gage, wife of Henry Gage, Lord Riley, owner of River's Bend Plantation and loyal servant of the king."

Edmond's jaw fell open. He'd risked their lives and sacrificed a fort protecting a Loyalist?

CHAPTER SIX

Tabitha knew not who looked more stunned, the Loyalist officer or Sergeant Lassiter. She dared not allow her gaze to linger on the Patriot scout who'd risked his life merely to avenge a slap—a gesture she couldn't rightly process just now but which did strange things to her insides. Judging by the outrage that now twisted his features, he'd not be repeating that mistake. She focused instead on the Florida ranger before her.

"You are Lord Riley's wife?" The flash of fear that accompanied his shocked expression lit an ember of hope in Tabitha's chest. If reprisal concerned him, he had not yet heard that Lord Riley was no more.

"I am. If you allow me to go free, I shall consider no damage done. 'Twas an honest mistake." She dipped her chin in a gesture of humility. He should reach around to undo her bonds at any moment now.

Instead, he asked, "And what of your companions here?"

Tabitha's gaze snapped up. "They may be rebels, but they acted honorably and for my protection. We were headed home when your scout there accosted us."

The Loyalist threw back his head and laughed. "I suppose home is Fort Howe, from whence they would shortly return with a regiment of rangers."

Tabitha spluttered. She hadn't thought of that. She hadn't thought this out at all, had merely gotten an idea while praying —that of leveraging her former alliance—that she'd thought had come from God. But truly, what made her think God would guide her? Even when she'd acted in her sister's interest rather than her own, she'd landed in disaster.

The man seized her arm so suddenly, she gasped and stumbled. The growl he emitted raised the hairs on her neck. "What kind of fool do you take me for, woman? One who releases his foes? Indeed, I just informed the commander of this fort that he must submit to unconditional surrender or suffer the death of his entire garrison."

A movement in the corner of Tabitha's eye told her the sergeant had stiffened. He'd already drawn himself up when the enemy officer grabbed her, as if he might challenge the man even with his hands tied behind his back—despite what he would see as Tabitha's betrayal. He spoke in a gravelly voice. "Captain Winn will not surrender the fort."

The Loyalist's eyes did not leave Tabitha. "Then you will all die with them."

"All?" The word escaped on a puff of breath. Except for her husband, Tabitha had yet to meet a man she couldn't charm or condescend into submission. Cold fear doused her from head to toe.

"Yes, you, too, *Lady* Riley." His expression hardened. "Do you think I believe that Henry Gage would let his wife go traipsing across the frontier in his manservant's garb?" He shook her so hard that she bit her tongue. "Liar!"

Tabitha gulped back a sob. "'Tis the truth. I am Tabitha Gage."

"Sit down and shut your clacker." He shoved her backward, and she fell into the men, who did their best to catch her.

Tabitha rolled the wrist she'd landed on and swallowed a whimper.

"Colonel Brown!" A young man with a turkey feather on his hat called from across the clearing as he pointed to the fort. "The gate is opening."

The colonel summoned the Indians standing nearby with a jerk of his hand. "Stay with them." As they drew closer, he pivoted and hastened toward the other officers under the live oak. When an emissary was sent to retrieve Captain Winn's answer, Tabitha chanced a sideways glance at Sergeant Lassiter.

His straight burnished brows created a slash above his glowing amber-brown eyes. "You little fool." His tone cut as much as his words. "Did you really think to bend Burntfoot Brown to your will?"

Tabitha drew back. "Who?"

"Have ye lived under a log the past year, lass?" Private O'Connor shook his head and peeked over his shoulder at their guards. They stood by, stoic, watching as the officers conferred over a piece of paper—the Patriot reply, no doubt. O'Connor continued in a low voice. "Thomas Brown is only the most feared Loyalist in the southern colonies. He refused to sign the Patriot Association. The Sons of Liberty burned his feet, tarred and feathered him, scalped him, and fractured his skull, but he wouldna renounce his loyalty to the king. He escaped to South Carolina and then to Florida. Now he has no mercy."

"Th-they scalped him? The Sons of Liberty?" What would her upstanding Patriot captain of a brother-in-law have to say about *that*? Even Temperance, former Daughter of Liberty leader, would not attempt to justify such abuse, pious Christian that she was.

"Aye, and I'd say the other one about our age is Daniel McGirth."

Sergeant Lassiter avoided her questioning gaze but explained, nonetheless. "And he possesses an equal thirst for revenge. He was with the Patriots here on the Satilla when an officer wanted his horse."

Dougal chimed in again. "Offered him a commission for it."

"He wouldn't take it. The officer threatened him, and McGirth decked him. They threw him in jail, found him guilty at a court martial, and had him whipped."

Tabitha's lips parted. Her secret reading of revolutionary pamphlets had added to her newfound hatred of harsh overlords, but if these tales were true, she could understand where these particular Loyalists came by their convictions.

Dougal rubbed his ear with his shoulder, satisfying an itch, then righted his head. "He broke out of the jail and rode away on his horse. A fast one, so they say."

"So it doesn't matter where your allegiances lie. Only a fool would trust those two." Sergeant Lassiter's eyes flashed.

"Yes. A fool. I got that part." Tabitha's chest burned. It shouldn't matter what he thought of her, just so long as they got out of this alive. And she had bargained for him when she appealed to Brown, had she not?

"And a liar?" He arched his brow at her.

Was that a touch of hurt in his tone? She stiffened. They did not know each other well enough for either of them to feel betrayed.

"I did not want to lie to you, but if you knew my husband was a prominent Loyalist, would you have helped me?" Defensiveness sharpened Tabitha's reply. Could he not see the position she was in? Did she really have to explain?

"Yes, Mrs. *Gage*." The sergeant never looked away. "We would have helped you."

"'Bound in honor to not comply!'" The exclamation drew their attention to the conference of Loyalist officers. Colonel

Brown slapped the paper against his thigh. "Treat them like prisoners of war, over my dead body!"

"We resume the siege." The response of the youngest of the three officers also carried to them. "Once the British Regulars arrive, they will rue the choice they made in this hour."

"Wait." Brown held up his hand and glanced toward Tabitha and the men at her side.

She sucked in her breath, caving her shoulders in as though she could make herself small enough to avoid his notice. He conferred with the other officers, occasionally looking their way.

"We're to be used as bargaining chips." Dread weighted O'Connor's statement.

Tabitha swiveled her head toward him. "Would they do that?"

"Did you not think of that either?" Sergeant Lassiter's accusation made her heart thud, but he sighed and added, "Whatever happens, we will do our best to protect you, Mrs. Gage."

"Thank you. I—" Heavy footfalls curtailed the explanation the man's noble offer made Tabitha willing to supply.

Colonel Brown marched straight up to her and lifted her by her upper arms. He positioned his face a few inches from her own. "It seems Colonels Cunningham and McGirth do not trust my conclusion about you." His sour breath smelled of rum. "On the off-chance that you are indeed who you say you are, they declined to use you as bait. But as I will not take prisoners, you shall relay our response." His gaze swept over to include her fellow captives. "On your feet. You are all to be returned to the fort. Whatever its fate, so shall yours be."

"We accept that fate wholeheartedly." Confidence strengthened Sergeant Lassiter's reply as he got to his knees.

"I wouldn't be so pleased if I were you." The colonel's hard fingers bit into Tabitha's arm, and he propelled her forward. A harsh chuckle broke from his throat. "By tomorrow, Colonel Fuser will arrive from St. Augustine with two hundred British Regulars and Cussuppa's Creek warriors." He twisted to address Sergeant Lassiter, who had risen and now stumbled along beside O'Connor and the Indian wearing the sergeant's hat. "Give that message to your valiant Captain Winn."

Colonel Brown waved his white handkerchief again as he approached the fort, which resembled the one at the Altamaha —a square enclosure of upright logs, sharpened at the tips, bastions on each corner. They stopped in the middle of the clearing, and the Indian's knife flashed out. Tabitha gasped and retreated several steps, but Brown caught her, turned her to face him, and held her arms out. The rope around her wrists strained, then fell to the ground. Tabitha rubbed her tender skin as the warrior freed the Patriots.

The colonel slowly walked backward, his eyes on Sergeant Lassiter. A wicked grin cracked his face. "I will see you again. In this battle...or after."

The sergeant's hand went to his empty belt. Obviously, they had known better than to ask for their arms—or horses, though Tabitha's heart ached at the thought of her dainty Cora the mount of a rough-riding East Florida Ranger. Sergeant Lassiter gave a grim nod. "I shall count on it."

A cry drew their attention to the ramparts. "'Tis Sergeant Lassiter! Open the gate."

The gate creaked open, and the sergeant took hold of Tabitha's arm. "Hurry."

She ran with him into the palisade, Private O'Connor just behind. No sooner had the gate shut than firing resumed from the Loyalists. Men garbed in the rough, drab-colored material of the frontier returned fire from the fort walls.

A man about Sergeant Lassiter's age with the quality of clothing and bearing of an officer leapt from the ramparts and jogged over to meet them.

The sergeant released Tabitha to salute him. "Captain Winn, sir."

The commander's gaze raked Tabitha, and his eyebrows shot up. "Come into the blockhouse and give me your report, Sergeant."

Tabitha could've cried from relief. The boom of muskets and zip of lead shot reduced her knees to the consistency of Annabelle's mayhaw jelly.

Captain Winn led them into the strange-looking square building the top floor of which extended beyond the bottom floor all around. The darkness inside, relieved only by high square loopholes, forced Tabitha to stop a moment and blink. When her eyes adjusted to the lower light, the gleam of a couple candles drew her gaze to a paper-strewn table in one corner. The captain led them toward it, past a ladder that led to the second story and a youth with light blond fuzz on his jaw packing wads of powder and lead balls at another table, rougher hewn.

After reaching the corner that must serve as his office, Captain Winn pivoted to face them, eyeing Tabitha's attire and frayed braid. "Who is this, Sergeant?"

"This is Mrs. Tabitha Gage, wife of Lord Riley, a prominent Loyalist who owns a plantation on the Altamaha. Her cattle were among those stolen by the Indians we were tracking. We were attempting to escort her home when a native scout came upon us in the swamp."

"Mrs. Gage." Captain Winn folded one arm over his waist and proffered a brief bow. At last, a gentleman bred. But when he raised his eyes to her again, they were hard. "You are a Loyalist?"

"My husband was a Loyalist."

Sergeant Lassiter's quick intake of breath cued Tabitha to her lapse even before his captain repeated, "'Was'?"

Her companions might well see this as something else she'd

withheld from them—no doubt having taken her reference to her spouse being gone as off to the war—and would trust her less than they already did. And admitting she was without a husband's protection put her in an even more vulnerable position. But there was nothing for it now but to tell the truth. Still, Tabitha's throat worked to produce the words. "Lord Riley died just above a week ago."

She couldn't look at the sergeant. Would he judge her less harshly now that he knew necessity had forced her onto the frontier? No. He probably still expected she had a bevy of servants to do her bidding.

"My condolences, madam," the captain said. "Whatever your allegiances, 'twould seem your fate is entwined with ours for the time being. No doubt, you have been through a harrowing ordeal."

"Indeed, sir." A week ago, no one could have told her she'd find herself in a fort full of strange men, under siege by the British forces. As the room spun around her, she propped herself on the corner of the table.

"Please, take a seat." The officer indicated one of three rush-bottom chairs, which she gratefully sank onto. "Private O'Connor, serve the lady some cider."

"Aye, sir." O'Connor moved toward a pitcher, a decanter of what appeared to be whiskey, and a tin cup on the corner of the desk. "Then, with your leave, sir, I will see about replacin' our arms the Loyalists took." Bitterness laced his words as he poured from the pitcher.

"Do that." Captain Winn turned to the tall man whose presence seemed too big for the low-ceilinged room. "Sergeant, I would know everything you know."

Tabitha downed the cider Private O'Connor handed her while Sergeant Lassiter gave Captain Winn an accounting of the day prior, concluding with the threat of reinforcements Colonel Brown had rendered before leaving them at the gate.

Across the room, O'Connor made his selection from a small store of muskets, pistols, and knives.

Winn's face grew grave. "By that count, we will soon face five hundred of the foe. We are only eighty. Even with the strong walls of this fort, we can only hold out so long against those odds."

Tabitha shuddered. Thomas Brown had promised to kill every man here when he overran the fort. What would he do with her?

She eyed the whiskey decanter. Perhaps she ought to fortify herself with some Dutch courage.

"We must have reinforcements." Winn banged his fist on the table, making Tabitha's cup rattle and her hand fall back into her lap. He sank into one of the other chairs while Sergeant Lassiter remained standing.

"'Twas my intention to seek help from Fort Howe before the native captured us in the swamp." The sergeant hung his head as if ashamed. Bereft of his hat, his queued brown hair glittered with auburn strands in the dim light. He wasn't going to blame her, even when doing so could have redeemed him in the estimation of his commander? Before Tabitha could own her shortcomings, Sergeant Lassiter's chin lifted. "But sir, last I was aware, Colonel Harris has only forty at Howe. Even if he sent every man he had, we would still be outnumbered. And chances are good that most of them will already be out scouting to the south."

"Then we must pray that, in light of the incursion on our southern border, General McIntosh has dispatched more troops to Fort Howe." Captain Winn ran his hand over his chin, producing a rasping sound. "You can still make that run for us, Sergeant Lassiter. After dark, you shall set out for Fort Howe."

Sergeant Lassiter stiffened, and his gaze shot to Tabitha's— so quickly that she failed to hide her panic in time. The notion of remaining here without him filled her with terror. And why should that be? She had met him the day prior, a meeting he'd been none too pleased about. Private O'Connor had showed her more kindness. And yet there was something about the sergeant's solid presence that made her feel less alone. Indeed, less alone than she had felt in a long time.

His jaw tightened, then his gaze softened. He looked back at the captain. "Sir, I gave my word to Mrs. Gage."

Captain Winn stared at him a moment. Tabitha half hoped he would demand an explanation of what type of word Lassiter had given. Indeed, she'd like to know above anyone exactly how far the sergeant's protection extended, but the captain merely dipped his head. "Very well. I will send Sergeant Owens. If he returns with reinforcements, they can strike from behind while my men mount a frontal assault."

Horror at those words mingled with relief that Sergeant Lassiter would not be leaving, but Tabitha had no time to examine either reaction before the door to the blockhouse burst open and two figures in buckskin and linen burst into the room.

She shot to her feet.

The boy wrapping powder spun around.

The newcomers were soldiers. One leaned heavily on the other, a dark-red stain marring the shoulder of his ecru hunting shirt.

"Clear the table." Sergeant Lassiter hurried forward to assist the youth in transferring the prepared shot into his cartridge box. "Put him here." They had no sooner done so than the sergeant ripped open the neck of the wounded man's tunic. "Tabitha, bring the whiskey."

Before she could process the fact that he'd used her given name, he turned with his hand out.

"The whiskey. Now."

She grabbed the glass container and scuttled to his side.

The man groaned as blood ran from a hole just beneath his collarbone.

The soldier who had brought him in stepped back and adjusted his linen haversack, his eyes dark with concern. "I fear the shot is still in him."

"Thank you, Private. He will be taken care of to the best of our abilities. To the wall, then. All of you." Captain Winn waved toward the door, and the two privates scampered out, O'Connor leaning a musket for his sergeant near the exit before he disappeared into a haze of light and smoke.

When Tabitha extended the whiskey to Edmond—for she might as well get used to his Christian name also, especially if they were trapped in this fort together—he shook his head. "That means me too."

"Here." Stepping closer, Captain Winn untied a linen pouch and unfurled it to display a selection of tweezers, needles, sinew, and bandages—a medical kit. "We have no surgeon, but this may help."

As the commander laid the supplies on the table, Edmond pushed the decanter back at Tabitha. "You will have to take care of him. And any others who might come."

Her eyes went wide. "But I have no idea what to do." Why did they think that, just because she was a woman, she ought to know how to nurse a wounded man? She'd never seen a battle before. Not even a hunting accident. If she had, she would have been shielded from the unseemly results as her servants offered the care.

"Then you must do your best." Edmond touched her arm. "I know you have the strength to face this."

"I don't." Blood gushed from the dark entry wound, and Tabitha swallowed hard.

"The woman who stood up to Burntfoot Brown?"

She wrapped her shaking hands around the cool glass of

the decanter, clutching it tightly to prevent it slipping through her fingers. "I knew not who he was then."

Edmond's chuckle drew Tabitha's gaze. His held...admiration? He wasn't angry at her for not telling him she was a widow. Something warm trickled through her, infusing her with strength.

He nodded to the wounded man. "Pour a little whiskey over the wound, then you must fish the shot out."

When her mouth fell open, Captain Winn groaned. "I could do it myself faster. When you finish mollycoddling the lady, Sergeant Lassiter, will you join me for tea on the ramparts?"

"Yes, sir."

The quick grin that flashed over Edmond's face was the first Tabitha had seen, and she sucked in her breath. Those laugh lines around his mouth would slay any lass, Loyalist or no. And she would do anything to see that smile again.

CHAPTER SEVEN

Edmond rammed another charge into the breach of his musket, handling the hot barrel carefully even while wearing woven mitts. What he would not give to have his rifle back, though smoke hung so thick over the ramparts, he could scarce see what he was doing. His ears rang, his eyes watered, he could barely draw breath through his nose, and his throat scratched as though lined with sand when he swallowed. After exchanging fire with the Loyalists until dark the day before, they had been at it for almost six hours today.

Still, this was a far cry from face-to-face combat, which he'd seen last year here on the Satilla, south on the St. Mary's, and again when Fort Barrington had fallen under attack in October. He'd take fighting from behind strong pine or cypress walls over that any day.

"Hey." Edmond nudged Dougal. "Got any more shot?"

The private eased down from firing his musket and thumbed open his empty cartridge box. "Down to my last. Ask Shelton or Bailey."

Edmond looked down the line at the two other rangers who frequently scouted with them. "Got anything?"

Both shook their heads, their unshaven faces begrimed. Their expressions reflected the lost hope of all those manning the wall that reinforcements would arrive. Just as Edmond had feared.

"I will go see if there's any left in the blockhouse." 'Twould give him a chance to see how the Loyalist widow fared.

They had carried several wounded men in to her yesterday. At twilight, Edmond had volunteered to assist with the last who'd fallen nearby. He'd found Tabitha with her shirt sleeves rolled up, wisps of hair loose from her braid, hands and arms smeared with blood. When she turned to him, he expected the pleading in her eyes. What he did not expect was what she'd said.

"I used all the bandages and the geranium you gave me." He carried a supply of the powdered root in his haversack, as 'twas needful for slowing bleeding. "I have nothing else that will help these men, not even honey. They suffer terribly."

The moan from a soldier who cradled his linen-wrapped arm near his chest punctuated her statement.

"I know. I'm sorry," Edmond had said. 'Twas all he could do not to thumb back the strand of hair stuck to her cheek.

"That one did not make it." She'd tipped her head toward a blanket-covered form in the corner. Then her eyes searched his. "Edmond, if the British come tomorrow and this siege continues, no one is going to walk out of here."

The way she used his name made him want to move heaven and earth for her. Even more so that she pleaded not for herself, but for the men. Evangeline would never have displayed such strength. He couldn't be angry with Tabitha for leading them to believe her husband was alive, not when a man's name was all that might protect her. Edmond could even understand her bargaining with Brown. But that still did not explain her desperation in hunting down lost cattle. And had she shared her husband's sentiments? Her reply to his captain, clarifying that her husband had been a Loyalist but not mentioning herself, had cast doubt on that.

His questions would have to wait.

"Hold up, Tabitha. You are doing well." He'd allowed himself to squeeze her arm, reassurance she soaked up with an immediate softening. "This will be over soon."

One way or another.

During the night, Colonel Brown had drawn his forces back into siege position. And come daylight, the expected reinforcements had arrived, British Regulars in red and white with the sun flashing off their bayonets and painted Creek warriors with bows, tomahawks, and muskets. They approached far too near for comfort and hid behind stumps and logs, keeping close watch on the loopholes.

Edmond cocked his musket's dogshead and sighted a particularly vexing brave, waiting until the eagle feathers moved above the downed tree he lay behind. At last, Edmond got the shot he wanted, and the man fell backward. Edmond stepped down from the loophole and wiped his face on his sleeve. This wasn't the first man he'd killed, and it wouldn't be the last, but the day the sight of death failed to clench his chest with regret was the day he'd fear for his soul.

"Cease fire! Cease fire!" The cry echoed from without and within.

A messenger approached with a white flag.

∾

"We're to *walk* to Fort Howe? *Tonight*?" Clutching her chest, Tabitha faced Edmond and Dougal just outside the blockhouse a couple of hours after Captain Winn and Colonel Fuser had met halfway on the field outside the fort.

"Aye. Unarmed." Dougal's wry comment escalated her terror to a whole new level.

She'd known the fort being overrun as Brown had threatened was the worst that could happen. All she'd heard from the men in the blockhouse had been of the bitter quest for revenge shared by the trio of East Florida Rangers commanders. Apparently, the backstory of the youngest, Colonel William Cunningham, bore strong resemblance to Daniel McGirth's. While she was thankful Colonel Fuser's nobler sensibilities had prevailed over the ranger officers' bloodlust, marching without defense to Fort Howe could mean massacre outside the fort walls rather than within. "What will prevent them from attacking us on the road?" Especially the Creek allies. Would the sole British commander, Fuser, be able to hold them in check?

"The lieutenant said Captain Winn requested an escort from the 60th Royal Regiment." Edmond held the barrel of his musket, its butt planted on the ground. Powder darkened his cheekbones, a shadow of auburn whiskers his strong jaw. He had spoken with the superior officer as the men emerged from a lengthy parlay with Winn in the blockhouse, where he reported the officers had sworn to die to a man, but the dwindling powder supply had forced the captain to seek terms— ones better than those Colonel Brown had offered the day prior.

Tabitha curled her hand at her breast. "But why can we not go in the morning?" The sun already slanted in from the west, and they were still waiting on the British colonel's response. By the time they had it and set out, it could be full dark. The thought of traversing the tangled wilderness at night wrought shivers down her spine.

"'Tis not the way of things, lass." Dougal spoke with regret. "Even with us leavin' now, they will likely require hostages."

Edmond answered her alarmed glance. "To ensure we do not mount another assault."

She blinked. "How will the hostages be chosen?"

"From among the officers." When her chest heaved with a deep breath, he added, "Higher-ranking ones. And if it helps, I asked Colonel Winn if he could request your horse. I doubt even they will refuse to let a lady ride."

Tabitha held out little hope for such a courtesy, given the way this experience had reframed her expectation that Loyalist officers would act as gentlemen. No, the men before her, with their rough clothing and stoic manner, had proven themselves more deserving of the label. How thankful she was that Edmond should not be among those held by the British. And how thoughtful that he had extended himself once again on her behalf. Her mare would provide such comfort—though not near as much as this man's presence would.

After they got to Fort Howe, Sergeant Lassiter would fade into the background of her life. They would have no call to cross paths except perhaps on rare occasion. Until then, she would enjoy the comfort of someone watching out for her.

Her shoulders relaxed, and she offered him a small smile. "Thank you. I want you to know, I'm cognizant of the honor you do me. The trouble you have gone to." Tabitha allowed herself to reach for his hand, intending to give it a brief squeeze, but the moment her fingers brushed his strong, callused palm, heat licked up from her midsection and set fire to her face. Not to mention, Edmond's eyes went wide. She quickly dropped her hand to her side and included Dougal in her glance. "Both of you. If ever there is something I can do for you in the future..."

"Thankee, ma'am." The Scot tipped his head.

Edmond remained silent, his presence next to her a palpable force.

At that fortuitous moment, Captain Winn strode toward them from the gate. He stopped in front of them and removed his cocked hat. "Colonel Fuser has agreed to the terms. He requires but two officers remain behind and will provide an escort to Fort Howe." His gaze swept Tabitha. "Mrs. Gage, your horse will be delivered once we surrender our arms."

She blew out a little breath and thanked the Patriot officer.

Dougal grumbled about sacrificing yet another firearm.

Edmond frowned and stepped away from her, speaking low to Winn but in a tone she could yet hear. "How can we be certain the Regulars will not abandon us on the road?"

Captain Winn resettled his hat on his head. "We can't. I read of Indians killing prisoners between Montreal and Albany. So I suggest you stay close to the lady." As he glanced back at her, Tabitha wrapped her arms around herself. "Pack your things, Mrs. Gage." A forced smile stretched his lips. "You shall be home soon."

His reassurance rang hollow.

It took little enough time to gather her belongings when she'd arrived with aught but the coat on her back. While the officers packed papers and accoutrements, Tabitha helped some of the men piece together stretchers for the wounded soldiers.

By four o'clock, the South Carolinians and Georgians had stacked their arms and vacated the blockhouse. Tabitha's heart beat hard at the red-and-white uniforms of the British officers who waited in the stockade. One of them demanded the Patriot commanders surrender their swords. Rather than hand his weapon over, Captain Winn placed it on a stump, and the other officers followed suit. The swords were collected and presumably taken to the Loyalist officers.

As Winn formed his men to march out, Tabitha kept to the shadows, avoiding the curious and speculative stares of the English officers.

An older man with polished brass buttons and gorget who could only be Colonel Fuser strode into the fort bearing an armload of swords. He approached Captain Winn and returned the weapons. Tabitha released a breath. If Fuser was honorable enough for such a gesture, surely, he would not send his Creek allies after them.

Sight of her mare coming through the gate provided further reassurance—until she saw who led her. Thomas Brown. As he approached, Tabitha's legs started to shake. Edmond stepped out of line and stood beside her.

The Loyalist colonel halted a few feet away, his mouth a slash across his stiff face. "Your horse, madam." After a jerk of a bow, he presented the reins.

When Tabitha hesitated for fear of her fingers brushing his, Edmond took hold of the leather lines for her.

Brown cut a glare at him before sweeping Tabitha with a disdainful look. "Twice now, you have been the recipient of my grace." His thunderous expression and begrudging tone belied his outlandish statement. "Should our paths cross again, I shall expect the favor to be returned."

The old Tabitha would have told him she owed him nothing. But the old Tabitha wasn't widowed and destitute on the border of a war zone. The current Tabitha silently took Cora's reins from Edmond, her gaze downcast.

Brown scoffed, pivoted on his heel, and stalked away.

She let out her breath, then gathered the mare's head against her breast and kissed her ear.

"Let me help you mount." Edmond's voice behind her soothed her frazzled nerves.

"I think I shall walk a bit." She turned to offer him a wobbly smile. "But thank you." She wouldn't share that she felt safer at his side than up on her horse.

She did not need to ask him to stay close. And the captain hadn't either. He remained a foot from her as they exited the fort and followed the troop north, the wounded borne on stretchers in the middle. Loyalists and Indians bracketed the Old Post Road. Thank goodness she had not mounted Cora. The men stared enough as it was, their eyes glittering dark in the rapidly encroaching shadows, weapons bristling at their sides. A column of British Regulars fell in behind them.

They had traveled less than a mile when the last rays of weak winter sun splintered through the trees. The underbrush rustled along the silvery thread of the sandy road. She pulled Cyrus's coat tighter and shivered in the cool dankness of the February evening.

Again, the urge to pray came over her, more strongly than it ever had. But she no longer remembered the liturgy from her youth when she'd attended Christ Church with her family. And talking with the Almighty was the practice of pious women like her sister. She settled for a silent plea.

Dear God, keep us safe.

A new thought stopped her in her tracks. Had God sent Edmond and Dougal? What about the steer stuck in the hedge? If not for the steer, if she had not come upon the men, would she have stumbled all alone into the Loyalist troops instead? And maybe met a much worse fate?

Dulcie would say so. She was always talking about the grace of God. 'Twas ludicrous for Thomas Brown to speak of grace. His return of her horse had been forced, not freely given. Not requiring nothing in return.

If God had arranged for Edmond to find her, *that* was grace.

"Are you all right?" Edmond's voice was filled with concern as he wrapped his hand around her arm.

She had slowed. She had best get moving, or the British Regulars would march right over her. Tabitha glanced over her shoulder to see how close they were and gasped.

Their escort was gone.

CHAPTER EIGHT

E dmond and the men went back a ways and searched the woods on either side of the road, but the Brits had blended into the night.

"'Tis a trap," cried one private, whose high-pitched voice suggested he was on the tail end of puberty, a notion his excitability only emphasized. "The lobsterbacks mean to leave us to the mercy of the Indians."

Edmond shushed him as murmurs and mutters broke out among the troop. A glance at Tabitha showed her clinging to her horse's neck. "We do not know that," he said. "It may just be that they rued a thirty-five-mile walk."

"One way," Dougal put in ever so helpfully.

"And the possibility of meeting resistance at Fort Howe." Edmond firmed his tone. "It behooves no one to panic."

The sole senior officer among them, a lieutenant of Winn's Edmond did not know, shouldered his way into the knot of anxiously shifting dark forms. "While I agree with that, it does behoove us to get off this road. Unarmed, on foot, we make ourselves a target. We must press on to Fort Howe, but we should do so through the forest."

"The swamp, ye mean," someone mumbled.

"Indeed," the lieutenant said. "'Twill not be easy, but the longer we tarry, the more open we lay ourselves to possible attack."

Tabitha shivered at Edmond's side, likely both from cold and fear. He was fighting the urge to place his arm around her shoulders when she took a quick breath and spoke out. "Sir, should someone not warn the commander at Fort Howe as quickly as possible that McIntosh has fallen? Mounted, I could surely stay ahead of danger."

Edmond stiffened. Yes, chances were good that Fuser would order his troops north with no delay, but just because Tabitha was the only one with a horse did not mean she need volunteer for such a perilous assignment.

Before he could protest, the lieutenant turned to her, his face in full shadow beneath his hat. "It was the next thing in my mind, though I hesitated to ask it of you. Is that a risk you are willing to take, madam?"

Edmond shook his head. "Someone else could—"

"If Sergeant Lassiter were to accompany me, it is." She stepped closer to him, and he startled at her suggestion—and the confidence in her tone.

Edmond's admiration for the woman warred with something else—a sickly sense of doubt. Anything could befall them between here and Fort Howe. What if he failed her, as he had failed Evangeline? He sought the first excuse he could seize upon. "Are you certain your mare could withstand our combined weight for that distance?"

Tabitha patted her mount's side. "Cora is stronger than she looks. And I am light."

Indeed, she was. Edmond's stomach muscles clenched at the idea of cradling her for the ride. It had been over a year since he'd held a woman. "We would need to set a fair pace." Though he argued with her, the wistful note that crept into his tone proved he also argued with himself.

"All the more reason to not stand about dithering." The lieutenant tipped his head. "The lady speaks wisely. The two of you shall ride to Fort Howe while we cut through the swamp."

"Aye, sir." He gave a brief nod. Tabitha would be safer on her horse than slogging through the swamp without it, should they send another rider. And if they encountered danger, he would stand against it while sending her away on the fleet mare. "But how will you find your way in the dark?" Edmond meant no disrespect, but the recently arrived South Carolinians had yet to grasp the lay of the land.

"We will help them, sir." Dougal wrapped his fingers around his belt. "I have a fair sense of direction in these parts."

The officer lifted the leather bag he carried. "And I have a compass."

"Very well." As loath as Edmond was to leave his men, they were right. This made the most sense. What made no sense was that proximity to a certain dainty widow affrighted him more than the tangled bog and all its wild creatures—possibly including the human variety. He grasped Dougal's arm. "God-speed. I will see you at the fort."

"That you will." Dougal slapped his shoulder.

Edmond reached for the saddle. After swinging up, he held his hand down to Tabitha, who took it and settled herself astride in front of him. He gathered the reins and called to the bay mare. "Ha." With a jolt of hooves, they were off.

A half moon illuminated the way before them. Dark shadows danced over the path, vying for his vigilance. An owl startled from a branch they passed under, its flurry of wings causing them to duck. Edmond kept the mare to a trot. At that pace, as Tabitha predicted, Cora maintained an unflagging tempo.

78

At length, the black hat in front of him swiveled as Tabitha asked, "Do you think we are safe?"

"As safe as one can be in these parts." He allowed a chuckle to rumble from his chest. "I would not have agreed to take the road otherwise."

"Yet you did so reluctantly." The flatly stated observation did not accuse, and yet Edmond felt the barb to his chest, nonetheless.

"I am ill accustomed to the role of protector." Despite the meaning of his name.

"Yet you fill it valiantly."

Her mirror statement sucked the air from his lungs. "When I give a promise, I aim to see it through."

Her head turned again. "You promised me nothing." Her words were soft, almost breathless.

Warmth started in Edmond's midsection and spread. "If I say I will do something, 'tis a promise."

"Fortunate for me." Tabitha's small hand slid over his forearm that held her snug in the saddle.

His heart rate picked up. He scanned the forest. He mustn't allow her to distract him.

Too late.

Tabitha shifted her weight, causing Edmond an uncomfortable awareness of her soft curves. "Is there no one in your life you watch over? No...woman?"

"My mother. She lives in Darien with her kin." His reply came out tight.

"Scots, then?"

"Yes." Of all the times for a getting acquainted chat...

Tabitha tilted her head. "But your last name is English, so I presume your father was English."

"That is correct. Mrs. Gage, 'tis best if we ride in silence. If we talk the whole way, we have one less sense attuned to danger."

She sniffed. "'Mrs. Gage' now, is it? Very well." She fell into what she probably presumed would be an accusing quiet. But Edmond's chest expanded with a strange urge—to laugh again. Flashes of her spirit only further pricked his admiration.

Finally, he whispered, "What of your family?"

After a moment, she swiveled to answer, also in a whisper. "My parents are in Savannah. My twin sister's husband is a captain of militia in St. George's Parish."

So she had no children. "Why did you not return to Savannah after your husband's death? Why stay in this lonely land?"

Her chest huffed above Edmond's arm. "So my father could marry me off again? No, thank you. No, I will make my own way now. With the help of Dulcie and Cyrus, of course."

"Your servants you lost in the swamp?"

"I did not lose them." Her reply sharpened. "They lost themselves. But I am concerned, wondering if they made it out. And if they search for me. I know you must hasten to the fort, but might we stop on the way? You can be rid of me and free to go about your duty."

Rid of her? The idea set like a heavy pudding in his gut. Somehow, they had formed a bond these past several days. And that brought about greater unease. For obviously, their paths must soon diverge. But not yet. "It makes no sense to take you east after we cross the ferry. Once we get to the fort, I'm sure someone can escort you home."

"I do not cross the ferry."

Edmond stiffened. "But everyone knows River's Bend lies adjacent to Fort Howe."

"River's Bend is no longer my home." Sadness leeched into her soft reply.

"Then where do you live?"

"Across the river. My husband sold River's Bend just before he died, as well as his house in Savannah. After sending the proceeds to his family in England, he most generously left me his cattle lands this side of the Altamaha." The tinge of sarcasm in her words conveyed her true feelings on the matter. "And the log cabin Dulcie and Cyrus live in."

Edmond pulled back on the reins without thinking, fixed as he was on her stunning revelation. He spluttered a good five seconds while Cora stood still. "What kind of man would do such a thing?"

Tabitha angled ever so slightly toward him. "One with a gambler and reckless speculator for a brother-in-law, though the esteemed Lord Riley covered it well."

"He left you destitute? To live with servants?" Had Edmond been fortunate enough to capture a woman of her caliber, back when he had allowed himself to desire such a thing, he would prize her above all else. And he would make certain she knew it, even after his death.

"As I stated, I can only assume he intended me to return to my father. After eleven years." She cringed, then shot a glance back at him as though embarrassed. Of her predicament? Or her age? Edmond would never have guessed it, even though her visage, her bearing, held a canniness the lack of which oft led younger women to err—women such as the one he'd once thought to take to wife. "Edmond?"

He snapped to attention. "Yes?"

"Ought we to ride on to Fort Howe?" Her soft breath fanned his face.

His midsection clenched in a visceral reaction, his heart in an emotional one. He stared into the dark pools of her eyes. "I'm sorry for what you have been through."

"Th-thank you." Her fingers tightened on his arm, then she turned abruptly, as if unsettled by his nearness. As he was by hers.

He snapped the reins, and Cora started forward. How quickly Tabitha Gage had made him forget his mission. That he could not allow, for another woman was counting on him. But his chest burned with hatred for men who used their power to abuse the vulnerable. He had just one more question.

"How could a man be party to dispossessing a widow in such a manner...buying her house and kicking her out?"

Tabitha's back rumbled with a mirthless chuckle. "It did not seem difficult at all for Hugh Jackson."

Edmond stiffened. She'd just spoken the name of the man who had wrought devastation on his own family and future.

~

The evening following their arrival at Fort Howe, Tabitha bent over one of the wounded men who had arrived with the others from Fort McIntosh that morning. Lieutenant Colonel Francis Henry Harris had insisted she rest on his own cot when she and Edmond had ridden in. She had been too tired to argue, falling asleep to the murmur of the men's voices as they discussed the fall of the stockade on the Satilla.

She'd awakened inside the dim blockhouse to the cry of the sentry as the party from the south arrived, filthy and bedraggled after beating their way through the swamp all night. Colonel Harris had declined an escort for Tabitha to return across the river, but upon sight of the wounded soldiers, he had agreed to send a man to fetch Annabelle from River's Bend. She'd arrived an hour later with her box of medicinal herbs and had since been instructing Tabitha in their application.

The slave woman gazed up at her from packing a private's inflamed arm wound with powdered goldenseal root. "You not faint at sight of such things?"

Tabitha blew a puff of air through her nose. "I've never been faint in my life."

Annabelle's dark eyes swept her with fresh admiration. "You just might make it livin' across the river, Miss Tabitha."

The wash of affirmation straightened Tabitha's spine. She actually cared what a slave woman thought of her? She, who had only craved the approval of Savannah's elite? And her father.

Annabelle nudged a roll of linen into her hands. "Then you want to bandage him up?"

With a smile at the soldier, whose expression bordered on worshipful, Tabitha bent to her task. She was just tying off the bandage when a shadow loomed from the open door.

"Mrs. Gage?"

She whirled at her married name spoken in Edmond's deep voice. He stood there holding his hat against his chest, and his lips parted as he took her in. Tabitha smoothed her hand over the striped linen short gown and petticoat Annabelle had brought her, correctly assuming she might be in need of fresh clothing. She'd also managed to subdue her hair beneath a mob cap.

"Uh...ah..." Edmond seemed to have forgotten what he'd come to say. As if to buy time, he gave a nod at Annabelle, whom he had met earlier, then refocused on Tabitha. "I would speak with you a moment."

Tabitha moved away from the man she'd attended and washed her hands with lye soap in the basin. "I'm listening."

So were all the soldiers Edmond perused. "Perhaps we might step outside?"

"Of course." She proceeded him through the door, blinking at the bright sunshine, then turned to face him in the yard. "Annabelle brought news that Dulcie and Cyrus made it home safely."

His countenance lightened. "I'm glad to hear that. Then you will be less anxious to cross the river."

"My mind is eased, yes, and the wounded men do need me.

Annabelle will have to hasten back to River's Bend." Mr. Long had granted her permission to attend the soldiers at Fort Howe, but should Hugh turn up while she was away, the overseer would be hard pressed to explain her absence.

Edmond's shoulders relaxed, and he slipped his hat back on. "You would not object to staying a while?"

"For a few days, no." She glanced around at the activity in the fort's yard. "Though I admit, being the only woman amidst so many men makes me ill at ease."

He grimaced. "I fear more are coming. And you might need to remain more than a few days."

"What?" The word squeaked out more loudly than intended. Some soldiers stirring something in a pot above a small fire a few feet away observed her with interest.

"Shall we walk?" Edmond waited until she gave a nod to take her elbow, guiding her toward the gate. "General McIntosh is sending reinforcements, men from Midway, Darien, and Savannah, hoping to prevent the Loyalists from crossing the Altamaha."

She shuddered as they passed out of the fort. "They are that certain the men who took Fort McIntosh will pursue?"

He nodded. "And when they arrive, we will ride out to meet them."

Tabitha swallowed hard at the notion of Edmond facing the enemy outside the fort walls. Of more men wounded—possibly him. "What if they besiege the fort?" This time, they might not show as much mercy, especially if Colonel Fuser was not in charge.

"We will not let them get that far." Edmond led her to the riverbank and turned to face her, but she couldn't smooth her frown away fast enough. "Do not worry. We will have enough men this time. But you see why 'tis best you remain here until they are driven away."

"I cannot argue with that." Annabelle and Mr. Long would

be safe this side of the river as well. Tabitha released a sigh, something in her chest twisting. She watched a songbird flit about the branches of a blossoming cherry laurel tree, pecking off tiny black berries. "But I must admit, I long for the comforts of home." Resting or performing the most basic personal care was nigh unto impossible with privacy so lacking. "Although..."

"What?" Edmond stepped closer.

She met his gaze. "The cabin across the river is not home. 'Tis River's Bend I long for." Her high-ceilinged room. Her washtub by the fire. Annabelle's cooking.

He frowned. "Could Mr. Jackson not be persuaded to sell you the house?" His face twisted as he said the name, as if he'd eaten a crabapple. He'd gone silent when she told him about Hugh Jackson the night before. Doubtless, the man's reputation preceded him even to Fort Howe. Or maybe 'twas her neediness that repelled him.

"As if I had the money to buy it." Reaching up to pluck some fragrant white blossoms from the cherry tree, Tabitha laughed without mirth. "No, though he will give it to me—if I marry his son." She turned back to him. "Julian."

He grabbed her arm so abruptly that she almost dropped the flowers she'd been gathering to brighten the sickroom. "You cannot do that. Ever. Promise me, Tabitha."

She drew away from him, her heart pounding. "Why? What do you know of Julian Jackson?"

"Only that he is the worst sort of snake you shall ever find in these wilds. Worse than his father. At least Hugh's threats are direct. Julian is the viper who charms before he devours."

At the haze of anger that darkened Edmond's voice and countenance, Tabitha retreated a pace. This was more than a cruel planter's reputation. "What did he do to you?"

Edmond ran his hand over his face, falling silent as he looked away. Finally, he said, "My family had business dealings with theirs, back when my father was a factor—the sales agent for cotton and rice planters."

"Was?" Tabitha blinked.

"Let's just leave it at that." His gaze seared hers. "Trust me when I say you should stay away from them."

Her chin went up. "I already planned to do so, which was why I was out in the swamp chasing cattle—cattle which are now gone. I must find a way to make up the income they would have brought at market."

Edmond cocked his head to one side, brows drawing into a flat line. "Your husband had extensive holdings. I would assume he possessed more cattle than the ten the Loyalists stole."

"You would assume correctly. Originally, two hundred head."

His eyes brightened so quickly, she almost thought she'd imagined his previous ire. "Then I've an idea. All the men coming to Fort Howe will need to be victualed. What if Colonel Harris would purchase cattle from you? Obviously, it would have to wait until the Loyalists are driven back, but after that, he might send men to herd some cows with your brand back to the fort."

She sucked in a quick breath. "You think he would do that?"

"Why not?" Edmond shifted his weight, and a muscle in his jaw twitched. "I think the question is more whether you would be willing to supply the Patriots."

Tabitha stiffened a moment, then relaxed her shoulders as understanding dawned. "Ah. The question Captain Winn posed to me at Fort McIntosh…I never answered it."

"I think it would be fair to say I've seen you play both sides." He watched her closely.

"A matter of survival. Being a man, you wouldn't understand." Tabitha dropped her head and closed her eyes for a moment. What *did* she truly believe? She looked back up at him. "I never had to speak or decide for myself before. Because my father was a Loyalist, I was a Loyalist. Because my husband was a Loyalist, I was a Loyalist. I accepted that because that brought the most comfort in my life. When my sister threatened that comfort with her Patriot ideals, I was angry with her. But I understand now. I've seen power abused one too many times. Yes, Edmond, I will supply the Patriots."

There was that smile that stopped her heart. He cupped her arm and ran his hand up and down her sleeve, and blood rushed through her limbs. "Then I will speak to the colonel."

"That would be..." Tabitha sagged. "An answer to prayer."

Again. And again, Edmond had been part of it.

CHAPTER NINE

MID-MARCH, 1777

E dmond helped Tabitha out of the ferry boat that had just brought her across the Altamaha River about two weeks after their arrival at Fort Howe. He had swum their horses over and met her on the other side. The mounts now waited on the bank.

Tabitha looked back at the stockade as Edmond paid the ferryman. "I cannot believe I tended Lachlan McIntosh himself. And he was pleased with my care."

The fifty-year-old general, brother of the man who had commanded Edmond's troop last year and acknowledged head of the clan that had settled around Darien, as well as a tax collector, surveyor, and justice of the peace, held thousands of acres south of River's Bend. 'Twas no wonder Tabitha had found his gallantries flattering. But now her glowing brown eyes swung to Edmond as if she sought his approval too.

He did approve. Tabitha had handled the fresh wave of wounded men—including their fearless general, who had been struck by a musket ball in the heel—with as much fortitude as the slave woman she'd again summoned from River's Bend. She'd not even quailed at helping prepare for burial the twelve soldiers they lost defending the river crossing. But if he wanted to shield his heart, he couldn't afford to show his admiration. Not when he'd just been consigned to helping her again, once again placing him in close proximity to her.

He'd thought after arranging the contract for her cattle, Tabitha would be taken care of. That at least the income would buy her enough time to make a plan to get back on her feet. Instead, rather than being promoted for taking down three Loyalists in the fray—including the officer proudly mounted on Maximus—Colonel Harris had assigned him to aid the widow in rounding up a dozen head of cattle to fill the soldiers' bellies. At least Edmond had retrieved his horse.

The way his pulse raced as Tabitha laid her hand on his arm gave testament to the dangers of remaining close to her. Women weren't to be trusted. And ever since she had revealed her unfortunate connection to the Jacksons, Edmond had been torn between a fierce urge to protect her and the desire to ride as far away as he could as fast as possible. The memories the mere mention of the Jackson name stirred made him sick. How could he embroil himself again with such wicked men?

"I cannot thank you enough for speaking to your colonel on my behalf." Her lashes fluttered, and she looked away as if embarrassed by her own gratitude.

"I'm just thankful the new commander agreed to honor his predecessor's commitment." Lieutenant Colonel Harris had been relieved by Colonel Stirk with fifty of his men from the Second Georgia Battalion. While the British had retreated toward St. Augustine, an increased number of scouts would patrol the area south of the Altamaha for some time, making it possible for Tabitha to return home—and Cyrus and Edmond to round up some of her cattle. For which he was less than thankful. Why couldn't Colonel Stirk have sent someone else?

Tabitha scanned his face. "But you would rather be with your men."

How did she do that? He thought himself stoic, but she seemed to discern his every thought. He led her to their horses. "If it means helping you make a start here, I am happy to oblige."

"A start that does not include Julian Jackson." Her gaze fixed on him as he secured her stirrup and held out his hand. She took it.

"Yes." He tightened his jaw and boosted her up, only releasing his breath once she was mounted. He swung onto Max, and they started down the Old Post Road. But he couldn't let the subject go. "He has an ulterior motive, you know."

"What?" She shot a glance over her shoulder.

"Julian. Everything he does is calculated. If your husband already sold his father the plantation and he did not leave you an income, what does Julian stand to gain?"

Tabitha huffed. "Me?"

Edmond gave his head a quick shake. "The man is a notorious womanizer. Why would he settle down with..." His voice trailed off as Tabitha's scarlet countenance evidenced his blunder.

"A penniless widow half a dozen years his senior?"

"That was not what I was about to say." And he never would have guessed she had passed thirty.

"But it was what you were thinking, was it not?" She tossed her head. "You must consider me a fool to boot. Of course, it already occurred to me that the Jacksons are playing some sort of long game...probably having to do with the land. Maybe they want the cattle. They have neither south of the river, after all."

"I would never think you a fool." Impetuous, perhaps. Headstrong, no doubt. But never a fool. "It sounds as though you have already discerned the focus of his motives. You must guard against giving him any leverage, Tabitha."

"Yes, *Sergeant.*" Her narrowed eyes shot daggers at him, then she tapped her heels on Cora's sides and trotted ahead.

Edmond released a heavy sigh and followed her onto a path through the woods. Words had always been his shortcoming—written, but even spoken ones. She could tie him up with her tongue and render him defenseless in about five seconds. He should have heeded his own inner voice of caution and refrained from expressing any concern for the feisty widow. He would find her cattle and leave her to her own devices.

Then why did he fight to urge to apologize all the way to her cabin?

A mulatto woman in linsey-woolsey clothing with a kerchief on her head came running from the porch as they rode up in the yard. Chickens scattered at their approach, some flying up into the nearby trees with a squawking and fluttering of russet wings. Tabitha swung down from her mare before Edmond could dismount to assist her. As he led Maximus closer, Tabitha and the young woman embraced with cries of greeting. Tabitha's obvious affection for her servant softened Edmond's resolution to remain detached.

"I'm so glad you are all right." The woman held Tabitha's arm. "I knew we should never have split up to cover both sides of that ridge."

"I'm glad *you're* safe. I was so worried until your mother told me you'd made it home."

"And you got caught in a siege? Oh, Miss Tabitha!" The woman covered her mouth.

"All is well. Sergeant Lassiter here came to my rescue." Tabitha turned to him as he led Maximus closer, but her manner was stiff, and her tone held an edge. "Rather unwillingly, as I recall."

Edmond frowned. "You had my man at gunpoint."

"So I did." Tabitha chuckled.

"I think I've proved my trustworthiness since." Was she that irritated by his questions about Julian that she would revisit the enmity of the day they met?

"And so you have." She proceeded to explain to her servant, whose widened gaze swung between them. "Sergeant Lassiter has arranged a contract for us to supply beef to Fort Howe. He is here to help Cyrus round up a dozen cows. Edmond, this is Dulcie."

Edmond lifted his hat. "Ma'am."

Dulcie shook her head and cast a slightly censorious glance at Tabitha. "Sounds like the Lord's provision to me."

Edmond stiffened. She thought God had sent *him* to help them? Could the instinct to protect mean he was being given a second chance to prove himself?

"I knew you would say that. I'm not sure the sergeant agrees." Dismissing both him and God, Tabitha glanced toward the cattle pen where a single wiry stallion nibbled grass on the other side of a split-rail fence. She spoke again before Edmond had a chance to respond. "Where is Cyrus?"

"Burning off some land he be clearing. He be back soon. Come in. I just set some squirrel stew to simmer."

To Tabitha's credit, she did not so much as wince.

Edmond took Cora's reins. "I will see to the horses."

Dulcie jerked her chin. "There's a creek just past the house, if you want to water them."

When Tabitha walked toward the cabin without acknowledging him, Edmond tugged the horses toward the water, his chest tight. Was Tabitha that offended over his comment about Julian, or did she feel just as ambiguous about relying on him as he did about being relied upon?

No, that wasn't right. He did all in his power to convince his superiors, his men, and what remained of his family of his trustworthiness. It was his inexplicable connection to a woman that had him rattled. And not just any woman, but one who stirred him in unexpected ways. One he admired.

A woman Julian Jackson wanted.

He let the horses drink, then allowed them to forage along the banks. He could stand a few minutes to collect his thoughts. He couldn't risk a repeat of the past. He was right to guard his heart.

He sat on a fallen log in the sun and lowered his head into his hands, releasing a heavy breath. He'd just closed his eyes when the leaves rustled and a sharp pain shot through his ankle.

His eyes popping open, Edmond jerked and yelped. Then he leapt up—for slithering away into the saw palmettos was a two-foot-long gray-and-tan snake with segmented rattles on its tail.

~

"That sergeant seems nice." As she stirred the stew, Dulcie smirked over her shoulder at Tabitha. "And handsome."

Tabitha had no call to notice—much less, remark on—Edmond Lassiter's appearance. The way the sunlight struck the red in his hair and the amber tints in his brown eyes. Those laugh lines beside his mouth. His broad shoulders, trim hips, long legs. Indeed, none of that. If marriage to her father's peer had not taught her to pay no heed to younger men, Edmond's disbelief over Julian's interest in her should.

Tabitha sniffed as she placed several clay mugs on the rough pine table and began to fill each with cider from a pitcher Dulcie had given her. "He is only here because his colonel ordered him to be. Once he gets shed of his duty to us, he'll be gone."

She'd known from the first that duty and chivalry motivated Edmond's protectiveness. But after they had faced down the Loyalists together, she thought she'd glimpsed genuine admiration in his eyes. She had dared to assume his intervention for the beef contract arose out of personal regard, but Edmond's reserve this morning even in the face of her gratitude had revealed where his true motives lay. He'd clearly resented being saddled with her. And the moment she grasped that, she'd chided herself for her error in trusting him.

"Do not be so sure of that." Leaving the ladle in the pot, Dulcie went to fetch a stack of wooden bowls from the sideboard. "I see the way he looks at you. And if he be the way the Good Lord intends to provide—"

"How does he look at me?" Tabitha hastened over to take the bowls—all but one, which Dulcie kept to fill with stew.

"When you walked away from him earlier? Like a lost puppy." She chuckled and handed Tabitha the serving.

That couldn't be right. Dulcie must have mistaken regret for yearning.

"I jus' wish I could remember why his name sounds so familiar." A dimple of concentration tucked into Dulcie's smooth cheek.

"Perhaps you have met him before." On her comings and goings across the river, 'twouldn't be so unusual.

Dulcie shook her head. "No, but his last name...it seems I have heard it. But I cannot recall..."

The door banged open, and Tabitha almost dropped the stew.

Edmond braced himself on either side of the frame, his face ashen.

Her heart nearly stopped. "Loyalists?" It was all she could do to transfer the bowl to the board.

"Pygmy rattler."

"What?" The word whistled from her constricting throat.

"Where?" Dulcie beat her to the sergeant's side, supporting him as he stumbled forward. She helped him to the bench, where he collapsed and extended his left leg.

"My ankle." He reached for the black leather gaiter buckled over his stockings between shoe and breeches but quickly sat up again, squeezing his eyes shut.

"He is going to be sick." Dulcie snatched a platter from the table, brushing off the cornbread that had been on it, and held it out in front of Edmond.

He leaned forward and heaved, but only thin juices came up. He groaned.

Dulcie put her hand on his head. "We need to get that gaiter off, Miss Tabitha."

Jerking into motion, Tabitha knelt before Edmond and unbuckled the leather wrap. It fell away to reveal a spot of blood soaking his stocking between the boney protrusion and the tendon that ran up the back of his leg. She removed Edmond's heavy leather shoe and let it drop before rolling down his stocking. When he sucked in his breath, she removed the woolen garment as gently as possible. Casting it away, she studied his discolored skin.

"I see but one mark. And his ankle is swelling."

Dulcie had put aside the trencher and now moved over to the sideboard. "Good thing he had the extra covering. It may be that saves him."

"I'm right here, you know." Edmond's wry comment might have elicited a smile under different circumstances.

"And that is where we want to keep you." Tabitha intended no double meaning, but if he assumed one, she would hardly pause now to correct him. She took his heel onto her knee and looked up at the servant, who returned with a wet cloth. "What do we do?"

"First, we wash it." She bent toward Edmond, but Tabitha extended her hand.

"Let me do that." He wouldn't even be here if it weren't for her. The least she could do was tend his wound with as much care as she'd given the soldiers at the fort. Dulcie passed her the cool cloth, and Tabitha held it over the swollen flesh, wincing as Edmond stiffened. "Sorry."

"You have to cut it." His tight voice drew her alarmed gaze upward. "Let the poison out."

"No." Dulcie's sharp retort made them both startle.

Edmond glared at her. "'Tis what a soldier said who got bitten by a cottonmouth."

She shook her head. "My mother doesn't hold with that. She has herbs for snakebites the Creek people used."

The muscles in Edmond's neck strained. His knuckles whitened on the bench. "The venom has to be bled out."

"A poultice is your only chance. A man might not die from the bite of a pygmy rattler, but you could lose your foot. Maybe part of your leg." Dulcie's gaze swung to Tabitha, who had frozen in cold horror at her words. This was the world she'd been dropped into from her coddled perch high in society— one of lethal enemies and venomous serpents. Where one must be on daily alert merely to survive. "I will ride for the medicine."

"You can hardly sit a horse, much less swim one across the river. And there are so many soldiers in the area and no telling how they would treat you. They will leave me alone." Tabitha got to her feet, handing the cloth to Dulcie. "If I need to, I can tell them who I am." Or who she had been.

Edmond's hand shot out and grasped her wrist. "No. You cannot go." The statement was no less forceful for its wheeziness. He was shaking, and perspiration popped out on his forehead.

Tabitha drew her lower lip up. He worried about her encountering the Jacksons. Gently, she pried his fingers from her flesh. "'Twill be fine. I will be in and out so quickly no one but Annabelle will know I was there."

CHAPTER TEN

In the warm kitchen of River's Bend, Tabitha patted first her right pocket tied beneath her petticoat, then her left. "St. John's wort root for poultice. Virginia bugleweed for tea. Thank you, Annabelle." She would hug the older woman, but it might shock her into a faint, and they were standing awfully close to the big brick hearth where a turkey roasted over small orange flames. The hem of Tabitha's petticoats still hung heavy with dampness after her crossing of the river, even atop Cora, but she had no time to linger near the warm fire.

Dulcie's mother eyed her, her brow winkled beneath her turban. "What you gonna do 'bout them cows now?"

"I have no idea." She had not thought past getting the herbs back for Edmond. Thankfully, Cora had still been saddled in the cabin yard. She now waited at the hitching post at the back door. "I must go."

"Jus' a minute." Annabelle swung around and took up a thick cloth. She slid a paddle beneath a loaf of her crusty, fragrant bread and removed it from the beehive oven. After wrapping the loaf in the cloth and putting it into a canvas sack, she held it out to Tabitha.

She stepped back with her hands raised. "I cannot take that." Nothing here belonged to her anymore. It all belonged to Hugh Jackson.

"Yes'm, you can. You got extra mouths to feed." The cook's pitying expression reminded Tabitha that she was reduced to charity until she could bring in that payment from the fort.

She took the bread. And she did slip an arm around Annabelle then. "Thank you."

The cook's eyes widened, then she patted Tabitha's arm as she pulled away. "I be prayin' for the sergeant...and for you."

Her words slowed Tabitha's steps to the door. She'd once thought herself magnanimous for reading the Bible to the River's Bend workers. At Dulcie's urging, they had appointed an hour every week for Tabitha to share Scriptures from the front porch. But she had read the words without listening to them, thinking only of the favor they purchased. The slaves had absorbed them more than she. Now she had to rely on Annabelle's prayers. And Dulcie's.

And she had to come and go by the back door, like a slave herself. She jerked it open and gasped.

On the stoop stood Julian Jackson.

His handsome face broke into a grin. "I thought I recognized your mare. What are you doing here, Mrs. Gage?" He wore a green woolen frock of a country gentleman with striped waistcoat, brown breeches, and riding boots.

Tabitha clutched the neck of the sack against her waist. "I was just visiting Annabelle. I'm going now."

"Nonsense." He swept off his cocked hat. "Our meeting is fortuitous, for 'tis you I seek."

She lifted her chin. "I no longer reside here. As I said, I must be leaving now." She sought to cut around him, but he blocked her way. Her pulse accelerated.

"I know. When last I came, Mr. Long told me you had taken

a trip, but he pretended not to know where. Not very far, it would seem." His dark eyes gleamed.

"I'm afraid I'm in something of a hurry."

"As am I." He planted himself squarely in her path. "To hear your answer."

"My answer to what?"

"To my request to call upon you, of course." He gave a slight bow. When he straightened, the amber stickpin in his stock glistened in the midafternoon sun—like Edmond's eyes. "How can I do so if I know not where you are?"

"There is no need. I am not ready to receive callers. I'm sure you will understand." Gritting her teeth, Tabitha pushed past him and hurried down the steps. She must get to Edmond.

Julian followed and caught her arm. "When will you be ready?"

Tabitha pulled back. It took everything in her not to jerk away and to maintain her decorum. "If you must know, I do not anticipate ever marrying again."

His eyes narrowed. "You may wish to rethink that."

His presumption made her forget she no longer had the right to be haughty. She strode over to Cora, who stood beside Julian's sleek stallion. "Why would I do that?"

"Because if you are uninterested in the honor I bestow upon you, my father will have no choice but to call in the loan."

Tabitha froze in the act of securing the bread in her saddle-bag. "What loan?"

"The one your husband took out from a lender in Darien when he purchased your land south of the river from the original grantee." Julian watched her without an ounce of compassion lightening his expression or his matter-of-fact tone. "It seems he grew delinquent with his payments. Interest does accrue."

Tabitha gaped at him. This could not be. How many other

surprises had Lord Riley left for her? "What has it to do with your father?"

Julian tucked his long, slender fingers in the edge of his waistcoat. "My father has dealings with the same man, who, it seems, was in a panic upon learning of Lord Riley's death, knowing he would not see another shilling. Father purchased the note as a favor to you, so the man would not be breathing down your neck. As I said, he is prepared to forgive the sum should you reconsider my suit."

Tabitha's resolve hardened. This was a bribe, not an act of benevolence. "I will pay you." With jerky movements, she stepped forward to untether Cora. The mare snorted and blew, sensing her agitation. "I just need a week or so."

Julian tipped back his head and laughed. "You have three hundred pounds buried somewhere? Jewels to sell, perhaps?"

"Three hundred pounds?" Tabitha mentally flailed on the cusp of a black abyss. The sale of a dozen head of cattle would not even cover half that sum. Cyrus had told her she might expect ten pounds for each cow. As for jewels, those had slowly been sold off to prop up Henry's crumbling family estate in England.

What had her husband done to her? She turned her face away. She couldn't, wouldn't, let this man witness her distress.

"Your land south of the river..." Julian's tone had assumed a speculative undertone. "Tis undeveloped wilderness, not worth much, but my father might be persuaded to take it in settlement of the debt."

She snapped her head back toward him. "And leave me homeless?"

His brows elevated. "Ah, so that *is* where you are staying. I thought as much. Well, as you know, you can have both home and husband, should you choose." He tugged on the narrow waist of his frock coat and straightened to his full height. The magnanimous expression vanished—in its place, a glimmer of malice. "Most women would be grateful."

Tabitha took hold of the saddle. "I will get your money." One way or another.

She mounted up and rode out of the yard as though the hounds of hell were after her. Because they just might be.

$\sim$

On the crinkly mattress of the cot that the women had helped him to before Tabitha left, Edmond alternated between chills and sweats. Dulcie kept a cloth on his ankle that must be cold, though he could hardly say given the numbness and tingling radiating up his leg and down into his stiff foot. His stomach and guts clenched, and he had cast up his accounts twice now. Dulcie kept sending him concerned glances. She blurred a bit around the edges.

Cyrus had come in with the smell of wood smoke and peeked at his ankle. He seemed a good sort, not put out with finding a strange Patriot ranger recumbent on his bed. "I think this a dry bite," he had said as he rewrapped the bandage. "That means not much venom. I seen something like this before on a slave clearin' a rice field." His pronouncement had lifted some of the weight from Edmond's chest. After downing some stew, Cyrus had gone back out.

Where was Tabitha? That his need had sent her into danger left a bitter taste in his mouth.

He had been foolish, distracted by her, or he never would have sat on that log without checking the area first.

At last, footsteps clambered up the front steps and across the porch, and the door flew open. Tabitha's dark hair straggled down from her bun, sans cap. Her wild gaze cut to him. "How is he?"

"Worse. But Cyrus says it might not be too bad. Did you get the herbs?" Dulcie cleared a spot on the table.

"Yes. Your mother gave me instructions for a poultice and a tea." Hurrying forward, Tabitha slipped her hands through the slits in her over-petticoat and tugged out two pouches.

Edmond's awareness swam in and out as the women conferred over the table, mixing and stirring.

"I know you be worried, Miss Tabitha, but take a deep breath." Dulcie's sharp whisper cut into his consciousness. "You're trembling. You can't help him unless you stay calm."

She was that concerned for him? Edmond lifted his head.

"Of course I am worried. But 'tis not just about the sergeant." Her voice wavered.

"What, then?"

Tabitha shook her head. "I will tell you later."

Edmond's neck muscles gave out, and he fell back against the pillow. Dulcie came over a few minutes later, explaining that she would apply a poultice and bandage to his wound. She worked at the foot of the bed while Tabitha approached with a mug.

She bent over him, a tentative smile on her face. "I made a tea that should help. Can you rise up enough to drink some?"

Edmond struggled to find leverage, but his arms failed him. Dry bite or no, enough of the foul poison had entered his system to make him helpless as a babe. Cursed weakness.

"'Tis all right. Let me help." Tabitha slipped her hip onto the edge of the cot and her arm beneath his shoulders.

With her assistance, he was able to raise his head enough to sip the bitter brew. He made a face.

She chuckled. "Apparently, it needs more honey."

When he had swallowed enough to satisfy her, she rested his head back on the pillow, but she did not leave. She asked for a cloth from Dulcie, who was finishing her own ministrations, and wiped his forehead.

He was finding it hard to get a good breath. "Thank you. Thank you both." Hopefully, he whispered his gratitude loudly enough for Dulcie to also hear before she moved away, greeting her husband as he came in the door.

Tabitha laid her hand on Edmond's temple—checking for signs of fever? Her brow puckered. "I am just sorry this happened. You would not have been here if you weren't trying to help me."

Edmond caught her gaze. "What happened at River's Bend?"

"Why...?" She drew her hand back, a flash of wariness crossing her face. "I saw Annabelle and got the herbs, of course." When she moved to stand up, Edmond tangled his fingers in her petticoat, keeping her beside him.

"Tell me what happened."

Tabitha's lips parted as she drew in a quick breath. Dulcie and Cyrus stilled beside the table, looking their way. Tabitha glanced between them and Edmond. Slowly, she sank back down on the mattress.

"I saw Julian."

Edmond's chest tightened even more. "Did he threaten you?"

"He said..." Her fingers massaged the mug she held, and her gaze skittered away. "He said his father assumed Lord Riley's land debt of three hundred pounds."

Dulcie gasped. "I thought this land was paid for long ago."

Stepping forward, Cyrus balled his fists. "He demanded payment?"

She glanced at him. "Payment or courtship."

"No." Edmond's protest rasped so harshly that Tabitha drew back.

"I told him I would pay him, but I have no idea how."

Edmond licked his dry lips. "Send to the fort. Tell the colonel what happened and ask for a man to replace me on the cattle drive." When he struggled to sit up, she slipped another pillow behind his back. The room spun, but he pressed his eyes closed until his vision cleared. He had to do what he could to help these people.

"I can go." Cyrus brought over the bench from this side of the table so he and Dulcie could sit close to the bed. He leaned forward, forearms on his thick legs, clasping his hands. "I will go tonight."

"And then what?" The despair in Tabitha's face twisted Edmond's heart. "Even if we sell the cattle, it shan't nearly be enough."

"We will think of something." Dulcie touched her shoulder. "And we will seek wisdom from above. When we pray, God promises to answer."

Tabitha dipped her head and spoke so softly, Edmond strained to hear. "Julian suggested I might trade this land to settle the debt."

Dulcie snatched her hand back, her eyes going wide. "You mustn't do that, Miss Tabitha."

Tabitha's gaze pleaded for understanding. "I know this is your home, Dulcie, and the only one I have now, too, and I told Julian I would find a way to pay him instead. But short of a miracle..."

"Then a miracle is jus' what we should pray for." Cyrus's deep voice rumbled with conviction. "Not jus' because this is our home, but because I heard on the grapevine that the Jacksons wanna clear this land up to the river. Plant rice. Buy more slaves. Lots more slaves." He shook his head. "More of our people in bondage, and under the worst conditions."

Dulcie groaned.

Tabitha blinked at Cyrus. "I guess I should not be surprised."

"There's something else." Edmond frowned as he attempted to pin down the elusive threat that had been dancing around his awareness. One that required him to trust that Tabitha had meant what she said about supporting the Patriot cause. He shifted on his pillow.

Tabitha's brows bunched together. "You should rest."

"The Jacksons are the only Loyalists left in these parts." Edmond leaned on his one shoulder. Swallowed back the bile that rose to his throat. "If they owned this land next to the river crossing, it would give the Brits a foothold."

Cyrus put his hands on his knees, his eyes flashing. "They could try again to take the fort."

Tabitha's hand fluttered to her chest. "You mean work with the East Florida Rangers?"

"Do you not think it possible?" Edmond sought her gaze.

Her slender throat bobbed as she swallowed. "Not only possible. Probable. They were active in politics whereas my husband was not. I had not even considered the military angle. If they take Fort Howe, they could launch an invasion into the settled lands north of the river."

"Exactly." He sagged back on the pillows with a small nod.

Her slight frame shuddered, and she ran her hand over her face. "I cannot let that happen. But how? How am I to stop them?"

Dulcie straightened and lifted her head. "Miss Tabitha, you are not alone. We will find a way together."

Cyrus gave a grave nod.

Tabitha's lashes fluttered, and tears filled her eyes as she studied the faces of her servants, more resolute than many a man Edmond had battled beside. And Tabitha's battle to trust them was equally evident. As was his, to trust *her*. But if they were to defeat their common enemies, they must work together.

"Count me in." Edmond slid his hand across the covers to nudge hers.

"But this isn't your fight." Tendrils of dark hair skimmed her shoulders as she shook her head. She wiped her sleeve across her eyes.

Oh, if only she knew. He couldn't tell her why it mattered so much that the Jacksons be held to account. That history not repeat itself. His failure was too shameful to share. Edmond settled for the simplest answer. "Their loyalties make it my fight."

A spark lit her eyes. "Then we'd best get you well."

His heart thundered a warning, but he pushed it aside. He would find a way to help her while keeping his emotions out of it. This was his second chance to see justice done. This time, he would not be too late.

CHAPTER ELEVEN

E dmond drifted into an uneasy sleep in the wee hours, dreaming a bullet nicked his heel. No, that was wrong. That had been General McIntosh. But his ankle alternately ached and shot sharp pains. Then someone dropped their ramrod with a clatter that shot him upright.

He blinked in the lingering darkness—not of the forest, but of Tabitha's cabin. A dark shape froze near the fireplace.

"Sorry. I dropped the poker." Tabitha's tone hinted at a grimace.

Edmond fell back against the pillows with a groan. He'd barely managed to nod off after being awake most of the night, listening to rain on the roof. "What you are doing?" That someone was about this early was not the surprise, but for the past two mornings, it had been Dulcie, coming across the dogtrot around dawn to start their morning meal. The servant had moved into the other room of the cabin with Tabitha, leaving this one to Edmond two days prior, when Dougal came from the fort and departed with Cyrus in Edmond's stead.

"Letting Dulcie sleep. She has worked much too hard since we have been here." She retrieved the poker, and the curfew over the embers clunked in the fireplace as she used the tip to move it aside. "I shall warm the hasty pudding. And I thought I would make coffee."

"Coffee?" Edmond perked up at that. How long had it been since he'd had a cup?

"I brought some with me from River's Bend." With a lift of her skirt, she got down on her hands and knees in front of the hearth. "Too bad I did not also bring a bellows." Tabitha began to blow on the embers, her breath coaxing them to life.

"Have you any idea what a long process it is to make coffee?" He'd seen the officers about the task at the fort. They had always grumbled over the lack of servants to do the chore.

"Yes, which is why I'm up—" Her response terminated in a fit of coughing and choking, and she sat back on her haunches, waving her hand before her.

He leaned up on his elbow. "What happened?"

"The ashes...blew back on me." Tabitha ran her hands over her face and hair, then brushed them down her bodice, mumbling as she did. "Good for nothing...stupid...useless..."

The bitterness in her voice brought Edmond's brow down. She was talking not about the ashes, as he'd first thought—but about herself. "'Tis a mistake easy enough to make, even for someone accustomed to the task. What matters is that you're here to give your servant a break. 'Tis more than most mistresses would do."

"Well, I cannot be most mistresses anymore, can I?" She rested her hands on her knees, her face turned toward him, though he still could not make out her features. "If we're going to survive, we're all going to have to pull our weight. I still think I should have gone with Cyrus. Two men are not enough."

Edmond scoffed. "And get captured again by the British? Is that what you want?"

"Of course not." She dropped onto her hands and blew

again, more evenly this time. Finally, the embers sparked to life, and she added kindling to encourage the blaze.

"You have done a lot here. Helping Dulcie plant the garden…" Two days ago, they set out peas, beets, beans, cucumbers, and radishes in the drizzle while Edmond had watched from the porch, simmering over his invalidism. Yesterday, they planted corn. "Not to mention all you have done around the cabin."

The growing light flickered on Tabitha's homey touches. Of an evening, she'd laid out embroidered linens and adorned the table and shelves with blossoms in pottery mugs. A framed sampler she had stitched leaned on the rough wooden mantel, its precision and brightness a bittersweet reminder of her former life.

Her hand pressed to her back as she rose gave evidence of the more painful result of her labors. "Yes, and it will be another long day getting the flax in. And on not much sleep. At the very least, I need a cup of coffee first."

Edmond struggled to a seated position. At the sharp pain that darted up his leg, his breath whistled in. "You cannot work in that far field without someone on guard."

With a grunt, Tabitha lifted the heavy black pot that held the porridge onto the iron arm over the fireplace. "Dulcie says it can wait no longer." She moved the kettle over the now-crackling flames.

Would she learn to spin the flax into clothing too? Was it truly possible for a woman bred to comfort and exalted station to transform herself into a frontierswoman? Or would her industry flag under tedium and her determination break under trials?

"I've had no coffee in weeks." Tabitha brushed off her petticoat. "'Tis a small comfort, but a comfort, nonetheless."

Edmond wasn't letting the previous topic go that easily. "I will go out to the field with you." The least he could do was sit with his rifle on a log—one without a serpent lurking beneath it this time.

She faced him, shaking her head. "Tis too soon. You shouldn't be walking."

"I should make it just fine with the crutch Cyrus cut for me." He tipped his head toward the heavy branch with a split in the top leaning against the wall.

Tabitha pursed her lips. "How *do* you feel?"

The ready lie on Edmond's lips died the moment his gaze swung back to her. He couldn't help it—he spluttered out a laugh.

"What?" Her hand went to her hip.

"Your face..." He encircled his own with a wave of his hand. "You have ashes..."

Her mouth tightened, and she snatched up a cloth from the table and ran it from forehead to chin. "Better?"

"Well, yes, but your hair..." Edmond rubbed his jaw in an attempt to hide his smile, as his amusement only seemed to irritate her more.

She flung down the cloth and barked out a laugh. "I must look ridiculous."

"Like a spirit from the netherworld." How refreshing—a woman capable of laughing at herself. She surely had possessed a vibrant sense of humor in better times.

Still chuckling, Tabitha pulled on the tie that held the end of her braid and shook her dark hair loose. It fell over her shoulders in rippling waves, softening her face, making her look like a girl, and Edmond forgot all about ashes. And humor. As she ran her fingers through the tresses, he averted his gaze.

"You were telling me how you feel."

"Well enough." Apart from a quickly increasing need to answer the call of nature—which he could hardly do with her present.

"Truly?" Her nimble fingers worked her hair back into a braid.

Even though he did not sense much change, he could hardly say so if he intended to accompany them to the field. "The swelling seems down this morning."

"I will check soon as I light the candle." Another thing she had brought from River's Bend. Edmond couldn't say he missed the smoking and stink of the pine knots poor settlers oft-times burned as a cheap source of illumination.

"No need. I'm sure Dulcie will be in soon." He shifted.

Tabitha stiffened and dropped her hands. "I am just as capable with herbs as Dulcie."

"You are, but you're busy." And Dulcie's nearness did not make him lose his breath the way Tabitha's did. The fresh, lemony scent of her hair simultaneously twisted his gut and reminded him that whatever her current circumstances, she was far above him in station.

With a sniff, she caught up a tin candleholder. "I would hardly prioritize the coffee above your health." She leaned closer to the fire to light the wick, set the candle on the table, and gave the hasty pudding a quick stir. Then she wet a cloth in the basin on the sideboard and hurried to his side. Tabitha opened the shutters over the bed, allowing dawn's gray light, the twitter of early songbirds, and cool, damp air smelling of the river into the chamber.

Edmond sighed as she sat down beside him, the curve of her hip pressing into his leg.

Holding his foot up, she gently unwound the bandage and extended the candle toward his ankle. "'Tis still discolored, though a bit less swollen, perhaps. It needs a fresh poultice."

"It can wait until after we break our fast." Anything to get her off his bed. Did she not even think of the impropriety of them being in here alone?

"No need." In her hurry, she clunked the candle down on

the upturned stump that served as a bedside table. Wax splattered, and the flame flickered.

Edmond caught her arm. "Not now. Pass me that crutch." When she gave a little huff, he added, "Please."

She lifted her brows to enhance a pointed look. "You ought not to be walking around."

Edmond's patience thinned. "Would you prefer I use the chamber pot?"

"Oh." Her eyes widened. "I will step out."

"No. Hand me the crutch." He did not mean to sound that brusque, but she wasn't listening.

Tabitha stood and held out the crutch, gaze averted. And thankfully, this time, she let him get up on his own. But the pain shooting up his leg made him pause and swallow a moan. Her eyes shot to his. "You are not better."

"I am fine."

"I'm going to help you to the door. And you will not argue." Tabitha whisked under his left shoulder, wrapping her arm around his waist.

He hated to rely on her. She only let him go after opening the door into the dogtrot. He made it to the end of the breezeway, but that was far enough, and thankfully, Dulcie did not come out while he was about his personal business.

By the time he returned to the main cabin, green coffee beans roasted on an iron spider over the flames and Tabitha was mashing something in the mortar with the pestle. She jerked her head to the bench, which she had pulled out. "Sit there."

He did so, leaning the crutch against the table. The thing inflicted as much harm as it helped, gouging out a deeper groove in his armpit.

She brought the mortar around to his side, along with a fresh strip of linen, and bent to unwrap the old bandage.

When she smoothed some of the salve onto his wound,

Edmond sucked in his breath and gripped the sides of the bench. "If this was a dry bite, I cannot imagine what a real one would have felt like."

She shot him a knowing glance. "Mm-hm. I knew it still hurt."

"I cannot sit about while you women work yourselves to death." A sizzle accompanied his words.

Tabitha wiped her fingers on the cloth, grabbed a wooden spoon from beside him, and whirled to stir her coffee beans, which were beginning to turn yellow and expand. "Very well. I have a job for you."

"What is that?" Anything to help—and keep his eyes off her pleasing form as she scurried about, striped bodice laced tight and petticoats swaying.

"You can grind my coffee beans. I have no grinder here, and I am loathe to mash them in that mortar." She turned back, putting the spoon down and taking up the length of linen.

"Happy to oblige." Edmond held himself stiff as she wrapped his leg.

She shot him a relieved look. "Thank you. Too bad Mary Musgrove still doesn't have a trading post just across the road. I have thought of so many things I need, and I can hardly keep going back and taking things from River's Bend."

"'Tis no problem. I daresay it will take me half the time it would take you."

"And will not cost me money I do not have." She tied off the ends of the linen with a satisfied purse of her lips.

"Cyrus and Dougal should be back soon."

He prayed they had not run into any British stragglers. But even if they returned today with a dozen head of cattle, Tabitha would need a much larger sum to settle her debt and get the Jacksons out of her life. And then she'd need a steady stream of income if she was to make it on her own.

Edmond rubbed his chin, whiskers rasping beneath his

fingers. He needed a shave. He was as bristly—and probably as pungent—as a bear. What he wouldn't give for a good dunk in the creek.

A sudden burning scent made him straighten. "I think your coffee beans are ready."

Tabitha turned from packing up her herbs to check the contents of the spider. "You have a nose for coffee, Sergeant Lassiter. They are just right." She wrapped a rag around the handle of the flat skillet and raked the crackling, steaming beans, now a golden brown, into a wooden bowl. "I will let you transfer the proper portions." She wiped off the mortar and pestle and placed them in front of him, then slid him the wooden bowl.

While Tabitha set the board, Edmond crushed the beans, but he'd barely cracked the shells before he wrinkled his nose. "I still smell something."

"Oh no!" Tabitha's hand flew to her mouth. "The porridge!"

She leapt over to the hearth and reached for the iron arm that held the pot. With a small scream, she jerked her hand to her chest.

"Tabitha! Did you burn yourself?" Edmond lifted himself off the bench. Ignoring the fire shooting up his leg, he hobbled to her side and encircled her wrist, drawing her hand toward him. Indeed, angry red slashed across her palm. "What were you thinking? You need to slow down." Even the simplest injury could quickly turn fatal this far out in the country. Did she not know that?

Tears filled her eyes, and she jerked her hand away. "I was thinking of you—and c-coffee." She darted for the basin on the sideboard and immersed her hand in the water. "I just wanted something that actually tasted *good*."

Compassion squeezed his chest. "I understand, but you must stop going like a house afire. It's too much. You're doing too much."

Rather than conceding as Edmond expected, Tabitha straightened with an indignant breath. "Too much, am I?"

"I said—"

"Yes, I suppose you *would* think so. After all, if I had not been where I ought not to be in the first place, you would not be saddled with me now with aught but injury to show for it."

He blinked, and his step faltered at her acidic tone. "That is not what I think at all. I just meant that you are unaccustomed to this type of life. It will take some time to get used to."

"No need to remind me that I'm spoiled and pampered and useless, thank you. I'm well aware." Snatching her hand from the water, she strode past, nearly upsetting his precarious balance on her way to the fireplace. "Otherwise, I might be able to do something right."

What was going on? Everything he said to mollify only inflamed her more. "Tabitha, please just stop a minute. You're not hearing me."

As it was, she jerked the pot forward—thankfully, using the cloth this time—and uncovered the hasty pudding. A horrible stench filled the cabin.

Tabitha wailed. "I've ruined it!" Batting her lashes, she reached for the spoon, but Edmond caught her hand. She gasped and flinched back.

"I'm sorry." He'd grabbed the one with the hurt palm. With a grimace, he released her. "I did not mean to hurt you, only to stop you from stirring it. 'Twill make it inedible."

Tears poured down her face. "You must think me a bumbling idiot."

"Not at all." Edmond touched her elbow. "Sit down. The porridge matters not."

"It does matter. What else are we to eat?" She waved her hand at the fireplace. "'Tis not as though Annabelle is here to bake us a loaf of her delicious bread. Even if she were, we can hardly bake without an oven." She spluttered out a bitter scoffing sound.

"We can probably salvage enough of the pudding." He'd eaten worse on campaign.

Tabitha wiped her face with her sleeve and sniffled. "I cannot believe I let it burn. All I had to do was warm it."

Edmond braced himself on the table and redirected her to the more pressing matter. "Have you any honey?"

She raised an incredulous expression to him. "You want honey now?"

"For your hand." He tipped his head to her fingers curled in her lap.

"Oh." Her face slackened. "No. Only molasses, and not much of that." Then her back straightened. "But Dulcie has herbs for burns."

"I will get them. Use this for now." Edmond step-hobbled over the sideboard and brought back the basin without sloshing quite all the water out. He plunked it down in front of her.

"Thank you." She lowered her hand into it again and pressed her trembling lips together.

"First..." Biting back a wince, Edmond eased himself down next to her, his leg extended toward the fireplace. When she still did not look at him, fighting another round of tears, he touched her chin, gently turning it toward him. Her gaze reluctantly followed. "You are not spoiled. Or useless. Or a bumbling idiot. You should not be so hard on yourself."

"You say so only because I'm crying." Another tear trembled on the edge of her dark lashes before spilling over.

Edmond was quick enough to halt its descent with his thumb. He brushed it away, then tucked a strand of ashy hair behind her ear. "I'm saying that because you are brave and hardworking and compassionate." He owed her that much, did he not? After his humor at her expense, followed by his own *ill* humor? Though the way she was looking at him set his insides aquiver. He sought to relieve the awareness that suddenly hummed between them with a chuckle. "Besides, if anyone is useless, 'tis me."

Tabitha laughed, but then she did something completely unexpected—she dove her cheek into his hand, nestling against it. "Thank you."

She had soaked up his stingy bit of praise like tallow on a dry hide. And her cheek was the softest thing he'd felt in over a year. He couldn't help but caress it. When her lips pressed a kiss onto his palm, he sucked in his breath. She turned her head toward him, gaze alight with...fear? Hope? What did she see on *his* face?

He had no time to find out, for the door opened, and Dulcie entered.

CHAPTER TWELVE

When Tabitha went back into the cabin after scrubbing out their supper bowls on the front porch with a corncob and a bucket of water, Edmond sat in Cyrus's rush-bottom chair by the fireplace. A matching footstool supported his feet, but judging from the way his jaw tightened when he wasn't sipping the raspberry leaf infusion Dulcie had made him for his pain, he ought to have returned to his bed. Doubtless, the stubborn man would refuse to do so until they retired to the other room. He'd insisted on remaining with them in the flax field all day—and he would hardly stay seated as he scanned the woods around them with that stoic vigilance of his. Tabitha had held her peace. She had said too much already, and eventually, Dulcie had given up too.

It was not that Tabitha feared his displeasure, not as she had her husband's. Even in his worst moments of pain and frustration, Edmond had never said the spiteful things to her that Henry had. Indeed, his affirmation after she had botched their morning meal had come so unexpectedly that her defenses had crumbled.

But *why* had she kissed his hand? Tabitha cringed over that even as she wiped the board clean. Had it really been so long since she had found a man appealing that she had completely lost her senses? She'd made a fool of herself. Perhaps Edmond's silence now attested to his discomfort in her presence more than his discomfort from a day out of bed.

She needed to set things straight. Let him know she had meant nothing by that impulsive gesture. She might have been vain and foolish once, but she was no fool now. A man of his years would never consider her a catch, not unless he wanted something—like Julian. But Edmond did not want her land. And Tabitha still had her pride.

Dulcie looked up from preparing a fresh pot of corn porridge for tomorrow morning. "Miss Tabitha, you brought your Bible from River's Bend, did you not?"

Tabitha squeezed her cloth out at the basin. "I did." It was actually Henry's big family Bible from England, the names of centuries' worth of Gages written in the front. How ironic that it should rest in her possession when she had been the one who'd ended their line.

"Might we read a passage tonight before bed?" Dulcie's eyes glowed in the firelight.

Tabitha glanced at Edmond, who remained facing the flames. Tired as she was, she would not give him the impression she cared nothing for the Holy Scriptures. "I will fetch it."

She went across the way and dug the Bible from the bottom of her trunk. Its weight reminded her of all the heavy expectations she'd failed to meet. Re-entering the common room, she laid the book on the table. "What shall we read?"

Dulcie cocked her head. "When I was little, Pa would read to us from Psalms."

Psalms...where was that? It had been a long time since Tabitha read to the slaves on the plantation, and she had mostly flipped about until she found a passage that looked good. Usually something about contentment and hard work that would please Lord Riley should he happen along. Sensing Edmond's gaze on her back, she turned to him. "Would you like to read?"

He almost dropped his mug. "Me?" His eyes went wide, and he raised his other hand. "No."

"Please?" Tabitha offered him the Bible.

"A wonderful idea," Dulcie chimed in. "'Tis something so soothing in a man readin' God's Word aloud."

"I said no. Thank you." A flush stole upward from his linen stock.

Awareness struck her. "You *can* read, can you not? 'Tis no shame if you were never taught." Lots of people were illiterate —just not the men who frequented Tabitha's former circles, which was why the possibility had not dawned on her earlier.

"Of course, I can read. I attended university." Challenge flared in his eyes. Setting his mug on the floor, Edmond reached for his crutch. "I think I will sit on the porch for a spell. You go ahead without me."

Over their protests and Tabitha's assurance that she did not mind reading, he clumped to the door, which they had left open to the early-spring twilight. After he pulled the door to and his steps retreated across the porch, Tabitha ran her hand over her mouth. She spoke in a low voice to Dulcie. "Perhaps we ask too much of the sergeant. He must feel trapped here."

A speculative gleam filled Dulcie's eyes as she gazed after him. "I am not sure that is it. From what I see, he wants to do more, not less."

"You think he has something against the Bible, then?"

Dulcie gave the mixture in her black pot a quick stir. "When a man run that fast from the readin' of the Good Book? I can only think maybe he be holdin' some anger against the author."

Tabitha sank to the bench with a sigh. She flipped the delicate pages in search of Psalms, but all she could think of was how she had made Edmond uncomfortable yet again. Why was she always demanding too much?

Finally, she found the beginning of the book Dulcie had requested and began to read. "'Blessed is the man that walketh not in the counsel of the ungodly, nor standeth in the way of sinners, nor sitteth in the seat of the scornful. But his delight is in the law of the Lord; and in his law doth he meditate day and night.'"

When Tabitha paused, Dulcie murmured a soft "amen." Had Tabitha not been scornful of those who sought to follow God, despite her upbringing in Christ Church? She had thought them too weak to navigate the challenges of life. But look where her attempts to do so in her own strength had landed her, while her sister was ensconced in her comfortable home with Ansel and their babies. Even Dulcie—dirt poor, scorned by whites and blacks alike—had a hardworking man who loved her and obvious peace in the face of prejudice, deprivation, and war.

Tabitha resumed her reading. "'And he shall be like a tree planted by the rivers of water, that bringeth forth his fruit in his season: his leaf also shall not wither; and whatsoever he doeth shall prosper.'"

Was that why Temperance and Dulcie were so content? God blessed them for their faithfulness? Even as she finished reading the psalm, Tabitha remained fixated on a conviction that she was somehow outside that blessing. But how did she get in? She wanted to prosper. She was more desperate for it now than ever.

When Tabitha closed the Bible, Dulcie rose from situating the porridge in the embers. "Thank you, Miss Tabitha. God's Word is more filling than the heartiest meal."

Tabitha nodded. "'Tis the least I can do. Losing your position at River's Bend, leaving your mother behind, and me moving in here—it cannot be easy for you either."

A knowing smile flashed across Dulcie's face. "The way I see it, good is already comin' out of this."

"How so?" As far as Tabitha reckoned, they still did not know where their next meal was coming from, much less how to settle her husband's debt to Hugh Jackson. Not to mention the ongoing threat of invasion from East Florida.

"Look at all you have learned. And how well you take to it."

Tabitha pressed her hand behind her hip, momentarily easing the ache there. "My back is not taking to it."

"But every day, you get stronger. You are smart, Miss Tabitha, resourceful. And already, you think of other people more than you ever did before."

Sudden moisture sprang to Tabitha's eyes. Once again, this humble mulatto woman's affirmation pierced her self-protective shell and fed something hungry within. "You and Cyrus still rely on me for income, Dulcie. I am well aware of that."

"The Good Lord provides what we need, even in hard times. Especially in hard times." Dulcie untied her apron and hung it on a peg near the sideboard. "And now, I will take myself off to bed. You coming?"

"In a minute. I think I will check on the sergeant first." Tabitha averted her gaze. Dulcie was right—she *was* thinking of other people more. But was her concern for Edmond purely altruistic? Or did familiar selfish motives lurk behind it?

No. She could not allow herself to develop feelings for the first man who came into her life after Henry's death. Had she not learned that only once a man had you did he show his true colors? She had gotten herself into this mess, thinking she could charm and manage her husband, only to have him turn on her when she had not given him what he wanted most. Well, she would not let Henry have the last word, even from the grave. And she would not repeat the mistake of believing she could subdue a man. She had been wrong to show Edmond her emotions earlier.

"Mm-hm." Dulcie's murmur challenged Tabitha's convictions.

"Tis not like that, Dulcie." Speaking softly, Tabitha led the way to the door. "Soon as he is able to ride and Cyrus returns, Edmond will be gone."

He sat on the bench on the front porch, his leg extended before him as he gazed toward the sliver of light lingering on the horizon. Dulcie bid them a goodnight before slipping across the dogtrot and into the other side of the cabin, and Tabitha perched onto the seat next to Edmond. For a moment, only the dripping of droplets from the trees and the peep of frogs from the creek broke the silence. Doubtless, he was waiting on her to leave so he could go to bed. She might as well get right to it.

"I know I can be too much."

"What?" Edmond turned toward her, his tone portraying his confusion.

"Earlier today when I was so stubborn, and again tonight, pushing you to read. I don't know when to back off. I've always been that way."

He chuckled softly. "I would have called it determined rather than stubborn."

Tabitha laughed. "A nice way of putting it. But I want you to know, I do not expect anything from you. You have already done enough." Ultimately, 'twould be a relief to them both to rid him of whatever responsibility he felt toward her. And herself of hope that would never be fulfilled. "But I should explain why I got so...emotional earlier." She swept her gaze over the floorboards.

"You do not have to do that. The strain you are under would break most women."

"As generous as that is for you to say, I want to explain."

"Very well." Edmond angled his shoulder against the cabin wall behind them and studied her in the dim light.

"The things you were saying...calm down, slow down, quiet down...I could never seem to do those things growing up. I had far too much energy. I always knew my father wanted me to be like my twin sister, Temperance—calm and ladylike and good." Tabitha placed her hand on the bench between them. "By the way, I understood when you did not want to hear the Scriptures tonight. I have never felt the need for God in my life either."

Edmond stiffened. "That wasn't it."

She drew her hand back into her lap. "Oh, so you *are* religious?"

"I would not say that. I grew up with faith in God. I just have not seen it do much good in my life." His voice tightened. Perhaps Dulcie had been right—Edmond held God responsible for some pain he'd experienced. Rather than explain, he relaxed some and prompted her to continue. "Your father did not approve of your spirit?"

"Hardly." Tabitha wrapped her arms around herself and shivered in the damp air. She gave a small, bitter laugh. "Which is funny considering I got my spirit from him. I suppose he did not find it an appealing quality in a girl. He should have had a son. Maybe that was what I was trying to be...to fill that role."

"Having a son is not a guarantee a father will be satisfied." Again, that grim tone. "But go on."

Tabitha took another breath. "When Temperance and I turned seven, Father got us both ponies for our birthday. We kept them at our plantation south of Savannah. After a month of us taking riding lessons, Father came out from town with his new cotton factor, and we wanted to show them our progress."

"What was his name? The factor?" Edmond's sharp inquiry drew a frown from Tabitha.

"I don't recall." Why would he interrupt her story for such an unimportant detail? Did he not realize she was laying herself bare? Tabitha hurried on before she could lose her courage. "Anyway...Temperance, of course, kept to walking and trotting her pony as our instructor had directed. But I had to show off. I tried to jump a split-rail fence. I was almost unseated, but I managed to hang on. Not for anything was I going to fall in front of Father. I rode back expecting him to be impressed with my courage. But he snatched me off my pony and switched me in front of his guest." Tabitha cringed, her chest tightening even at the long-ago memory of her shame. "He told me I was too much to be borne and sent me to my room."

"Too much..." His words soft, Edmond uncrossed his arms and straightened. "So when I said something that sounded similar to you..."

Tabitha dipped her chin. "I might have overreacted a bit. And then when you said you thought the opposite, that you thought I was *brave*..." Oh dear. Why did her voice give way like that? She swallowed and looked away.

Edmond nudged her arm. "I meant what I said. Dulcie said it earlier too. You are smart and strong."

"You heard that?" Tabitha's face heated even in the semi-dark. What else had he heard?

He gave a nod. "What's important is that *you* hear it. Your father was wrong not to prize your spirit. You will need every bit of it to survive out here."

Warmth flooded Tabitha's chest. But this time, she would not touch him. Or break down in tears. "Maybe there was something to what she said—about this place bringing out the best in me. Ever since I married, I felt so useless. I tried everything just to keep myself occupied and was good enough at most things—music, gardening, sewing, running the household—but nothing I did mattered. I was marking time. Now when I do something, 'tis for a reason. I have a purpose."

Each day she awakened, the drive to rise and go about her business had fair stolen her breath. Even back in Savannah, she had never felt that way. She had been a pawn to be used by the men in her life. Now she could set her own path.

"I can see that. Not all women thrive under adversity. 'Tis a trait to be much admired." The conviction with which Edmond spoke once again hinted at a story beneath the surface. "But your father...did you ever make peace with him?"

She blew out a scornful laugh. "By going along with him, yes. The next time he came, I was as sweet as pie. I begged him to take me riding and promised to do exactly as he said. Finally, he agreed. We left my sister at home." Tabitha's chest swelled at the remembered sense of being chosen. Favored. "He even admitted I probably got my risk-taking and sense of adventure from him. But I only maintained his approval by doing what he wanted. Eventually, that meant marrying Lord Riley."

"And how did *he* feel about your spirit?" Edmond's low tone hinted at his caution.

She cut him a sharp glance. "How do you think? He kept me at River's Bend to ensure I remained in check."

Edmond sat back and rubbed his chin. "Now I understand why you did not seem devastated by his passing." He flicked his fingers in her direction. "Forgive me. I should not have said so."

"Why not? You are right." And here was her chance to absolve him of any guilt he might harbor about leaving. "Marrying Lord Riley was my decision. My mistake. And now I must correct it. If you see spirit in me still"—she spluttered a laugh—"'tis something of a miracle. But this time, I must right my problems with hard work, not by cunning...or charm..." Not that such manipulations would succeed on a man such as Edmond, even did she remember how to employ them. "Or by putting the burden upon you."

His hand lowered to his lap, palm up. "You did not put it there. I offered to help carry it, remember?"

"Yes. And you did help by securing this cattle contract."

"That will not—"

"It will set us on our feet. What else can you do?"

"Actually, there may be something we can do together, if you're willing to hear me out." Edmond sat forward, speaking quickly before she could cut him off again. "I had a lot of time to think today."

He had been thinking, not brooding? Not trying to avoid her after she'd thrown herself at him? "What were you thinking about?"

"Timber. This land is full of massive yellow pine and cypress. Jack McMullan has a crew of reputable loggers in Darien. If I contact him now, I might persuade him to sign with you to harvest some this fall and float them down to the mill in the winter."

Tabitha's eyes widened. She had seen timbermen riding single trees and massive rafts down the Altamaha when water levels were highest, but it had never occurred to her that she might hire loggers to do the same. "Would they take their earnings out of the profit, or would they require some payment up front?"

"I don't know. I can ask."

That would only extend her debt to him when she already had enough to repay. "There's no need. I will talk to Cyrus, and we can look into it."

"It might be best if I go on your behalf." Edmond leaned down to massage his leg. How it must be paining him. "And you would likely need more than an introduction, but rather, someone to continue to act as your representative. A manager, as it were. Someone to transact your business and keep your accounts. I served as apprentice in my father's factor office and excelled there and at university at numbers."

The mention of his father's work tickled the edge of Tabitha's awareness, but she hastened to disabuse him of the notion that she needed an employee. As though she would have a pittance to spare in the near future—much less, enough to compensate a manager. "That is commendable, but I'm not afraid of a little math either. Between Cyrus and me..."

"The thing is, I'm not certain how McMullan would respond to a black man, even if he is free, or..."

"Or a woman?" Her eyebrows shot up.

Straightening, Edmond gave an apologetic chuckle. "Scots can be a bit, well...clannish."

"And I suppose these McMullans are friends of your mother's family."

He shrugged. "Maybe distant kin."

"Assuming they would work with me and Cyrus"—or they might find someone else who would—"lumbering is an excellent idea. Thank you."

"It might pay your debt to Jackson, but you will need a steady income after that. I pondered what you said earlier—about a store."

Tabitha blinked at him a moment. "A store?"

"A mercantile, this side of the river, such as Mary Musgrove ran. But a store rather than a trading post since this is now white man's land. There isn't another for miles around. It would not be hard to clear a patch of forest fronting the road and raise a log structure."

Was he serious? A high-pitched laugh escaped Tabitha. "Perhaps if I had a crew of slaves to command, 'twould not be hard. But Cyrus is not a slave, and he already has his hands full."

Edmond studied her a moment before he offered quietly, "'Twould be no hardship for me once I am fit."

"No hardship?" She tossed her hands up. "With your duties at the fort and a war on our doorstep? Even if you could make time, what would be in such an endeavor for you?"

"Keeping your land out of Julian Jackson's hands would be satisfaction enough."

She scoffed. "For some business dealing that went awry?" She had not taken Edmond as the type to hold a petty grudge.

"'Twas more than that." Even in the dim light, the tightening of his jaw was noticeable.

"I'm listening." Tabitha rested her hands on her knees and angled toward him.

"Talking about the past does not fix it. Taking action does. That is what I'm trying to do." His rapid-fire sentences made her stiffen.

"I don't understand. What aren't you telling me?"

He looked away. "Nothing that bears repeating."

Her heart shriveled as surely as if he had censured her. She had opened up about her past, but he did not trust her enough to share his, even if it explained his compulsion to help her. Confirmation that she was wise not to rely on him.

"We could discuss a partnership," he said. "I would consider my help an investment."

A partnership? She knew how those turned out. The man always had the controlling interest, no matter what the woman brought to the table. "I appreciate your suggestions, but I think it best that I find my own way in this."

Edmond drew his feet beneath the bench. "Do not allow pride to cloud your common sense, Tabitha. This is a good offer."

Tabitha stood up, her heart thudding. "'Tis not pride, Sergeant Lassiter. 'Tis self-respect. And if you cannot see that, we have no more to say to each other."

Edmond rose as she turned and headed for her room in a swirl of petticoats. "Tabitha, hear me out."

She closed the door on his entreaty—too gruff to be considered a request. Even so, regret flooded her chest. The magnitude of her desire to trust Edmond only served as a reminder that she should not.

CHAPTER THIRTEEN

The morning after Tabitha refused Edmond's offer of help, he hoed manure and compost in with the thick black soil for the melon patch while Tabitha and Dulcie prepared mounds for planting. Tabitha had protested his assistance, but Dulcie had supported his determination to resume some physical activity.

The frequent rains of the last week had given way to mid-April sun that warmed their backs while the soft, sultry breeze carried birdsong and cloying floral scents. The showy yellow flowers of the nearby tulip tree had begun to bloom, along with the Ogeechee lime trees and switchcane along the creek bank where Edmond had picketed Maximus. The stallion ripped up green grasses and chewed contentedly, flicking flies with his tail.

"If Cyrus has a froe, I could use it on some of those split logs to make new shingles for the roof." Edmond nodded toward the shed.

The full brim of Tabitha's straw hat remained downturned. "No need. He will be back soon enough." After breaking their fast, she had put off Edmond's attempt to draw her aside for a private conversation, and her continued refusal to even look at him made it seem unlikely she would allow another opportunity.

In her mind, he was already gone. What had caused her to withdraw after her unexpectedly affectionate gesture yesterday morning and the things she had said about her childhood last night? Things which made him want to help her even more? He could only presume he had presented his ideas too forcefully—and right after she revealed how her father and husband had kept her under their thumbs.

Once again, he should not have allowed his emotions to enter the equation. He could surely have persuaded her if he had stuck to logic. But somewhere along the way, the need to prevent the Jacksons' tyranny had turned into a genuine desire to help Tabitha. A woman as spirited and determined as she deserved independence just as much as this land did. The two goals were becoming entwined in Edmond's mind.

He would just have to speak his piece in front of Dulcie. Perhaps she would support him. Tabitha probably had not even told her of Edmond's idea to generate income. "Tabitha, I know you prize your independence, and perhaps I spoke too forcefully last night, but you have to allow me to help. Not just today, but in the future." Maybe if he explained about his mother, it would wring some understanding from her. "What I propose would benefit all of us."

She lifted her head, but rather than looking at him, she raised her gloved hand. "Listen."

Edmond cocked his ear. Indeed, underbrush cracked and hooves trod the path from the road. He tossed down the hoe and limped toward the side of the house where he'd left the rifle he'd been issued upon his return to Fort Howe. But a lowing brought him up short. Cattle!

"They are back!" Dulcie leapt to her feet as the first two brown-and-white cows came into view. A bull followed, chestnut-colored with black markings, maybe eight or nine hundred pounds, swinging his horned head in irritation. Cyrus edged his mount to the steer's side to head him off.

"We have to open the corral." Tabitha scrambled up, and she and Dulcie ran across the yard to remove logs from the fence so Dougal and Cyrus could drive the cattle into the muddy enclosure.

Edmond grabbed his crutch instead of his rifle and used it to help shoo the animals in the right direction.

"Get the rail back in place," Dougal called from atop his mount as the cows circled around the corral.

Dulcie dragged her end of a log toward the enclosure.

Tabitha, who had been staring at the livestock, jumped into motion to assist. Once they had both logs back in position, Dulcie ran to her husband. He dismounted and wrapped her in his embrace. Edmond and Tabitha approached Dougal as he slid down from his mount, his hair damp and his face streaked with dirt.

"Bloody beasts." Dougal swiped off his cocked hat and ran his sleeve across his forehead. "Herdin' a bunch of heathens would've been easier."

"Surely, a wee passel of cows did not cause you trouble, Private." Edmond clenched his friend's shoulder and gave him a light shake. "We were beginning to despair of your return."

"Good to see you, too, and fit enough to harass me, sir." It was Dougal's turn to grab Edmond by the arm, grinning. "When I left, you looked about two paces from death's door." His answering shake made Edmond chuckle and plant his crutch more firmly on the ground.

Tabitha turned back from assessing the corral. The log had left a smear of mud across her petticoat. "There are only six. Where are the others?"

Dougal's mouth went flat as he replaced his hat, and Cyrus drew near, frowning as he led his horse. "Sorry to say, Miss

Tabitha, but the answer to both your questions is six is all we could find. Folks are sayin' the Loyalists took two thousand head of cattle back to Florida with 'em."

"Two thousand?" Tabitha gasped. She stared at the bovines still jostling about the corral, churning up mud. "You mean to say, out of our original two hundred, this is all that remain?"

Cyrus dipped his head. "'Fraid so."

Dougal stepped forward. "We scoured every swamp and savannah from here to the Satilla, Mrs. Gage. Cyrus speaks true."

"But this will not be nearly enough..." Tabitha bit her lip as her words trailed off.

Dougal's face creased with compassion. "It may be that some turn up later from the canebrakes, but for now, this is the best we could do. We are sorry not to bear better news."

"I understand." She squared her shoulders. "I am thankful for the half dozen you were able to bring. I know it can have been no easy task." Her words made Edmond's chest expand with pride in her. "You men must be tired. Thirsty. Hungry. Come into the cabin."

"My horse is picketed near the creek, if you wish to use the line." Edmond gestured past the house.

Cyrus reached for the reins of Dougal's stallion. "I will take them."

"I will go with you." Dulcie shot her husband a soft smile as she rubbed his horse's nose.

"And I will warm the remainder of this morning's porridge." Tabitha turned toward the cabin, but before she could hurry away, Edmond caught her arm.

"Tabitha, now more than ever, you must reconsider my offer." Edmond did his best to keep his tone low, persuasive but not overpowering. When she pulled away, he released her, but he rushed his words. "Let me go to Mr. McMullan on your behalf. You will need the income from timbering. If Mr. Jackson knows how you will get the money, he may give you more time."

Tabitha's gaze swung from him to Dougal, who watched them with his brows knit and an expression of intense curiosity. "Thank you, Sergeant Lassiter, but after today, I believe our paths must diverge."

Stubborn woman. He wanted to shake her as he had shaken Dougal. To make her see reason. But any further urging from him would only make her an enemy. "Very well." He stepped back and dipped his head. "Should you change your mind, you will know where to find me."

~

EARLY MAY, 1777

Two weeks had passed since Tabitha had last seen Edmond Lassiter, and she couldn't help but think of him as she and Dulcie ferried across the Altamaha on their way to visit Dulcie's father at River's Bend. Spring floods carried extra sediment and debris downriver, making the crossing difficult. 'Twas with relief that they spied Cyrus awaiting them on the opposite bank, his stallion and Tabitha's mare in hand.

"You made it across safely." Dulcie kissed his cheek after Tabitha paid the ferryman. "I was praying the whole way."

"Thankfully, these two are strong swimmers." Cyrus handed Tabitha Cora's reins.

Tabitha stroked her mare's brow and murmured words of appreciation and comfort. Then she said, "Thank you, Cyrus. I should not have allowed my indecision to put off this trip." While she had stood firm about not involving Edmond in her plans for the future, she had remained torn about the best way to secure Hugh Jackson's money. Finally, she had decided she and Cyrus would travel to Darien in search of Jack McMullan while Dulcie visited her mother at River's Bend.

Dulcie eyed the log walls and bastions of Fort Howe. "I still think we should see if Sergeant Lassiter is free to ride with us to Darien."

"I am certain he is too busy with duties. It seems there is an unusual amount of activity at the fort." As Tabitha spoke, in fact, a company of mounted rangers turned off the main road for the palisade, riding past an encampment of soldiers that overflowed the fort walls. Tents had sprung up like ecru-colored mushrooms in the green field where horses were pick-eted, swirls of smoke from a dozen campfires twisting toward the glary gray sky and hanging heavy on the damp air. From inside the stockade, a snare drum rolled and sharp orders echoed.

"He would not be too busy for you. I daresay he has been waitin' for you to come to him."

Tabitha turned away. Dulcie had made her opinions clear in more than one hearthside evening discussion. She insisted the sergeant harbored some special admiration for Tabitha, but Tabitha sensed a darker, more personal motive beneath his benevolence. Whatever he concealed, it could not be good. "Never again will I make myself beholden to a man I do not know. Besides, if this Mr. McMullan doesn't want to work for me, I will find someone who does." With a grunt, Tabitha hoisted herself into the saddle. She straightened at the ache in her back from too many hours bending to weed the flax field.

As soon as Dulcie was mounted behind Cyrus, they rode toward River's Bend, putting Fort Howe—and talk of its occu-pants—behind them.

At the driveway to the plantation, Cyrus pulled up his reins. "Maybe you should wait here, Miss Tabitha, while I check an' make sure the Jacksons aren't up at the house."

"'Tis a good idea, Cyrus." She smiled her appreciation, and

she and Dulcie waited while the man trotted his mount ahead. What would she do without these two faithful servants?

In about five minutes, he appeared at the end of the lane of Spanish-moss-draped live oaks and waved his arm for them to come on. They urged their horses forward, and Tabitha stifled a surge of yearning as the house came into view, the white porticoes gleaming among flowering hedges. While she might miss the comforts of wealth, her years at River's Bend had been empty. She had played a part here, a shadowy actress in a half life that brought more pain than pleasure. Now, her body might hurt, her stomach might growl, but she was free. She just had to figure out how to remain that way.

Cyrus led them past the main house to Marcus Long's cabin at the head of the row of slave cabins. They had timed their arrival in hopes of finding him at home for his noonday meal, and Tabitha relaxed a bit when he came out onto his porch. He greeted them, hugged his daughter, and helped Tabitha to dismount.

A few minutes later, he saw them settled around his board with servings of succotash and Annabelle's crusty white bread, which Tabitha devoured as though it were the finest European pastry while Dulcie filled her father in on their plan. Tonight, Tabitha would soak in a bath, wash her body and hair with scented soap, and sleep in the feather-mattress embrace of her old bed. Tomorrow, she would ride to Darien refreshed and dressed in her smart navy light-woolen habit to call upon Mr. McMullan. He would see she was a lady of quality and good for her word, even though she no longer had her husband's name and title to back her. Ha. As if she ever truly had.

"The only thing we could not decide was whether we should take the payment from the sale of the cattle with us in case the logging crew required earnest money," Tabitha told the overseer after Dulcie concluded her summary, "or leave it with you in case the Jacksons come to call while we are gone. It might go some distance in easing our request for an extension on payment of the debt."

"Hm. As to that..." Mr. Long sat back, rubbing his beard. "You can rest easy for a bit. They have important company from Savannah and shan't come in search of you just now."

"Oh, praise be," Dulcie murmured, spooning up a bite of stew.

"I would not sing your halleluiahs yet. Mr. Hugh Jackson came to see me a couple days ago. Asked me to make sure you knew his expectations. I was going to ride out tomorrow to see you." Mr. Long's gaze slid to Tabitha, wary and regretful.

She shrank back on the bench. "What expectations?"

"A reminder that he had given you through spring to make a decision—payment, the land south of the river, or betrothal to Mr. Julian. He put a date on it. The last of May."

Tabitha struggled for a deep breath. "But we cannot pay him three hundred pounds. Not until the end of the year."

Mr. Long's mouth pulled into a grimace. "He will say that leaves you two options."

Dulcie sat forward. "Perhaps if you gave him the fifty pounds we can spare from the sale of the cattle and we showed him a contract with Mr. McMullan, Mr. Jackson would agree to wait for the rest once the timber is logged."

"Perhaps. But you will never get that contract from McMullan, not the two of you." Mr. Long's gaze toggled between Tabitha and Cyrus. "They despise Negroes and would put no stock by doin' business with a woman."

Just as Edmond had said. Tabitha smacked her hand on the board. "That is absurd. Surely, the proper arrangement would persuade them."

Tabitha's heart fell as the overseer shook his head, his expression grim.

"What about someone else?" Dulcie glanced between

Tabitha and her father. "There must be someone else in the parish capable of loggin' some trees."

"The McMullans are the only experienced loggers not gone off to fight." Mr. Long withdrew a flask from inside his coat and sat forward to splash some strong-smelling liquid into his pewter tankard. "Besides, the Jacksons were firm. I fear you stand no chance of convincin' them to defer payment unless you can give them some official guarantee."

Dulcie turned a pointed look on Tabitha. "We must ask Sergeant Lassiter to accompany us."

Tabitha remained focused on Dulcie's father. "Would you go with us instead?" She knew better than to hope, but she had to ask.

Wrinkles radiated out from his lips as he pinched them together. "I'm sorry, Miss Tabitha. I cannot risk word of that gettin' back to the Jacksons. This sergeant, is he the one who came to your aid on the Satilla? Who was goin' to help you round up the cattle?"

"The one who stayed with us after the rattler bit him, yes. He sent one of his men in his place while he recuperated at our cabin."

"He is the one who suggested hirin' Mr. McMullan in the first place." Dulcie lifted a brow as she voiced Tabitha's omission. "His mother's family are distant kin to the loggers."

Her father took a sip of spirits before plunking his tankard on the table. "Then I suggest you fetch him at once. From what I hear, the Patriots are mobilizing for another invasion of Florida. Militia floatin' down from Sunbury while a mounted contingent will cross the Altamaha any day now to rendezvous with them on the St. John's. Then onto St. Augustine. 'Tis Button Gwinnett's idea. He has been doing all he can to discredit the McIntosh brothers and seize power."

The breath left Tabitha's lungs in a rush, and her back sagged. "Then we cannot possibly ask Edmond for help."

"It may be that he will remain at the fort," Cyrus pointed out. "Some will. Or he might have time to go with us tomorrow while the troops muster. 'Tis worth askin'. It sounds like our only chance."

Tabitha met Mr. Long's eyes, and he gave a firm nod. "You will not get Jack McMullan to sign on with you without him."

"Very well." She sighed. "Perhaps you would ride back to the fort to inquire, Cyrus?"

"Yes, ma'am." Cyrus plucked his hat off the bench and rose. "I will go straightaway."

As he left the cabin, a frown tugged down Mr. Long's brows as his gaze slid to his daughter. "Where did you say this sergeant was from?"

Dulcie sipped her cider from her pewter tankard. "His family is from Savannah. His father was a factor for cotton and rice planters on the coast."

Mr. Long's hand fell onto the table with a thump. "That is where I know the name from."

Dulcie straightened and set down her cup. "I thought it familiar too. He was your factor?"

"He was. A while back—maybe almost two years now— Lord Riley transferred his business to a new factor. Mr. Jackson —Hugh—had told him some unsavory things about John Lassiter. Implied he was dishonest, dippin' into the profits, if I recall correctly." He scratched the silvery bristles on his cheek.

Tabitha gasped. "No wonder Edmond hates the Jacksons. Did you learn if it was true...about his father being dishonest?"

"Never did find out." Mr. Long started stacking their bowls. "But I cannot imagine a man workin' to stop a man like Hugh Jackson so hard if the rumors about his father were true. Seems like somethin' a man would do to clear his name to me. Now, we should walk over and get you both settled. Annabelle will be eager to see you."

Questions swirled in Tabitha's mind as she followed Dulcie

to the big house. Was the harm Hugh Jackson had done to Edmond's father the source of the pain she had often glimpsed in his eyes? The impetus for his willingness to help her? If he did so out of a desire to prevent the Jacksons from hurting her as they had hurt his family, how could that be bad? Or did he operate from a desire for revenge?

Edmond had avoided speaking of his family, almost as if he'd had no life before he joined the rangers. What had happened to his father? Where was his mother? Before Tabitha considered any sort of partnership, she would require some answers, even if she risked losing Edmond's help with obtaining a contract with Jack McMullan. She had learned her lessons about trust. Any man she allowed close to her from here on out would have to prove himself worthy of it.

Even so, when horse hooves sounded on the driveway, her heartbeat clipped into double time. She ran to the front entrance as Cyrus climbed the front porch steps...alone.

Tabitha held the door open. "He could not come?"

Cyrus swept off and clenched his hat. "He was already gone, ma'am."

Gone without a word. Riding into danger in the Florida swamps, maybe never to return. Something twisted in Tabitha's chest, and she clasped her hands.

She knew now she had to manage this on her own.

CHAPTER FOURTEEN

"Miss Tabitha, you cannot go in there." Cyrus sought to deter Tabitha from entering the weathered gray building with sky-blue trim by planting his considerable girth between her and the door.

"Well, good thing for me, neither can you!"

Cyrus clenched his fists. Of course, he would never dream of physically deterring her. A black man touching a white woman? He did not even presume to stare her in the eyes as Dulcie was now wont to do. But he stood his ground. "No ma'am. We should wait for Mr. McMullan to come out and head home."

"Which will be what time, the middle of the night?" Tabitha placed her hand on her hip. Already, the long wait for the timberman outside his favorite watering hole would force her to procure lodgings for herself and Cyrus. The tang of salt and marsh drew her eye toward the rigging of schooners poking up above the river bluff, seagulls cawing as they circled overhead. She could not add the danger of lingering this near the dock after twilight fell.

"A lady cannot go into a taproom, an' that be where the owner told me Mr. McMullan is meetin' with his crew."

"Then I will merely go into the hall and wait there while the owner fetches him for me."

Cyrus's bottom lip turned down on the sides, and he tilted his head. His expression put Tabitha in mind of that stubborn steer he'd herded to Fort Howe.

But she was more stubborn than a steer when it came to their survival. She had not ridden thirteen miles from River's Bend to return emptyhanded. At one time, she had been able to bend any man to her will. The common laborers of Darien were a far cry from Lord Riley. Surely, if she mustered a show of confidence, enough of her charms remained to gain her an audience. She would follow that with the logic of a sound business proposition. She squared her shoulders and trod past Cyrus to the door.

Raucous voices accompanied by the scents of unwashed bodies and hard liquor hit her the moment she crossed the threshold. The next second, conversation ceased. Tabitha gazed past the slack-jawed proprietor standing in the walk-up bar to the taproom where a long tableful of roughly garbed men paused with pipes clenched between their teeth and tankards halfway to their lips, all staring at Tabitha in her blue riding habit and cocked hat. Suddenly, she felt like the brightly plumed hummingbirds that had whirred around the tubular red flowers of the buckeye tree outside the parlor window at River's Bend. She ought to be wearing black in public. She ought not to be here at all.

Her courage almost failed.

"Madam," said the owner, a gangly man with wispy silvery hair who appeared to be in his sixties, "you cannot be in here."

And unescorted—the words he did not say but clearly thought. Tabitha cast a furtive glance toward the exit. Cyrus wavered in the open doorway, then stepped inside, seemingly deciding that supporting her was more important than his safety.

She could do this. Tabitha lifted her chin a notch. "I have urgent business with Mr. Jack McMullan. If you would be willing to fetch him, I will wait here in the hall." She did, however, step out of view of the taproom.

"And just who might you be?" The man put down the glass he had been cleaning.

"Mrs. Henry Gage, wife of Lord Riley."

Whether the owner had heard of the death of Tabitha's husband or not, speaking his title did the trick. He dropped his polishing cloth and opened the gate in the bar, passing through the portal to the taproom.

"Well, now." Tabitha forced a smile at Cyrus before she took a seat on a hard wooden bench against the wall. He remained standing. Her hopes plummeted when the proprietor returned alone.

He tucked his fingers into the bib of his stained apron. "I regret to say, Mr. McMullan is unavailable, madam."

She stood with a swish of petticoats. "Nonsense. He will want to speak with me. Go back and tell him I am here on important business. I wish to hire him to log my land."

Drawing a slow breath as if to quell his impatience, the man dipped his head and pivoted once again for the next room. Tabitha remained standing this time, tapping the toe of her buckled black leather shoe.

Please, God. Please.

Then he was back, frowning and firmer. "Mr. McMullan sends his apologies, but he is not acceptin' new jobs."

She could not be defeated this easily—before she even got a chance. "Did you tell him who I was?"

"I did. And he replied very clearly that he does not work for women, no matter who their husband *was*."

Tabitha's chest clenched at the words.

The man extended his arm toward the door. "Now, madam, I beg you take your leave before the men get the wrong impression about your presence here."

Tabitha blinked at him, frozen in a paroxysm of dismay.

"Come, Miss Tabitha," Cyrus murmured close to her side. He took a step toward the exit.

"Fine." Heat flooded her face and neck, and she jerked her chin at the tavern keeper. "But you can tell him he will regret not meeting with me. I shall find someone else to log my land." As the man's brows rose and a skeptical smirk twisted his thin lips, Tabitha pivoted and stalked to the door.

Outside, her shoulders sagged. Who was she to make threats? A woman alone, with no money, no title, and no family. Well, not exactly *no* family...

Cyrus removed his hat and slapped it against his leg. "What are we to do now, Miss Tabitha?"

She inhaled a painful breath, then let it out in a huff. "Tomorrow, we go back and get Dulcie. And then we must journey to Savannah."

MAY 17, 1777

"Ye're awfully quiet this morning." Dougal's observation from atop his stallion next to Maximus drew Edmond's attention from the lush green forest encroaching the path along Thomas Creek. "Not still thinkin' of the widow, are ye?"

"Not just her." Edmond had dismissed his friend's suggestion that Edmond send a note to Tabitha before leaving Fort Howe. "No, if she didn't reach out in the two weeks since I bid her farewell, she does not want my aid."

A mind like Tabitha's 'twould not be easily swayed. But

somehow, that did not lift the sense of responsibility that insisted on settling over his shoulders whenever he thought of her. It had not helped that Muscogee Indians had harassed their expedition just the other side of the Altamaha, far too close to Tabitha's cabin.

Dougal shifted and readjusted his hat, which had already left a sweaty ring around his bright hair, even before nine in the morning. Whatever sultry breezes the residents of Florida's coast enjoyed must never penetrate these tangled bogs. "I found with me sweet Faith that she is most like to let me into her life when I share my mind with her. You know, *talk* to her?" Dougal shot Edmond a lopsided grin, almost apologetic. "Did ye tell the widow why you wished to help?"

"Of course." Edmond scowled. Of all times to discuss such matters... "I told her my family ran afoul of Hugh Jackson in matters of business."

"Ah, but that told her nothin' of the real story, did it?" Dougal cocked an eyebrow.

"It told her all she needed to know." He was regretting taking the private into his confidence, even though he now considered the well-meaning Scot a friend...and even though Dougal did not know all the details. This sort of prying was the very reason he preferred to keep personal matters to himself.

"Is that so?" When Edmond did not reply, Dougal rode on in silence, the creaking of leather, snort of horses, murmur of low conversation, and cries of exotic birds filling the lapse between them. "Ye should go see her when we return. If she knew how ye wished to spare her the hurt that befell your betrothed, 'twould soften her heart. And I wager, it doesna need much softening."

"Why would you think that?" Edmond cut him a glance.

Dougal laughed. "A woman doesna fight a man with that much fire unless she has feelin's for him."

Edmond frowned. Surely, the private mistook Tabitha's

independent streak for attraction. Even if she was attracted to him, what did he bring to the table, besides his youth and strength, things which most every other man under forty could offer? He had no fortune to lift her out of her difficulties, and only her isolation had kept her from knowing his name was tarnished. His one chance at making something of himself came from this army. This war. He would do well to stay focused on that. "I am more concerned about the proximity of the enemy and the anger the men may have stirred with what they did to the Seminoles they killed."

"Aye. A bad business, that." Dougal scanned the forest with fresh vigilance.

Earlier in the month, and again a few days ago, Indians who had attacked their party had been not only killed but mutilated by the Georgians. And they called the Muscogees, the Creeks and Seminoles, the savages. If only Edmond had possessed sufficient rank to stop the desecrations the rangers committed.

But then, things had not gone according to plan ever since they set out. After crossing the rain-swollen Satilla and St. Mary's rivers, they had reached the point where they were supposed to rendezvous with Lt. Col. Samuel Elbert's flotilla at Sawpit Bluff near the mouth of the Nassau River on May twelfth, as scheduled, but the militia had not been there. Neither had the supplies Colonel John Baker's horsemen had counted on. They had proceeded cautiously south, morale wilting and tempers shortening in the oppressive heat.

The morning of the fifteenth, they had awakened to about forty of their horses missing. They followed the tracks about four miles to find the mounts hobbled beside a swamp. Suspecting an ambush, Colonel Baker had left some men in plain sight and sent two other parties around to cut the hobbles. When the natives had popped up from the brush with their chilling war cries, the Georgians had held firm, driven them back, and recovered the horses, but the body of another

Indian had been left mutilated. The Indians had set fire to the woods to conceal their retreat. Baker had ordered his men to head back to Georgia and moved them to the banks of Thomas Creek, a tributary of the Nassau, where they had camped the night prior.

"The colonel heard from a local man that the authorities knew we were coming." Edmond tipped his head toward their superior officer, rounding a bend near the sandy creek bank just ahead. "That means the East Florida Rangers are probably not far away."

"We can take them." With a straightaway before them, Dougal relaxed in the saddle. "The sooner we do, the sooner we get out of this swamp."

"I would rather do so with Colonel Elb—"

Cries from the front of the column cut into Edmond's sentence. Past the line of mounted men, a flurry of movement drew his eye. Then a flash, a volley of musket fire, and a cloud of smoke. Shouts. Screams. Horses neighing, rearing, their owners turning them back—toward Edmond and Dougal. Ambush!

"Dismount!" Colonel Baker waved toward the forest floor, urging the rangers to take a stand and fight on foot according to their training rather than flee. He set the example by swinging down, followed by one of his lieutenants and several rangers close to them.

Pulse racing, Edmond drew his dragoon pistol and kneed Maximus off the path, Dougal beside him as their compatriots fled past. Edmond remained astride in an attempt to rally his handful of men. "Stand and fight!"

But when he glanced back ...three columns of British Regulars in red and white appeared, muskets leveled in their direction. Gunfire and smoke exploded from the front and the rear. Men fled into the forest on either side.

War cries whooped from the underbrush. They were

surrounded! A pop to Edmond's left, and a lieutenant sagged on his horse, a red spot blossoming on his shoulder. A tomahawk in the chest halted another man running into the woods. Chaos broke loose on the path, some rangers firing back, some fleeing, some dismounting, others taking whatever horse they could find. Shouts and conflicting orders mingled with the rattle of rifles and muskets.

A roached head popped up behind a fallen tree, the muzzle of the Indian's gun aimed at Edmond. He fired his dragoon pistol. The man jerked and fell.

Laid low over his stallion's neck, Dougal yelled in his direction. "We should dismount."

"No!" Their horses were their only chance of escaping this disaster. Edmond urged Maximus into the heavy curtain of the forest and drew his other pistol. A movement behind a tree signaled a foe ahead, which he dispatched with another click of the trigger. Holstering that weapon, he slid his long rifle from its sheath on his saddle.

A painted Seminole took aim from behind a massive stump to Edmond's right—at the lieutenant who had attempted to make a stand with Colonel Baker. Edmond fired a millisecond before the brave did. The native's shot went wide, clipping the officer's arm, and the Indian sagged over the stump.

"With me!" Edmond waved to Dougal and rode hard for the lieutenant who stood stunned, clasping his wound. With no chance to reload, Edmond fired his first prayer in over a year. *Cover us, God.*

CHAPTER FIFTEEN

MID-JUNE, 1777

Tabitha's black silk dress rustled as she descended the stairs inside her parents' house on St. James Square. She was already regretting agreeing to a supper with guests this evening—just an old friend of Tabitha's, her husband, and her brother, as Tabitha's mother assured her. But it had required Dulcie to dye one of the few silk evening gowns Tabitha had held onto for her forays into town. And she had no idea how to play the grieving widow. Neither could she reprise her role of spirited coquette. What was her public persona supposed to be?

When voices rose from the foyer, Tabitha paused on the landing and lifted her hand to her suddenly racing heart. She glanced up as Dulcie passed in the upper hall, hoping for a smile or nod of encouragement. But the servant's expression— eyes sad, mouth drawn tight—clenched Tabitha's chest with regret.

Dulcie and Cyrus had not wanted to come to Savannah, and the longer Tabitha remained, the more they withdrew. Being here forced them back into the role of servants...slaves. Tabitha regretted that but did not know how to change it. Three days prior, Cyrus had returned to the Altamaha, unable to leave his crops untended any longer. Tabitha had convinced Dulcie to remain with her a few more days.

When Tabitha and Cyrus had returned from Darien to River's Bend to fetch Dulcie and gather what remained there of Tabitha's finer attire, the couple had entreated her to come home with them and await the return of Sergeant Lassiter. But every day she might tarry in hope of aid from a man she did not even know if she could trust—and who might not return—brought her closer to another call from Julian Jackson. She was now past his date of reckoning, though 'twas doubtful he would come to Savannah seeking her. At least, not yet. Before he did, she had to persuade her father of the wisdom of investing in timbering.

That was another thing. Dulcie did not approve of Tabitha allowing her parents to believe she still owned and lived at River's Bend. Tabitha had told her parents that Lord Riley had sold his townhouse, but she hadn't told them what he'd done with the plantation. She had not lied directly...just not offered up the full truth.

Father would never invest his finances into what he would consider a dying cause. Only if she did not appear weak or desperate might she convince him to partner with her, sending his lawyer or clerk to gain an audience with Mr. McMullan and providing earnest money if necessary. So far, she had dropped casual suggestions into his ear, but pressing the matter would only reveal her hand.

Meanwhile, Mother kept finding reasons for Tabitha to extend her stay. No doubt, with her daughters both living far from Savannah, her mother was lonely. At least Temperance was not here to complicate matters.

Tabitha took a deep breath, willing herself to descend the

final flight of stairs. She had faced down painted natives and Burntfoot Brown himself. Why should she fear a few of Savannah's elite?

From the entryway, Tabitha's old friend Meg Collins gave a squeal when Tabitha came into view. The petite blonde broke away from greeting Tabitha's parents and hurried forward to embrace her. "Oh, my dear, my deepest condolences." She kissed Tabitha's cheeks. "'Tis so good to see you at last."

"Thank you. You look well." Tabitha forced a smile. Meg's form had taken on new curves that overflowed the bodice of her burgundy silk gown. Rouge highlighted her impeccably pale skin.

Meg waved and leaned close to whisper. "I can barely fit in my clothing. Three children and counting." She touched her abdomen.

Tabitha's lashes fluttered as the unintended barb hit the mark. "Congratulations."

"But you...slender as ever. You always did make a robe à la francaise look stunning."

Tabitha drew her arms close to her sides. She had always loved the way the box pleats of the regal style fell from the back of her shoulders to her hem and sailed behind her when she walked, but next to Meg's new polonaise gown with its looped swags and ruffled under-petticoat, she felt like a relic of the past decade. When had fashion changed so much?

"And your color is good. Does she not bloom of the countryside, Charles?" Meg turned to her husband, who approached with a tentative smile.

"Like an English rose." The debonair lawyer cut a bow over Tabitha's hand.

"And you remember my brother, Ezekiel." Meg indicated a ruddy-cheeked, fair-haired man of about Tabitha's height who turned from handing a servant his hat and walking stick. "A partner in Charles's law firm."

"Of course." Tabitha curtsied. "But where is your lovely wife this evening?" Several years before, Ezekiel had married a meek young woman Tabitha had never taken much notice of. Even now, she failed to recall her name.

Tabitha's mother glided forward and placed her hand on Ezekiel's elbow as the man dipped his head. "Sadly, Mr. Whitmire lost his dear Caroline to childbed last year."

"I'm so sorry." Heat flushed Tabitha's cheeks. "I have been away from town too long."

"'Tis all right. I would not expect you to know." Ezekiel flashed her a glance, almost as if afraid to hold her gaze. Before her marriage, he had never had the gumption to speak with her. Now, a certain wary hope lit his face. Surely, 'twas only the kinship of loss he expected.

But Tabitha's stomach swirled at the smiling glance her mother spent between them, the ever-present mouchet, or beauty mark, trembling on her cheek. Marjorie Scott now powdered her hair to cover the gray lacing her black tresses. "The two of you should have much catching up to do over supper." She fluttered her lashes and patted Tabitha's shoulder. She turned to the company assembled. "Shall we go in?"

When Ezekiel offered his arm with an almost apologetic smile, Tabitha swallowed and slid her fingers onto the bend of his elbow. So this was her mother's plan. Her father's too? Apparently, for Judge Scott gave her an encouraging nod before he led her mother into the dining room with golden light from bayberry candles gleaming off china, silver, and mahogany furniture. A centerpiece of sugared fruit and roses crowned the table.

Ezekiel seated Tabitha and cast her several sideways glances as servants brought in the first course of roast chicken, veal pie, carrots, cabbage, and pickled cucumber. "Do you entertain much at River's Bend, Mrs. Gage?"

"No, not very much." Tabitha adjusted her ivory-handled fork next to her plate.

"I hear 'tis a beautiful place."

"Yes, very beautiful." She grabbed her glass as soon as a servant filled it and took a swallow of the spirits within, stronger than the cider she had grown accustomed to. She covered a cough. Did Ezekiel think he would become master of a rice plantation if he won her?

"But no doubt, not very safe." He picked up his fork and cut into his veal pie. "We have heard of the raids along the border."

"Indeed." Father spoke from the head of the table, his forehead furrowed beneath his white wig. "Lachlan McIntosh moved his family to a house across the square last fall. 'Tis ironic that his plantation was ransacked not by Loyalists, but by Patriot troops searching for food. The house, barn, all the outbuildings were destroyed. Two dozen slaves escaped."

Charles speared a bite of chicken. "The rebels are disorganized and will turn on themselves. The feud between Button Gwinnett and the McIntoshes is evidence of that."

Tabitha sat up straighter. "I heard that Mr. Gwinnett authorized this latest invasion of Florida." The reason she had to worry daily over the safety of a man she shouldn't care so much about. "Why does he dislike the McIntoshes so? They are greatly respected near Darien."

"Oh, my dear." Meg tittered and laid her hand on the table. "You speak in present tense. That must mean you have not heard of the duel."

"What duel?" Tabitha shook her head. The ringlets Dulcie had arranged slid over her shoulder.

"The duel between Lachlan McIntosh and Button Gwinnett." Meg's eyes widened. "It happened last month after General McIntosh called Gwinnett a scoundrel and a lying rascal. When the two men met on the field of honor, McIntosh took a bullet in the arm but recovered while Gwinnett sickened from his wound and died."

When Tabitha's frown of confusion lingered, Ezekiel expanded on his sister's comment. "Georgia's new constitution called for a governor, not a president, and Gwinnett was defeated for the post."

Tabitha's head began to ache. The type of drama and gossip that had once fed her now seemed petty and convoluted. "But why call him a scoundrel and a rascal?"

Her father's grim expression reflected his disapproval of women participating in political discussions. He must have felt the need to curtail it by supplying the necessary facts, for he said, "Gwinnett wanted McIntosh's appointment over the Georgia battalion. And he made accusations about a rice shipment some in the Continental Congress believed Lachlan's younger brother George diverted to England. He was proven innocent, but Gwinnett had him arrested. Even now that Gwinnett is dead, the House of Assembly plans to send George to the Continental Congress to stand trial."

Meg leaned forward with her brows raised. "Can you believe all the excitement you have missed?"

Tabitha resisted the urge to laugh out loud. But she had even less desire to reveal her run-in with Burntfoot Brown and his Indian allies to her old friend than she had to her parents. Because that would necessitate explaining why she had been all the way down on the Satilla River in the first place. She was more than happy to focus on the second course of baked apples and potato pie with sides of watercress and nuts while the men lamented how many sons of prominent Loyalists—such as the three Habershams, James Jr., Joseph, and John—now involved themselves in the Patriot government.

But when the discussion circled back around to how Lachlan McIntosh would be returning to Savannah to recruit and to honor those from the recent campaign, her head snapped up. "They are back from Florida?"

"Indeed, and there is to be a military ball for the officers who receive promotions. Not that we will be going." Meg gave a disdainful sniff but managed to look faintly disappointed at the same time. "Though I imagine your sister and brother-in-law will be there."

Mother dipped her head. "I daresay they will. Temperance and Ansel arrive tomorrow." At Tabitha's wide-eyed glance, she added in a low tone, "I was sure you would want to see your sister before you left."

Tabitha swallowed hard. Temperance would see through her little tableau that all was well in the first hour. Most likely, Tabitha would be no more successful in hiding her resentment for the role her sister had played in forcing her into such a position. If Temperance had heeded her many warnings all those years ago, Tabitha would never have had to step in and save her. Not only her, but the family honor.

No doubt, their mother had dragged out Tabitha's visit with the express purpose of reuniting her daughters, who had scarcely seen each other over the past ten years. Likely, she imagined some bond would be forged from the meeting.

But a more pressing concern was uppermost in Tabitha's mind. She turned to her father. "Did you hear what happened with the campaign?" With his political and military connections, he would be among Savannah's first to receive news

He frowned. "To my understanding, the Patriot flotilla was unable to rendezvouos with the mounted forces. Blown off course, 'twould seem. They ended up on Amelia Island, where some of their men were assaulted while stealing provisions. Colonel Elbert burned every house and killed all the livestock. He finally gave up trying to navigate the narrow passage around the island and came home in disgrace."

"And the mounted contingent?" Tabitha held her breath,

waiting for word of Edmond. Her heartbeat pounded in her ears.

"Got what they deserved as well—ambushed by Brown's Indians and Loyalists and the Regulars of Major Mark Prevost. They fled in a panic. Several were killed and twice as many wounded. Forty prisoners taken, half of whom the Indians later massacred." He chuckled over Tabitha's soft gasp, rubbing his hand atop his silk embroidered waistcoat.

Tabitha's stomach soured. Had any made it out alive? Was Edmond even now a captive? Or worse, had his body been left to molder in the Florida swamp? She shoved her knuckle to her lips.

Her father snorted. "Such a bumbling disaster could hardly be termed an expedition, if you ask me."

"Totally inept." Charles raised his glass of wine and swallowed the remainder.

"Your Loyalist friends *would* say that, would they not? And yet, none of you were there." Sliding her plate away with a shaking hand, Tabitha chanced a glance at her mother, who kept her gaze downcast. At the very least, the division in their family, with Ansel and Temperance serving the Patriot cause, must trouble her. Had Tabitha just given away that she now harbored similar worry for the Patriot soldiers? Especially for one in particular. Just how much worry surprised even Tabitha herself.

Suddenly, she had to get away from that table. From Ezekiel's admiring glances and the other men's scorn for those who risked their lives for freedom, hacking through the wilderness with a courage and determination those at this table would never understand. Even if she could not join their fight, she needed at the very least to belong to a place where people were honest and hardworking. Where she might learn if Edmond had returned safely.

She slid her chair back. When all eyes turned to her, she

offered an apology. "Pardon me. I find I am not feeling well. I beg your leave to retire early."

"Oh, my dear, we have not had time to renew our acquaintance yet." Meg's pleading expression stayed her. "And my brother...well, I was telling him of your unparalleled skill on the spinet."

"Yes, she was." Ezekiel shot her a hopeful glance.

"Indeed, daughter, would you not stay long enough to render a tune for our guests?" Mother looked truly distressed. Tabitha's failure to adequately entertain their company would shame her.

As much as she yearned to run, Tabitha forced her shoulders to relax. "Perhaps a song or two."

"Then let us adjourn before my daughter expires." Though everyone tittered at Judge Scott's teasing exaggeration, the implied rebuke lodged inside Tabitha's chest. If he knew her true circumstances, he would consider her every bit the failure her husband had, and far more disgraceful than the Patriot soldiers.

They made their way to the parlor, where Ezekiel seated her at the spinet while servants offered rum, coffee, and cake. Thankfully, Tabitha's musical ability was one area no one would find her deficient. Henry had purchased a spinet and had it delivered to River's Bend as a wedding present and had kept her supplied with the latest sheet music for her to play for him of an evening. Those hours had been among the few in which she found contentment. She knew a number of classical movements by memory and rendered several while Ezekiel looked on with rapt attention from a nearby chair and her parents and the Collins murmured amongst themselves.

When Tabitha finished a minuet portion of a Mozart serenade, Meg's brother applauded with far too much enthusiasm. "Bravo! That was sublime."

Meg straightened on the settee. "Have you the latest Bach keyboard trios, Tabitha?"

"I do." Setting aside her coffee, Mother rose and hurried to Tabitha's side. "I picked up a copy from the printer just last week in hopes that we might make use of it while Tabitha is home." She riffled through some pages on the music stand, then held out a small booklet. "Here we are."

Meg joined them, taking the score from her, but Ezekiel hovered over Tabitha with eyes solely for her. "I only pray I do not embarrass myself before such an accomplished musician." He reached for her hand, and before she stopped to think, she gave it to him.

But her fingers never made it to his lips. For he paused, frowned, and turned her palm over. "My dear lady! Whatever have you been doing with your hands?"

∽

An hour later, Mother wavered before the parlor fireplace, her dark gaze boring into Tabitha's. "And you have been living in a log cabin—with slaves?"

Father led her to the sofa opposite Tabitha's chair and helped her sit down. Her parents had remained standing since bidding their guests goodnight. Tabitha's explanation of working in the garden had failed to satisfy, her fumbling attempts to wave off their concern earning dismayed expressions and awkward silence. Finally, Meg had suggested they take their leave. And then Father had pulled the whole shameful truth from Tabitha.

"Dulcie and Cyrus are not slaves." Despite everything, it seemed important to point out this fact.

"Oh, my sweet heavens." Mother covered her face, then abruptly dropped her hands to her lap. "Why did you not stay here after the funeral?"

"I did not know then. And once I did, I did not want to run to you with my tail between my legs. I'd been married eleven years. I am hardly a girl to come back home to my father. I wanted to salvage a modicum of self-respect. After all, Henry left me three hundred acres of good timberland and two hundred head of cattle...though the Loyalists stole most of them." She snagged her lower lip between her teeth, then added, "I sold a handful to the army."

Father spoke over the moan that tore from Mother's chest. "The Patriot army?"

She quailed under his glare. "Of course. They are the ones at Fort Howe." Could he not be proud she had managed six months on her own?

"So this investment you speak of...it is not some idle whim as you have allowed me to believe."

Tabitha held her head up. "'Tis a matter of survival. Especially now that the cattle are gone."

Father jerked the hem of his waistcoat down. "I will not have my daughter living in such circumstances. Working the fields like a slave. Vulnerable to marauders and raiders."

"What would you have me do, Father? Wed Ezekiel Collins?" Though he would probably not have her now that he suspected she had fallen on ruin. They could consider themselves fortunate if Meg did not spread tale of Tabitha's decline all over town by the week's end, supposed friend or not.

"Julian Jackson would be a far better prospect."

She had known she should not tell him about the Jacksons' ultimatum. Tabitha clenched her hands together. "I shall *never* wed Julian. The Jacksons are cruel and mistreat their slaves. They have a terrible reputation with women. And they ruined Sergeant Lassiter's family."

"Who is Sergeant Lassiter?" Frowning, Mother cocked her head.

"The man who helped me when I went searching—helped

me round up cattle. Edmond..." She paused and swallowed the emotion that threatened to rise upon speaking his name. "Sergeant Lassiter was the one who recommended Jack McMullan's logging crew. They are friends of his family." Ignoring her mother's confused expression, she turned back to her father. "If you will help me secure the contract, I will not need to marry again or give up my land as payment to the Jacksons."

Her father stiffened his spine. "Financing this uncouth venture would only enable you to remain in base circumstances. No, if you will not marry Julian Jackson, you will forfeit your land in payment of your husband's debt and return home."

Tabitha spluttered, holding her hands out. "And what of Dulcie and Cyrus? Do they mean nothing to you?" Of course not. They were not even his slaves.

"They are free." He shrugged one shoulder. "They can find their own way. Elsewhere."

"But that land is their home."

"Then *they* can find a way to save it. It should no longer be a concern of yours." Father ran his hand over his face. "I acknowledge that this is partly my fault. I pushed you to marry Lord Riley. I had no idea of the financial troubles within his family." He cut her a sideways glance.

That admission was more than she could have hoped for. She softened a bit. "I know that, Father."

He raised his head. "What's done is done." Over a decade of silent suffering, dismissed in four words. "You will disentangle yourself from this situation and return to your family."

"And then what?" She could no longer imagine herself here, content with pointless rounds of visits, navigating the complex intrigue of local politics—even those of this household.

Her father flicked his hand. "Eventually, you will marry again."

"Please, Father. No. Give me some dignity. Some choice of

my own this time." Tabitha rose, holding her hands out. "Is not one loveless marriage enough?"

"Whether you marry for love or not is up to you. But I will not support this foolhardy endeavor. You are not a frontier-swoman, Tabitha. You are a lady. And you will behave as such. Now, I cannot imagine we have anything else to discuss tonight." Her father strode from the room. A chill descended in his wake that even the compassionate stare of her mother could not dispel.

Tabitha closed her eyes as the walls of her opulent prison threatened to close in on her just as they had a dozen years ago. She was out of options. If she wanted a solution, maybe it was time she looked outside herself.

CHAPTER SIXTEEN

T abitha could scarcely conceal her anxiety as she waited in her father's open landau with her mother and sister for the Georgia Battalion to march onto the commons outside Savannah. Other vehicles and pedestrians crowded around. Children played with Bilbo catchers and marbles, while a few families enjoyed picnics. The mid-June afternoon sun beat down on her black hat and widow's attire, causing sweat to trickle beneath her stays and shift. Her hair stuck to her temple. Her palmetto fan scarcely stirred a breeze.

By contrast, Temperance looked cool and fashionable in a white embroidered cotton robe à l'anglaise. Flowers and blue ribbon with a cockade on the side trimmed her straw hat.

That Mother was here was a wonder, given Father's Loyalist views, but she and Temperance had placated him by saying Temperance could hardly attend the review alone. Ansel and his men awaited the Georgia Line at attention with the other militia across the field.

Tabitha had planned to avoid her sister as much as possible, expecting that it would be too hard to witness her joy, surrounded by her doting, handsome husband and her two little ones. Not the mention, the third one on the way. Whereas she, Tabitha, had not been granted the love of husband *or* child.

But ever since Temperance's arrival the day prior, something strange had happened. Tabitha had fought tears every time she observed her sister's tender and joyful exchanges with her husband and children. And not tears of jealousy. Tabitha's long-held resentment melted away in light of the undeniable truth—Ansel and Temperance shared the kind of love Tabitha herself had been incapable of a decade ago.

She had done one good thing in her life when she had stepped aside for Temperance to live a happy life. That brought a surge of comfort, yes. But that did not mean Tabitha wanted her sister's pity. The pity that Temperance's spectacles seemed to magnify in her eyes as she watched Tabitha, revealing that someone had told her of Tabitha's plight—and making Tabitha want to burst from the carriage and run to...where? She could not stay in Savannah, and as soon as she showed her face in St. Andrew's Parish, Julian would demand payment in one form or another.

She had spent the night prior tossing on her too-soft feather mattress, wracking her brain for an idea. Dulcie's words had come back to her—that God would provide what they needed, especially in hardship. And the Scripture she had read... Maybe God had not helped her because she had sat in the seat of the scornful. Been too proud to call on Him for help. And yet, when trouble came, she wanted to be like the tree planted by the water. But would God turn away from her if she only came to Him as a last recourse?

Finally, Tabitha had sat up in bed. She wouldn't pretend to be pious by kneeling on her rug. She said aloud, "God, I've made a mess of things, and I have no idea what to do. If it is not too late, will You help me? If You show me the way, I will follow You."

There had been no immediate answer, but she had not

moved until her tangled thoughts unraveled and calm relaxed her limbs. She had lain back down and covered her head. For the first time in years, she felt secure, as she once had when her mother had tucked her into bed.

This morning, that newfound security had given her the strength to face the uncertain future. Besides, this was her chance to spy Edmond—if he was among the rangers. Although, if he wasn't, she must not panic. They would have left a contingent at Fort Howe, would they not?

"He will be here." Temperance's low statement drew Tabitha's attention.

"Who?"

"Your Sergeant Lassiter."

"How do you know about him?" And how did her sister know seeing him was Tabitha's goal?

Temperance's glance slid to their mother.

"I told her." The motion of Mother's fan ceased. "You said he was willing to introduce you to the man who could log your land. All I must know is, is he a good man, this sergeant?"

"A good man? Why..." Tabitha spluttered. "The finest." Whatever questions might remain about his background, she could swear to that much. "But why does it matter what kind of man he is?"

Mother tipped her head forward. "We might have been apart for some time, but I am still your mother. I can tell he means something to you."

Tabitha opened and closed her mouth, then met her sister's knowing gaze before her own skittered away. "He has helped me more than you know. Kept me from danger." Memory of riding through the night against his warm, solid form shot a shiver through her even in the heat.

"Do you think he would still help you obtain a timber contract?" Temperance touched Tabitha's petticoat. "And

Mother said something about you opening a store at the ferry. I think that's a wonderful idea."

"I...yes." If she had the money to stock a store. "I do not know if he will still help. I put him off. I was...hesitant to form an alliance with him."

"As well you should be." Mother sniffed.

Perversely, her mother's caution made Tabitha want to accept Edmond's offer. "Father has left me without options. But while I might discuss a partnership with Sergeant Lassiter, I would be a fool to nurture any personal regard."

"Because of the way Lord Riley treated you?" Temperance's dark brows knit. When Tabitha averted her face, her sister squeezed her arm. "Please do not be embarrassed. Mother and I ached for you, the way he kept you cloistered in the country. We saw the way his regard slipped—and loosened that sharp tongue of his—as the years went by."

Heat flushed Tabitha's face, and she pulled at her tucker. "Years I did not give him an heir." And they had no idea what she had endured.

"'Twas no cause for him to treat you thus." The indignation in her mother's tone went a ways to soothing the burn in Tabitha's chest.

"And that may have been his fault and not yours." Temperance huffed, drawing a wide-eyed glance from Tabitha. She had never allowed herself to believe what her twin suggested—because in some strange way, that would have made things worse. To be blamed for something that was not her failing. Catching her eye, Temperance gave a somber nod. "Pray, sister, do not allow Lord Riley's evil hold to continue even after his death. God would not want you to fear all men. I promise you, they are not all like your late husband. I want nothing more than to see you find the happiness you deserve."

Tabitha's throat tightened. Was God speaking even now, answering her prayer of the night before, giving her direction?

Did she deserve happiness? Had she not eloped with Lord Riley with the same selfish confidence she had approached everything back then? Had she not believed Henry adored her and she could manipulate him like a child? She'd even gone so far as to hope her sacrificial act would finally purchase her father's approval. What a little fool she had been.

Maybe she did not deserve a second chance.

"Of course, you're right, dear Temperance. Our Tabitha deserves happiness. I am not convinced, however, that this sergeant is worthy of her." Mother pursed her lips and searched in the picnic hamper on the seat until she came up with a ripe strawberry. "I would like to know more of his family."

"I had Ansel make some inquiries." Temperance pushed her spectacles up on her nose, her gaze roving to the road where the troops would enter the field. "Sergeant Lassiter has a good reputation in the horse rangers, and he distinguished himself in Florida."

"What?" Tabitha could not stop the word that rushed out with far too much relief. "He is well?" Her heart, which had seemed to pause in its courses, resumed beating with wild abandon.

A smile lifted Temperance's lips. "Not only well, but I have every reason to believe he will be at the ball tonight. 'Twill be the perfect opportunity for you to speak with him."

"I cannot go to a ball!" Tabitha spread her hands to indicate her black attire.

"As me, you can." Her twin's impish grin could've been a mirror reflection of Tabitha's a dozen years ago.

Their mother gave a slight nod, her lips tipping upward. She approved? Marjorie Scott had once lost all patience for her daughters' lookalike capers. The last time they had tried to pull one over on her, Tabitha had forfeited social privileges for a month.

"But surely, you wish to dance with your husband," Tabitha

said. And he would not wish to dance with her. 'Twas embarrassing to recall how she had once laid her cap for him.

The roll of a snare drum competed for her attention. The First Georgia Regiment marched their way from Fort Halifax.

"A lovely thought, but not so appealing when one considers that my morning sickness shows up at night. Captain Anderson would not thank me if I cast up my accounts all over his polished boots." Temperance laughed lightly. "But he does need to put in an appearance. Only long enough for him to pay his respects to his superiors and allow you a moment to see your sergeant."

Her sergeant. She had sent him away so coldly when last they met that she could not be certain he would even be civil to her, much less desire any further connection. Could she set aside her pride to find out? Should she?

Tabitha stared at the three regiments marching her way, most of them in the hunting shirts of frontiersmen, as formal uniforms had yet to be adopted save for some officers at dress occasions. Where were the rangers?

Temperance nudged her. "You were the one who loved dancing, anyway. I always wished I could be more like you when it came to the social graces."

"I do not socialize now." Her stiff lips conspired to keep the truth in. "Why are you doing this for me?" Once upon a time, Temperance had resented Tabitha almost as much as Tabitha had resented her, just for different reasons.

"I can understand why you do not want to come back here. I see you are not the same person. If I am not wrong, your values and loyalties have shifted."

"You...are not wrong." Tabitha glanced at her mother. Was this her doing? Because surely, perceptive as she was, Temperance could not have surmised so much from a couple of meals and an afternoon of knitting soldiers' stockings together.

"I owe you more than I can ever repay, Tabitha." Temperance's gloved hand slid over to grasp hers. "You sacrificed so much for me. I will do anything I can to help you. Ansel and I will support you, as will our mother, though as you know, we are not particularly well off since we choose not to own slaves. But you always have a home with us, should you need it."

"Thank you." Tabitha dipped her head. "I now see what it is to live under a harsh master, and I understand your case for freedom. But I would not accept a handout...or a home with you, unless all other options had been exhausted." Hopefully, her sister would take that not as an insult but as the bid for independence it was.

Temperance nodded. "As I suspected. So, if you care for this sergeant, if you see him in your future, the least I can do is send you to the ball in my place. Consider it our last switcharoo." The glimmer came back into her eyes.

Tabitha swallowed a knot of hot tears.

"She is right. You are not alone." Mother leaned forward to caress Tabitha's arm. "There is something I could never tell you before that I must now. I wanted this opportunity, the three of us together, to make things right between us. Between the two of you."

Tabitha shifted, unaccustomed to their affection, leery of what might come next. "What is it?"

"While it is true that your sister wrote some of the Townsman letters that threatened those suspected of enforcing the Stamp Act, she did so as an example for the Liberty Boys. She never meant them to be delivered to the recipients." Fiddling with her sheer cotton tucker, Mother let out a sigh. "I did that."

"You...what?" Tabitha blinked in the too-bright light.

"Your sister's maid was afraid for her and brought the letters to me." Mother patted Temperance's petticoat, and Temperance nodded. "Little did she know, I was a secret supporter of the Patriot cause. I sent them to your cousin Frankie, and he delivered them thinking that was what she wanted. So it was my fault when suspicions turned on the two of you girls."

Tabitha lifted her hand to her temple. The bright fife notes of "Yankee Doodle" pierced her head like needles through a pincushion. "Why are you telling me this now?"

"Because you also support the cause of freedom now. And I want *you* to be free. As I have not been. As you have not been. And that was partly my fault."

Tabitha shook her head. Here she had blamed her sister all these years, never knowing it was her mother's action that had set the events in motion which led to Tabitha taking the blame to clear her sister's name. And indirectly, to her disastrous marriage. "I do not know what to say."

"Say you can forgive us." Temperance squeezed her hand, her face earnest. "And say you will go to the ball tonight."

Tabitha licked her dry lips as she looked between the two women she had thought cared nothing about her. Her lungs expanded with a deep, hopeful breath. They were right that she wouldn't want charity, especially not Ansel's. And her mother could not help her financially without running afoul of Father. There was one man who could. Her gaze sought him out among the Georgia Regiment of Horse that followed the continental foot soldiers.

There! Tabitha gasped. There he was, sitting proud and tall on Maximus. And Dougal was beside him. God had spared him. Would Edmond give her a second chance? One way to find out.

She blinked tears from her eyes and nodded at her mother and sister. "Yes."

~

How had he gotten from the tangled wilds of Florida to here? Edmond stood stiffly beneath the many iron candelabras of Savannah's public long room as the notes of flute, violin, and viola swirled around him. Dancers sacheted past, stirring air heavy with beeswax and floral perfume. Edmond pulled on the scratchy red wool facing of the collar of his new blue coat, which he wore with buff breeches and red sash. He had avoided asking anyone to dance. Even if he knew the steps, he would be sure to tread on the ladies' slippers in his Hessian boots, not broken in as yet.

But when the tune ended and something called an Indian Queen was announced, Captain Josh Weldon's blond, blue-eyed wife gave a wistful cry at his elbow. "Oh, that is one of my favorites."

"You know I cannot dance, sweetheart." The man Edmond had saved at Thomas Creek, then a lieutenant, lifted his arm in its sling. "But perhaps the lieutenant will."

Had it not been for the expectation in his voice and the hopeful expression Mrs. Weldon turned on him, Edmond would have continued searching the men nearby for the officer in question. But oh...the officer was him. He stiffened. "I'm sorry, but I do not know the steps."

"'Tis just a country dance. I will teach you as we go." Mrs. Weldon's pointed chin tipped up with a smile.

Nothing sounded more terrifying. But Edmond could hardly refuse, especially after Weldon had insisted on Edmond's promotion, the tailor's commission for his dress uniform, and his appearance at the officers' ball tonight. One dance. God help him. He held out his arm. "'Twould be my honor, ma'am."

Mrs. Weldon talked him through the steps as couples assembled in long lines of women facing men. She even illustrated the harder moves. Edmond was still puzzling over the bit where he was expected to hop on one foot at a time while extending the other, knee bent, when the music began.

He managed to get through two rotations, working their way down the line without a major incident, though he felt more like a dancing elephant than the red-heeled dandies who made it look so easy. And then he made his diagonal approach to a new lady, one so stunning in a royal-blue gown with dark ringlets spilling onto one shoulder from an elegantly mounded style that he shuffled and started off on the wrong foot.

"Edmond?" The woman sounded as stunned as he was.

He looked a second time at her face. "Tabitha?" He froze, forgetting to twirl, and would have let the dance go on without them had she not grabbed both his hands and maneuvered them in a turn. "What are you doing here?" Why was she not at home with Dulcie and Cyrus? Had something happened to force her to leave?

"'Twould seem I am celebrating your promotion...unless I mistake the meaning of this uniform." The comment came out breathless.

"No mistake." But who was she with?

Mrs. Weldon came forward, beaming, to dance with Tabitha's partner, a tall militia officer who wore his brown hair unpowdered in a smooth queue—and whose sharp gaze assessed Edmond right back when the four of them made a star together, turning right, then left.

That done, Tabitha passed behind Edmond, back to back. "I was so thankful to see you at the review today. So afraid that..." The chain with their partners took them away from each other. She managed to speak again as she whizzed by. "Meet me after?"

Edmond gave a quick nod, but his head spun. She had feared for him? Thought of him? And now she wanted to speak to him. Would her partner allow her? Judging from the way he escorted her from the floor a few minutes later, a protective hand at her back, and took her to a corner near the open French doors as though he meant to sequester her all to himself, 'twasn't likely. But after Edmond returned a grateful and flushed Mrs. Weldon to her husband, Tabitha's eyes flashed something his way. Pleading?

Could it be? Tabitha's father had pushed her into an unwanted alliance before. Had the man already found a replacement for her dead husband? At least he had picked a Patriot this time. Though the notion sat like a boulder in Edmond's middle.

Edmond squared his shoulders, excusing himself to the Weldons. He made his way across the polished wood floor before another dance could obscure it. Stopped and bowed before Tabitha and her escort. "'Tis a pleasure to see you here tonight, Mrs. Gage."

"And you, Sergeant..." She fumbled, clearly uncertain of his new rank.

"Lieutenant." He could hardly believe it himself. He couldn't wait to tell his mother, especially because the promotion came with a raise in pay.

Tabitha's lips pursed over a smile, as though she might even be proud of him. "Lieutenant Lassiter." She indicated the man beside her. "This is my brother-in-law, Captain Ansel Anderson. Ansel, this is...*was* the sergeant I spoke of, Edmond Lassiter."

Her brother-in-law. Edmond relaxed and extended his hand.

The man shook it. "An honor. And congratulations on your promotion. From what I hear, 'twas by God's own mercy any of you rangers made it from the swamp. Eighteen of you, did I hear?"

"Thank you, sir. Yes. You heard correctly." Edmond glanced at Tabitha, who produced a silk fan and swayed it before her rosy face. The movement wafted that memorable scent of lemon from her hair, and his stomach muscles clenched.

Her wide eyes had latched onto him. "What happened, Edmond? We heard you were ambushed."

He nodded and told briefly of the attack, mincing his words in light of their festive surroundings. The war cries and blood and panic seemed like a lurid dream set against this glittering celebration. And Tabitha seemed like a different person. Surely, she could not be the same woman who had labored up to her elbows in blood after the attacks on Fort McIntosh and Howe. His voice lost momentum as he concluded his tale. "We beat our way through the bog for days until we found a local who directed us to Amelia Island, where we joined up with Colonel Elbert. We reached Fort Howe on June ninth. I wanted to come to see you, but..."

"But you were no doubt ordered here," Captain Anderson supplied.

"Exactly." Edmond chanced another glance at Tabitha. Something was different about her, besides her elegant appearance. "What brings you to Savannah?"

She fluttered a glance at her brother-in-law. "Ansel, perhaps you would get us all some punch? We can wait for you just outside the door there, where we might find a breeze."

He tucked one hand behind his back and gave a brief, stiff bow. After slanting Edmond a warning look, he pivoted for the refreshment table.

"I do not think he likes me very much." Edmond chuckled as he offered Tabitha his arm.

"I doubt that is it." Her fingers came to rest above his elbow, and he led her outside. Not much breeze to be had, just the cloying scent of roses and jasmine. Lightning bugs flashed here and there among the periphery of the garden, where couples strolled tabby pathways or murmured among the boxwoods. The splash of water from a nearby fountain almost covered low, sensual laughter. "I'm afraid my sister put him in a difficult position tonight—that of playing guardian to me while I came in her place. We are letting people think I am she."

"But why?" On the terrace just beyond the room, Edmond turned to her.

"So I could see you."

Tabitha's blunt honesty brought him up short. "I'm sorry. I fail to understand. When last we met, you seemed determined to go your own way."

Her lips pressed together a moment. "Something I have always done, and it has never worked out well for me. You asked why I came to Savannah. I went first to Darien, to convince Jack McMullan to work for me."

"Oh?" Edmond's brows shot up. "And how did that go?"

"Just as you predicated. He would not even meet with me. So then I came here in hopes of persuading my father to back me."

Edmond spluttered. "Tabitha, why would you do that? Did you not tell me how your father hurt you in the past? Why would you put yourself back in his hands?" And why her father rather than him?

She sighed and dropped her arm to her side. "Because I had no other hands to go to." When his brows pulled down, she glanced at him, then away. "Or so I thought. According to Dulcie's father, Julian Jackson had been to visit, and he intended to demand an answer by the end of the month."

Edmond's chest rumbled with a growl. "But that is already past."

"I know. I left before he could call again. I tried to convince my father, without revealing my true circumstances, that investing in timbering was in his best interest. But the truth has all come out, and I'm afraid his answer to my dilemma is the same as the Jacksons'." She pressed her fan against her dress and would not meet his gaze.

Her father would marry her to that...that scoundrel? "Oh, Tabitha. I am sorry." Edmond reached for her gloved hand and gave it a squeeze.

Her eyes swept up to his, a spark of hope igniting there. "I do not think it was all for naught. I believe I might have finally learned my lesson about running ahead of God."

"You did?" Edmond bent toward her. Tabitha's resistance to things of faith had stirred his concern—and an awareness of exactly how far he had strayed himself. That she had found peace with God renewed Edmond's desire for a partnership.

She nodded. "Then today, my mother and sister...they set some things straight about the past...and expressed their support for me. My mother is a Patriot, Edmond."

He smiled and cocked his head. "So maybe you were meant to come to Savannah, just not for the reason you thought."

"Exactly. It was they who told me to come tonight. Because I had told them about you."

He drew a soft, quick breath. "You did? What...did you say?"

"That you were a good man, one I should have trusted more. If you are still willing to help me..." Her gaze searched his. "Although...I do still have some questions, about your reasons."

"I can understand that." Edmond raised her hand to his lips and pressed a kiss on the back of her gloved fingers. He would never have dreamed Tabitha would come to him, her manner so changed. Her risk necessitated his. "I shall attempt to answer them, and I would be honored to accompany you back to Darien."

Her lashes fluttered. "To see Mr. McMullan?"

"Yes. But first, there is someone else I would like you to meet." It was time he did as Dougal had bid him and trusted her with a little more of who he was.

CHAPTER SEVENTEEN

"So ye are the widow Edmond wrote me about." The petite, redheaded woman Edmond had just introduced to Tabitha as his mother possessed a surprisingly strong grip for someone so wan and thin. The way her blue eyes bored into Tabitha's and the retaining and squeezing of Tabitha's hand suggested some special meaning. What had Edmond shared about her? "I am most glad to meet ye."

"And I you." Though she was still befuddled at how she came to be here, in the crowded parlor of this modest little house in Darien with children and youths running in and out and the ring of their father's anvil at his blacksmith forge echoing from the yard.

Edmond had escorted her and Dulcie here a couple days after the ball during his leave, accompanying them on the stage from Savannah. But he had not prepared Tabitha for meeting his family. Had offered no explanations in the public conveyance. She could only assume he meant to make those now, or after.

Standing beside her in his new dress uniform—which his mother had exclaimed over when he had hugged her in greeting only moments before—he cleared his throat. "I am escorting Mrs. Gage and her servant home on my way to Fort Howe, but first, we have some business here in town. And before I ask her to trust me with that business, I thought she should meet you. I wanted her to understand that you are one of my main reasons for wishing a partnership with her."

"Oh?" Freya Lassiter's ginger lashes fluttered as she released Tabitha's hands. "What type of business?"

"We should sit down." Edmond touched his mother's arm and gestured toward a frayed paisley wingchair near the blackened hearth, cold on this blistering late-June day.

"You sit down. I must serve tea," Mrs. Lassiter said and smiled as her brown-haired sister-in-law, Meg Grant, entered the room, followed by Dulcie, both carrying trays of refreshments. The two women had scurried to the kitchen moments after Dulcie, Tabitha, and Edmond arrived.

"*I* will serve tea." Meg, Dulcie, and Tabitha all said the same thing almost simultaneously. Everyone broke into laughter.

"Rest, Mother." Edmond took her arm with a gentle concern that confirmed what Tabitha had suspected the moment she met Mrs. Lassiter. The woman was unwell.

Edmond's aunt turned from settling the creamware pitcher and cups on a side table. "I shan't have guests pourin' in me home." She lifted the brace for the hanging front of the table, expanding it so that Dulcie could place her tray of cookies beside the tea. Meg narrowed her gaze on the servant. "That includes ye."

"Allow me to help with the cookies, ma'am." Dulcie dropped a tiny curtsy.

"Verra well. Then ye can sit over there."

As the woman indicated a rush-bottomed chair, Dulcie's brows flew up—no doubt in surprise she wasn't being sent back to the kitchen.

Tabitha smiled at the woman's kindness and moved toward the sofa, where Edmond's mother settled next to her.

Mrs. Lassiter patted her arm. "Edmond told me about the cattle contract with the army. Does yer joint business have to do with that?"

"No, ma'am. I fear the Loyalists absconded with most of my cattle." Thank goodness, Cyrus had rounded up another ten head in the weeks before Tabitha left the Altamaha. But she could never sell those—not if she hoped to rebuild the herd. "Your son had the idea that I might log my land for timber, and he offered to introduce me to Jack McMullan."

"Oh, yes. We know Jack well. He'll be delighted to meet with you."

Tabitha managed to swallow the unladylike guffaw which attempted to escape as Mrs. Lassiter's sister-in-law set steaming cups of fragrant tea before them.

Seated across from her, Edmond covered a smirk with a rub of his clean-shaven jaw. So handsome, with his hair and brass buttons shining in the sunlight from the window.

"My special apple cinnamon herbal blend." Mrs. Grant winked at Tabitha, turning the handle of the creamware cup toward her. "Heavy on the cinnamon for Freya's heart. And otherwise, a reminder that these insufferably hot days willna last forever. And the cookies are our Scottish shortbread."

"Thank you. Both sound wonderful." Her heart? So that was what was wrong with Edmond's mother. Tabitha chanced a glance at him when the older woman leaned forward to pick up her cup.

He gave her an almost imperceptible nod, but he addressed his aunt. "Has Mother been resting as the doctor ordered, Aunt Meg?"

Mrs. Grant turned from pouring herself a cup of tea. She peeked around Dulcie, who was distributing cookies on small plates. "Indeed, no, Edmond. I just about have to drive her from the kitchen with me broom."

Edmond angled a chiding frown on his mother, who sank into the sofa and hid her face behind her teacup. "Well, I cannae allow Meg to do all the cookin' mornin', noon, and evenin', now, can I? Not with me livin' under her roof."

"Ye're family, Freya. As I so often tell her, Edmond." Mrs. Grant shot him a look that enjoined his understanding as she settled into the wingchair.

Likewise finished serving, Dulcie took her seat at the side of the room, apparently too uncomfortable to assume she should partake of the refreshments herself. Tabitha wanted to urge her to sample one of the delicious shortbreads, but the conversation went on without pause.

"And I love bein' here, but I willna be a burden to ye." The firmness of Mrs. Lassiter's reply, coupled with the flush that stole onto her sunken cheeks, gave testament of her fiery Scottish heritage. No question, her inner strength far exceeded the outer.

"Never a burden. A blessin', 'tis what ye are." Mrs. Grant served up a scowl with her reassurance and delivered it over the top of her teacup.

Edmond sighed. "Maybe soon I can rent you rooms at Mrs. O'Reily's, Mother—close enough to visit as often as you wish but private enough to give you all more space. At least until I can get a place of my own. The promotion should help. As will this logging contract, should we obtain it." Edmond's glance at Tabitha confirmed his meaning. Helping his mother was part of his desire to help her. A reassuring reason, indeed. "Until then, you must do as Aunt Meg says, and I've arranged for another doctor to come down from Savannah next week. He may be able to suggest a better course of treatment."

"Ah, Eddie, you didna need to do that. I trust me doctor

here just fine." Mrs. Lassiter's use of Edmond's nickname and the adoring way she looked at him warmed Tabitha's heart.

"Nonsense, Mother. Why do you think I wanted this promotion so badly?" The same reason he wanted the partnership with Tabitha and McMullan, no doubt. "There is nothing I would not do for you. 'Tis little enough after..." His sentence strangling in sudden emotion, Edmond looked away.

Tabitha's chest squeezed at the pain that flashed across his face.

"Wheest, laddie. What yer father did had aught to do with ye." The fierceness was back in Freya Lassiter's eyes, like blue fire.

Edmond shook his head. "If I had not failed him in his hour of need...if I had come to him sooner..."

Tabitha sat up straighter, holding her breath. What was this?

"Nay. Dinna take that on yerself. Not ever. Y'hear me?" Mrs. Lassiter waited for a response, and when Edmond only clenched his jaw, she shook her finger at him. "That was his decision. Not yers. And if I lay responsibility at anyone else's door, 'twould be at that of Hugh Jackson."

Edmond swallowed hard. "That is another reason I want to help Tabitha secure this contract." At his use of Tabitha's name, his mother's eyes widened, and she looked quickly between them. Edmond failed to notice as he blinked away a sheen of moisture before he glanced at Tabitha again. "Her husband sold most of his land to Hugh before he died, as well as leaving her in Hugh's debt."

Mrs. Lassiter inhaled a soft breath, her gaze settling on Tabitha, who dipped her chin.

Edmond balled his fist on his knee. "Now Hugh wants the rest of her land. And we must find a way to stop him. I will not see another family ruined if there is anything I can do to prevent it."

His mother and aunt nodded, mouths compressed and eyes soft with compassion.

Tabitha curled her fingers over her beaded bag, which she had laid next to her on the settee. "Before I left, my mother and sister spared me what they could to alleviate the debt." She had told Edmond in the coach how Mother had used her own stash of coins she kept in her room so Father would not know. Tabitha had assured both of them she would pay them back. "Combined with the money I made from sale of the cattle, I can pay Mr. Jackson about half of what I owe. If he knows I have a way to pay the rest by the end of the year, it should satisfy him for now." After all, had the money lender kept her debt, the amount would have made her current on her payments.

"Then I will pray for your success." Mrs. Lassiter reached over to clasp Tabitha's hand.

"As will I," Mrs. Grant echoed.

"Thank you." Tabitha bit her lip. While she had the ear of godly women, she might as well take advantage, seeing as how inexperienced she was herself in such matters. "Please pray also that Mr. McMullan does not require a down payment for his services, which would cut into what I could offer Mr. Jackson."

"We will ask for just that, Tabitha." Edmond's mother patted her again. "But ye shouldna fash. Edmond will take care of Jack McMullan for you. Will ye not, Edmond?" Her expectant glance at her son produced a firm nod.

Now it was Tabitha blinking back tears. The warmth and support of this family was what she had been missing in her own—until recently. The evidence of it now gave rise to both regret and hope. Mainly hope, because she had more people in her corner than she had ever hoped she could—Dulcie, Cyrus, then Mother and Temperance, and now Edmond and his family.

His mother let out a soft, slow breath, set her tea aside, and eased back against the sofa. She tugged on her bodice as though in need of cool air.

"Are you quite all right, Mrs. Lassiter?" Tabitha fumbled for her fan. She snapped it open and leaned over to swish it near the woman's flushed face.

"Aye. 'Tis just the heat that gets to me."

And the emotionally charged topic, no doubt. Tabitha cast a concerned glance toward Edmond, but he was up, widening the cracked-open window in vain hope of a breeze.

"Perhaps yer mother should have a wee lie down before supper," Mrs. Grant suggested, coming to her feet. "But ye will stay to dine with us, will ye not? 'Tis been so long since we have seen ye, and she has been so worried for news of ye."

"Of course, we will sup with you. That is, if Mrs. Gage is willing." Edmond turned back from the window to seek Tabitha's reaction.

"I would love that." The bustling warmth of Edmond's family drew her. Made her so much more at ease than the stultifying formality of her own home, which had stifled her spirit. "Though perhaps we might find our lodgings for the night and come back later." Tabitha rose also, and Dulcie followed her lead.

"A good idea." Edmond came over to drop a kiss on his mother's forehead. "That will give Mother time to rest and me time to arrange a meeting with Jack McMullan for tomorrow."

And Tabitha time to find out what had made Edmond shoulder the weight of his father's guilt. She'd started to accept the arm he offered when his mother caught her other hand. Tabitha turned back to her with a smile.

"Me dear, I do so look forward to knowin' ye better. Any friend of Edmond's is a friend of ours."

"Thank you. I feel the same." Tabitha shoved down a swell of disappointment at that word...*friend*. But that was more than a business associate—and all she ought to allow herself to expect.

Yet Mrs. Lassiter went on. "I never dared to hope he would trust a woman again. But ye're not a woman, are ye, but a lady? And maybe just the one the Good Lord has sent to right the wrongs of the past."

CHAPTER EIGHTEEN

E dmond could practically feel the questions brewing in Tabitha's mind as he escorted her from the brown-painted saltbox on the outskirts of Darien, Dulcie just behind them. He waved toward the blacksmith shed where Uncle Ian, whom they had greeted when they first arrived, labored with his oldest son. They would speak more later. As much as he might want to put off Tabitha's curiosity, he could no longer afford to do so.

"I know it is hot." He settled his hat against the late-afternoon sun. "But I wonder if we might walk by the river a bit."

Tabitha seemed to understand his offer. "Of course." She turned to Dulcie. "Would you be comfortable to go ahead to the lodging house? I will join you shortly."

"Yes, Miss Tabitha. I will get everything ready for you to change for supper." With a dip of her head, the woman hastened down the street, past one of the many five-acre garden lots that surrounded the business district according to Lachlan McIntosh's 1767 redesign.

Edmond led Tabitha west toward the commons and the south channel of the river, deeper and wider than the north channel on the eastern side with its high bluff. They strolled through a field past a waist-high crop of indigo, its yellowing leaves and browning seeds indicating the approach of harvest. "Dulcie is a faithful servant," he said.

"She is becoming a friend."

Edmond squeezed Tabitha's hand. How quickly she had adapted to her circumstances. Never once had he seen her look down on those other people of her class would consider inferior—his family included. And the way his mother had warmed to Tabitha...well, she had always been a good judge of character. Mother had tried to warn him about Evangeline, had she not?

Edmond cleared his throat. "After the things my mother said, I assume you have more questions."

She dipped her chin. "Meeting her answered some but raised more. I understand that if McMullan agrees to log my cypress and pine and you act as my manager, 'twill help you take better care of your mother."

"For some time, I have longed to see her settled in a more restful place. As you saw, she will not stop doing so long as Meg's brood is about."

"We should speak of terms. I assume you would expect half." As they reached the shade of a live oak, she turned to him.

"What? Half?" He spluttered. "No. I was thinking of ten percent. After all, I will only be keeping your books and visiting the logging site and sawmill on occasion." Luckily, his family also knew the Scottish workers at the tide-powered mill near the former site of Fort King George.

"And providing the connection I could not have gained otherwise." She tapped her lips. "We should also speak of the store."

Edmond gestured her toward a limb that arched along the ground, so low and broad they were able to sit on it. With the

Spanish moss swaying above them, they had a place out of the sun and a view of the revitalized Fort Darien across the river. "It makes sense for me to build in the fall when the underbrush dies back. Then you could stock it after your timber goes to the mill."

Tabitha settled her petticoats around her. "Agreed. But we should set an amount for your labor. I can pay you as profits come in, if you are amenable to that."

"That is fine." He frowned. Did she still think he might not hold up his side of the bargain? "I am not here to take advantage of you, Tabitha. I am here to set wrongs to right."

"I'm beginning to truly believe that." She braced herself with her hands on the limb. "Hugh Jackson's harm to your family went deeper than undermining your father's firm, did it not?"

Edmond swallowed and settled his hat on his knee. Once Tabitha grasped the full extent of his ignominy, she might decline any further association with him, but she deserved to know all. Well, almost all. "Jackson turned most of my father's clients against him with rumors that he had cheated him and mishandled funds. Lies."

Tabitha did not express the surprise he'd expected. She must have heard something from someone already. "But why? Surely, even a man such as him must have some motive."

Edmond ran his hand over his face. It came away damp with perspiration, which he wiped on the leg of his breeches. "A couple of years ago, I had a fiancée. Evangeline Russell. She was from a good Savannah family. Only because my father had been doing so well did I have hope of marrying her. I couldn't believe it when she agreed to be courted. But Julian took notice of her. He wanted her for himself."

There was the surprise, observed in the twitch of Tabitha's brow, the parting of her lips. Did she now understand his warnings about Julian?

He cast his glance across the river. "At first, she spurned his interest. It galled him that she could choose a lowly factor's son over him, a wealthy planter. Then his father brought the pressure to bear. We lost our clientele while I was away at university. Father was utterly ruined." He forced his gaze back to Tabitha. "I wasn't in time to stop it."

Tabitha's furrowed brow showed her confusion. "Why was that on you?"

"Who else?" Edmond threw his hands out. "I am their only child. My mother has always had a weak heart. She knew nothing of the business or society world."

"But what could you have done?"

Edmond briefly closed his eyes. This was more painful than he had imagined. "I could have passed the final exam. Then Father might have believed I could have helped him reverse the damage Hugh had done."

Tabitha tilted her head. "I thought you said you excelled at accounting."

"I did, yes. I do. And I can build anything. That all has to do with numbers. But reading... Do you remember when you asked me to read from your Bible?" He waited until she nodded. "It shames me to admit it, but the letters and words jumble themselves, and I cannot always sound them out in my head. 'Tis not that I cannot read but that it takes me much longer. Too long for a timed examination."

"Oh, Edmond." He turned away from the pity in her eyes, but she rested her hand on his arm. "Can nothing be done?"

"I've had the finest tutors. They do not understand it. But that is not the worst of it."

"You do not have to tell me more. I know enough now." She withdrew her hand and sat up straighter. "I want you to represent me to Jack McMullan."

His chest clenched at her confidence in him, but... "You have to know the rest. 'Tis only fair."

Tabitha sighed softly, as if reluctant. "What, then?"

"I tarried returning home, in dread of his reaction to my failure, which is what led to his death. I was the one who found him in our warehouse. He had taken a rope and strung it over a rafter..." Edmond's throat closed, and he could not go on. He swallowed and blinked back tears. "Minutes too late."

With a cry that seemed to also lodge in her throat, Tabitha wrapped her arms around him. She laid her cheek against his shoulder, and he wrapped his arm around her and allowed her to nestle close. Having here there felt all too satisfying, although pity was surely the unwelcome motivator of her actions. The embrace knocked her wide-brimmed hat askew, and when she moved back to right it, he withdrew.

She studied him with her lips pressed together, as if sensing his withdrawal was emotional as well as physical. "Edmond, as your mother said, it was not your fault. For your father to have done that, to have left his wife and son in such a predicament, well..."

He finished what she would not say. "It was the coward's way out. I know. It does not lessen my regret."

"Of course not. But I hope you do not hold guilt over it."

There was nothing to say. He had done what he'd done. Father had made his choice. And nothing could change any of it now.

A boat slipping past Lachlan McIntosh's land opposite, lazing down the river without a care.

"And your fiancée?" Tabitha asked.

"What did I have to offer her? Nothing but ruin. Do you know what my name means?" He glanced at her. "Prosperous protector." A bitter laugh escaped him. "And yet, I had failed them all."

"No, Edmond..."

"That was when I joined the rangers." The compassion in Tabitha's brown eyes made Edmond's gut twist. "Needless to say, though I told her it was the only way I could make a living and asked for her forbearance, she did not wait for my return."

Her brow wrinkled. "But Julian—"

"He did not get her either." At least, that had been true in the end. Edmond had revealed all the sordid details of his past he could bear to for one day. "That is of scarce comfort. But I fear he has held it against me."

"And you against him." Tabitha's somber tone as she tightened the bow of her hat ribbons beneath her mob cap hinted that his fears about her not wanting to be associated with his family might have been founded. "I just need to know if this is about revenge or about making a better future where people like the Jacksons do not always win."

He turned his gaze toward the river and the contingent of men marching into the four-bastioned fort beyond. "I do not deceive myself that I have it in my power to give Hugh and Julian Jackson the comeuppance they deserve. I just want to see them stopped. And honest, God-fearing people succeed. But I understand if you wish you find another partner. I will still make the introduction to McMullan."

Tabitha let out a breath and pressed against him, wrapping her hand around his arm. "I want *you*, Edmond." At those unexpected words, spoken in a husky tone—at her warm, soft form so near, his eyes sought hers, and his heart raced. Did she have any idea how she affected him? He had steeled himself for rejection, yet she looked at him as though he was a kindred spirit.

But surely, that was all it was—a connection from their shared experiences. Their losses. He had just confessed his family's most shameful secrets to her. How could she hold him in any personal esteem? Though she had fallen on hard times, he'd seen the world she came from. She would always be a part of it. And that meant he could not allow a personal connection between them, even if her current vulnerability, her gratitude, made her imagine one.

"Then I will do all I can for you." He swallowed. "As a business partner. And hopefully, as your friend."

"Of course." Tabitha blinked and pulled back, a shadow snuffing out the light in her eyes. "That is all I expect."

Good. They knew where they stood with each other. Edmond rose and offered his hand to help her up. When she quickly dropped it and walked ahead of him back toward town, he stifled the ache in his chest.

~

By noon of the day following their arrival in Darien, Tabitha sat beside Edmond and across from Jack McMullan at a table in the Salty Seagull, the same tavern where she had attempted to ambush the logger a month earlier.

The tall, raw-boned Scot with gray in his dark beard eyed her as their server delivered a loaf of crusty bread and tin bowls of corn-and-potato chowder. "Why did ye not say when ye came callin' before that ye were workin' with Edmond Lassiter?"

"Because we only reached the agreement when we met in Savannah." Tabitha leaned back to convey her thanks to the serving girl before she departed with her tray.

"Ye just met in Savannah?" After ripping off the end of the loaf, McMullan held the chunk in one hand while he dug into his chowder with the other.

"No. We...have known each other for some time." Suppressing a twinge of exasperation, Tabitha exchanged a glance with Edmond. She held no desire to detail their unconventional relationship to this stranger.

"We merely met up in Savannah," Edmond clarified, "when

Mrs. Gage was visiting her family and I was in the city with the rangers."

Tabitha attempted to move things forward a bit more speedily. "As the lieutenant stated, my three hundred acres lie across and other side of the river from Fort Howe. We have worked together before, when he obtained my cattle contract with the army."

"But this is the first time ye've attempted to harvest yer timber." McMullan raised his one eyebrow at her. "No one else has been in there yet pickin' off the best trees?"

"That is correct. No trees have been harvested." Tabitha took a quick sip of cider to hide her nervousness.

"You would be the first," Edmond said. "And I have personally observed near the river several good stands of cypress and yellow pine, eighty feet tall and greater." As he went on to detail the attributes and location of the trees he had encountered while scouting and staying on her property, Tabitha ate her stew and prayed for favor.

"I assume ye have no bulls trained to pull the logs to the river." McMullan's sudden statement stopped her as she lifted her last bite.

Was that what other cattle owners did with their steers? She lowered her spoon. "No trained bulls. No."

"Then we would have to drive our own from Darien. Huh." He rubbed his hand over his mouth, then dropped it onto his thigh. "But 'tis good yer land is not so far up the river. The logs could be floated single rather than takin' time to construct rafts. Speeds up the process. Given that, me boys might could fit it in."

Tabitha straightened as relief spiraled through her. "That would be wonderful. Would you require a portion of payment up front?" She held her breath. *Please, God...*

McMullan leaned forward and scooped up another bite of chowder. "Lassiter's word is good as gold to me." He waved his free hand, his bread consumed. "We know his people. Mind, I'm not sayin' I will do it. I would need to come take a look first."

Tabitha relaxed a fraction as she flashed a smile at Edmond. "Of course. Come this week...or as soon as you can."

Edmond nodded. "We head home this afternoon. Call on me at the fort. I intend to explain the business to my commander there. Once he realizes setting Mrs. Gage on her feet will keep her land out of Loyalist hands, I'm certain he will support our endeavors."

"Loyalist hands?" McMullan wiped his mouth with his sleeve and cocked his head.

Once more, Tabitha explained her husband's indebtedness to Hugh Jackson and her determination to hold onto the acreage.

When she finished, McMullan slapped the table. "Well, why did ye no' say so in the first place? Anythin' to shorten the reach of the graspin', greedy Jacksons."

Tabitha broke into a grin. "Then we look forward to seeing you within the week, Mr. McMullan. After Lieutenant Lassiter shows you around, come to my cabin, and we can draw up our contract over a meal. You and your men can spend the night, too, if that would be helpful."

Rather than offering his gratitude as she expected, the timberman cast a puzzled frown at Edmond. "If this isna yer land, and ye're no kin to this lady, Edmond, why exactly are ye doin' this?"

Edmond stiffened. "The harm the Jacksons did my family is not reason enough for you? Not to mention, the fact that they are Loyalists?"

"Aye." McMullan sat back from the table and brushed crumbs from his hands into his empty bowl. "But look at it from my perspective, will ye? If there is no legal connection between ya, I'm not really givin' me agreement to ye, am I? I'm givin' it to her." He looked from Edmond to Tabitha. The pull of his upper lip illustrated his distaste. In his eyes, she was still just a woman, an outsider, the widow of a prominent Loyalist.

Panic surging, Tabitha sat forward. "Of course, I will be paying Lieut—"

"Mrs. Gage and I have an understanding." Edmond's statement cut into her explanation. "Her husband has only been gone six months. She is in mourning, as you can see." He gestured to her black attire. What was he implying? "She lacks the luxury of time to secure her land all proper-like, so for now, we share a business partnership. But I assure you, I speak for her in all matters. Do I not, Tabitha?"

Tabitha gaped at him. Edmond's words, his tone, his manner, made her want to shrink into herself the same way Lordy Riley's dictatorial edicts had. They took away her power, her choices. But Edmond's eyes pleaded with her to agree. If she did not, they would lose this contract. "Yes." She managed to squeak the word out.

Jack McMullan drummed his fingers on the table as he looked between them. Finally, he thumped the wood again. "Verra well. Saturday, I will come visit yer trees." He stuck out his hand, and rising, he and Edmond shook on it. When Tabitha rose, too, her legs shaky, the logger took her hand and bowed over it. "Madam. And may I be the first to offer me congratulations. Ye did well fer yerself, Eddie." With a wink at Edmond, McMullan fished a coin out of his pocket, laid it beside his empty bowl, and waved as he headed for the door.

It had scarcely closed behind him when Tabitha turned on Edmond. Heat flashed through her. "Why did you just allow him to believe we were courting?"

His brows pulled together. "If I had not, he would not have agreed."

"But what happens if we do not wed?"

Edmond flattened his mouth. Did her questioning him

provoke his ire? "His crew will have the trees harvested long before that would be expected."

"So I have no say in the matter." Tabitha sank back onto her chair. "I am simply to do as you say."

"You have *all* the say in the matter." Sitting next to her again, Edmond reached for her hands. "I am sorry if you felt circumvented, Tabitha. That was not my intention. If he had left the table without an agreement, we would have stood no chance of securing your income. You know that, right?"

Tabitha exhaled a shaky breath. His warm grasp worked to thaw her hurt. "I do know it. 'Twas just the manner in which you went about it." So painfully...familiar.

Edmond's eyes sparked with sudden understanding. "From here on out, I shall say nothing to Jack you have not approved first. You have my word."

How she wanted to stay angry, but when he lifted her hands and kissed the knuckles of first one, then the other—his lips brushing her bare skin this time—fire coursed through her that had nothing to do with her temper.

And his eyes, when he raised his head...light from the window accentuated the amber flecks in them. "Miladay...I am your servant," he said. "Will you forgive me?"

Tabitha gave a simple nod, not trusting herself to speak.

Edmond's lopsided smile carved a laugh line in his one cheek. The sight was so unexpected, so startling, she held in a gasp. Was he flirting with her? Tabitha's heart turned over. Every time she convinced herself she was better off keeping him at arm's length, he broke down another wall.

She wasn't quite ready to surrender to his charm. "You told me just yesterday this was a business arrangement. Now you want me to pretend we are betrothed?"

Edmond lowered their joined hands to his knees. "Let Jack think what he will. The important thing is that we get the contract. Right?"

"I suppose." When he grinned and squeezed her hands, Tabitha looked away.

Gossip had a way of spreading. Others might learn of her intimate association with Edmond Lassiter. Would that really be so bad if it got her what she needed? She no longer cared for her reputation in society—so long as their conduct was upstanding before God. The only risk would be to her heart. And she could manage that, could she not?

CHAPTER NINETEEN

The summer air was redolent with promise as Tabitha sat in the dogtrot with Dulcie, snapping beans they had picked that morning in the garden. For the first time since Lord Riley's death, Tabitha could take a breath—assuming she succeeded in inhaling the stultifying liquid one called air this time of year. Somehow, she did not even mind the heat.

The tropical splendor exploding around them went a long way toward offsetting the blistering temperature. Against lush green, everything bloomed in shades of pink and red—swamp rose, fewflower milkweed almost as tall as Tabitha in the marshes, rose gentian in the fields along the woods, and trumpet honeysuckle, the whorled flowers and berries both scarlet. Nature's bounty seemed all the more vivid when the weight of the world did not rest on one's shoulders.

The return to hard work felt good after the idleness of Savannah. Tabitha's chores gave structure to each day, and every evening, she read aloud from the Bible. Likewise, Dulcie taught her not only the homesteading skills Tabitha grew steadily more proficient at, but Scripture verses her friend had long ago committed to memory, especially from Proverbs, her favorite book. 'Twas at times annoying, the way they would pop out at inconvenient moments, such as when Tabitha was on the verge of losing her temper with the laundry or in the heat of jam-making. "'A man of understanding is of an excellent spirit.'" Spoken softly, eyes averted. Humbly yet clearly instructing Tabitha in the ways of the Lord.

Then there had been the Saturday evening two weeks before when Edmond had ridden into her yard with Jack McMullan and his foreman, another big, dark-haired Scot named Alastair. The grin on Edmond's face had seared joy through her and assured her that her and Dulcie's labors on the supper of wild turkey with sage and cranberry dressing, peas, summer squash, and blackberry cobbler had not been in vain. He told her they had marked the trees Alastair and his crew would return in the fall to harvest. After the hearty meal, Dulcie had cleaned up while Tabitha printed three copies of a contract. She, Edmond, Cyrus, and Jack signed, then Alastair took a fiddle from the case strapped on his horse, and they celebrated.

Tabitha smiled even now as she sat in the spot where she and Edmond had danced to the Scottish tunes. Their wild sweetness against the tawny twilight sky and his warm, firm touch as he whirled her around and around, both of them breathless with laughter at their unscripted caper, had filled her bones with honey. Had she imagined the heat in his eyes, or had it flared there for Jack's benefit? Or in triumph at their shared success?

"You thinkin' of the lieutenant?" Dulcie shifted on the bench to toss a handful of snapped beans into the bowl, the ends into her discard pile.

"What makes you think that?"

"That dreamy look on your face." Her full lips flattened a

rebellious smirk. "He sure did come through for us, did he not?"

"He sure did. Sending Cyrus with a hundred and fifty pounds and a signed copy of the timber contract to your father last week for Mr. Jackson felt pretty good too."

"Mm-hm." Dulcie paused to swat a fly. "You reckon Jackson got it yet?"

"I expect so." Mr. Long had promised to take the money straightaway to his employer rather than wait for him to visit River's Bend.

"You reckon he gives us to Christmas to pay the rest?"

Tabitha snapped an extra-long bean into three sections. "If he wants to be fair about it, he will."

"Fair is not what men like him be known for." Dulcie pursed her lips.

Tabitha managed to quell the unease her companion's observation stirred—until horse hooves echoed up the path. Cyrus was out in the cornfield, and she was not expecting Edmond today...although his captain had given him the leeway he needed to oversee her timbering, just as Edmond had said he would do in support of the cause, since no new campaigns loomed on the horizon. But logging would not start for at least a couple more months.

She set aside her bowl of beans and rose for a better view.

When the trees disclosed a trim, erect figure atop a black stallion, Tabitha stiffened. Julian Jackson.

"Guess that answers my question." Dulcie's statement was as heavy as the stone in Tabitha's stomach. She sighed and brushed stems off her apron. "I can fetch cider."

"No." Tabitha clutched her arm. "Pray, do not leave me."

Mouth in a grim line, Dulcie settled back on the bench while Tabitha went to the edge of the porch.

Julian dismounted at the hitching post. His choice of clothing reflected the need for practicality in the heat rather than his usual panache—white cotton shirt, long, striped linen waistcoat, and buff breeches with his riding boots. From the moment his straw hat tipped back and his eyes met hers, though, a chill invaded the sweltering day.

"Mrs. Gage." Even her name held an edge.

"To what do I owe the honor of this call, Mr. Jackson?" Tabitha pressed her work-roughened palms against her linen petticoats. No doubt, sweat stained her underarms and glistened on her face, but she took a perverse pleasure in greeting him in such a state—refusing to even remove her apron.

"I came to discuss your loan payment."

She tilted her head. "It was not necessary to come all this way to thank me, sir." What a relief to be able to say what she wanted again. To reclaim just a modicum of self-respect.

"To thank you?" He barked a laugh. "To warn you. Indeed, I could not ride here fast enough to enjoin you to flee the danger to which you have unwittingly bound yourself."

"What danger is that?" Did he know something about Jack McMullan that she did not? Likely, he only sought to scare her, to force her back onto the defensive.

"If you will invite me on your porch, I shall tell you." Despite his request, his gaze swept the double-pen cabin with unveiled distaste.

"Of course. I was not certain you could abide our humble surroundings long enough to tarry." Gesturing him up the steps, Tabitha turned to Dulcie. "Will you fetch a proper chair for Mr. Jackson?"

Her brows a flat line, Dulcie went into the main room. She returned a moment later and placed the rush-bottom chair in the middle of the dogtrot, facing the bench where they had been working.

Patting her face with her apron, Tabitha returned to her spot.

Julian stepped around Dulcie and sat on the chair. When

she remained standing over him, he looked up at her. "And some lemonade."

Lemons? Tabitha laughed.

Dulcie answered through stiff lips. "We have cider."

"Well, go fetch it, woman. Or are you not in the habit of obtaining refreshment for your guests?" Tossing his hat onto the bench next to Tabitha, he swiveled to face her without waiting to see if Dulcie would obey his instructions.

Dulcie's narrowed gaze met Tabitha's, but Tabitha gave a slight nod. While Julian might be a guest of the most unwelcome variety, it would hardly do to anger him—especially when his sharp tone and abrupt gestures already conveyed a barely restrained temper.

As Dulcie turned, she spoke under her breath. "'If he be thirsty, give him water to drink.'"

"What was that?" Julian shot her a sharp glance.

Tabitha hid a smile behind her hand. "Dulcie was just agreeing with you that the Good Book enjoins us to offer hospitality." She suffered no temptation to add that the first part of that particular verse in Proverbs referenced showing kindness to one's enemies.

Julian scoffed but let the moment go.

Tabitha folded her hands in her lap. "Now, do I take it you and your father found something amiss with my payment? I did not think my request to settle the balance in December unreasonable given the fact that we supplied all we would have owed to the lender through this month, as well as offering a written guarantee for our means of obtaining the rest."

"Timber. That was smart." Though Julian's eyes slitted, the ire left them. A glow of admiration replaced it. "I should have thought of that myself."

"Then it was not my agreement with Mr. McMullan you objected to?"

"Not with him. With Edmond Lassiter." Julian straightened as he fairly spit out the name.

"Ah, yes." Why had she not expected that he would learn of Edmond's involvement, even though they had forbidden Mr. Long to mention it? "I did hear you had some unsavory business with his family once." She kept her face impassive and her observation vague. The less he thought she knew of his past association with the Lassiters, the better.

Julian's handsome face twisted. "He was cheating my father. Skimming off the top of our earnings."

"There are two sides to every story, Mr. Jackson. And that was Edmond's father, not Edmond."

"Edmond, is it?" He scoffed. "So the rumors are true?"

Tabitha kept her hands relaxed, though her pulse started to race. "What rumors?"

"That Lassiter is helping you because you intend to marry him." The hatred for Edmond in Julian's eyes—an obsessive envy that had existed long before she ever entered the scene— warned Tabitha not to feed his jealousy.

"You, of all people, ought to know better than to pay heed to the grapevine."

"So 'tis *not* true?" Julian leaned forward, the scent of sweat and spice invading her space. "Answer me straight, Mrs. Gage."

Tabitha's back stiffened. "I do not see what concern it is of yours."

"Do you not? When I am still waiting on your answer myself?"

"I thought my payment provided my answer." She rolled her lower lip between her teeth.

Thankfully, Dulcie appeared in the doorway with two pewter cups. Julian glared at Tabitha, refusing to release her gaze even as he took his drink from Dulcie. When she lingered, casting Tabitha a concerned glance, Julian finally looked at her.

"Do you not have something to do in the house? This is a private conversation."

Dulcie lifted her chin. "I answer to Miss Tabitha, not you."

The incredulity that momentarily contorted Julian's face made Tabitha lift her hand. "'Tis all right, Dulcie. We will be in hearing range."

Dulcie hesitated. After a moment, she dipped her head. "Call if you need me, ma'am." She went back into the cabin but remained in view of the open door as she worked at the table.

Julian's disregard for Dulcie gave Tabitha the courage to speak her mind. Cradling her cool tankard with her lashes lowered, she drew a deep breath. "Mr. Jackson, if your attitude toward my servant is any indication, the rumors of the poor treatment of your slaves are true. I saw enough cruelty and neglect at the hands of my husband. Why would I wish to subject myself and my servants to that again? Why would I wish to subject my land to rice cultivation, which requires heavy slave labor? For the first time in my life, I can be the mistress of my own destiny. Why would I forfeit that?"

Julian stared at her, and the tension left his broad shoulders. Perhaps her direct approach had disarmed him. He sat forward, but entreatingly this time, not threateningly. "Mrs. Gage...Tabitha...I fear we have been operating out of misunderstandings on both sides. Will you allow me to attempt to set things straight?"

She gave a slow nod. "I will hear you out."

"First of all, it grieves me deeply that a woman such as yourself would have suffered cruelty and neglect at the hands of any man, especially her own husband. Lord Riley was a fool. To take out his own failings on you rather than tapping into the resource at this side..." Julian shook his head. A damp tendril of hair fell onto his glistening temple.

Tabitha tipped her head. "Resource?"

A muscle in his cheek twitched. "Only a weak man is intim-

202

idated by an intelligent woman. 'Tis clear you could have helped him out of his financial troubles had he only invited you into his confidence."

Stalling a moment, Tabitha sipped her cool, tangy cider. This was not how she had forseen this conversation going. The loss of control left her fumbling. "What makes you say that?"

Julian spread his hands. "Well, for a start, he overlooked a fortune in timber."

"I doubt the Scottish loggers would have contracted with a known Loyalist."

His dimple flashed. "I bet you could have persuaded them, for you have done just that."

She pressed her back against the logs behind her. "Not as Lord Riley's wife." As Edmond's *betrothed*.

"Even as his wife, I daresay you would have. And then Mr. Long told me of your idea of a store. Brilliant! You have done the impossible—succeeded without a husband."

She had done nothing as yet, but better to not point that out either. Tabitha set aside her tankard and folded her apron between her hands. "If that is the case, why would I need to take a husband? Admittedly, marriage has not been good to me, and if I become financially independent..." She shrugged.

Julian's lips turned up in a slow smile, and he looked around. "Because while you might survive, Mrs. Gage, you are far from thriving. You? Here? Working like a slave?" He flicked a fold of her dirty petticoat with his pointer finger. "This is not what you were born to. You are a lady and should be treated as such. There is a beautiful house setting empty across the river, in need of a mistress's guiding hand. You could have back all your foolish husband squandered and much more—including a younger mate who can give you what Lord Riley never could." Julian's languid expression left no question as to his intended meaning.

There it was again—the intimation that the stain of barenness lay not on her, but on Lord Riley. Could it be? She might yet become a mother?

The sudden image of Edmond with a child upon his knee made heat climb like trumpet vine on Tabitha's cheeks. But she was too old for either him or Julian. They might not mind it now, but they would in ten years, especially if it turned out she *was* to blame for the lack of children. "If you are suggesting yourself as a husband, there are many much younger ladies who would be delighted to become the next Mrs. Jackson."

"Insipid girls, easily won, quickly tiring, who would have no idea how to help me run an empire."

Tabitha's lashes fluttered. "I am certain your father would take exception to that idea."

Julian flicked his fingers. "His role is waning. Already, he entrusts me with more and more. You guessed rightly that he would plant this acreage in rice, but I would diversify. And you would be just the woman to help me do it."

If Edmond had not shared his story of ruin at the hands of this man's family, Julian's fine words and charismatic presence might have swayed her. Might make her wonder if he could actually hope to plot a better path for his future, to overwrite his father's reputation for debauchery and cruelty. After all, anyone could change under the right circumstances. Hadn't she? A decade ago, she would've been more than Julian's match in pride and snobbery.

As it was, as long as she owed him money, Julian had power over her. She could send him away with a lofty rejection, but she would also feed an enemy's hunger for revenge. Against herself *and* Edmond.

Tabitha lowered her head in a show of submissiveness. "You honor me, sir. But you will understand why I struggle to believe what you are saying when I have seen firsthand how hollow the promises of powerful men such as yourself can be."

Julian went still. "But you will accept promises from—and

make promises to—a common man like Edmond Lassiter?" A hint of a growl rumbled from his throat. "Believe me when I say, he does not come from honorable stock. Do you know he once left the woman he claimed to love?"

Tabitha's gaze shot up. She widened her eyes in pretended innocence, but...could Julian be telling a part of the truth Edmond had left out? Had his fiancée asked him not to leave her rather than joining the rangers? But what choice had he had?

Seemingly encouraged by her doubt, Julian warmed to the story. "She begged him to wed her and try to salvage his father's business rather than flee like the coward he was, but instead, he abandoned both her and his mother, leaving them to face the shame of his father's deeds. I see you know what I am speaking of. But I am not here to impugn a man who is clearly beneath both of us. Only to offer you another option."

Tabitha sought to deflect the bitterness emanating from the man opposite her, despite his denial. "My arrangement with Lieutenant Lassiter is of a business nature. He agreed to help me to benefit both of us in a time of need."

Julian's gaze locked on hers. "Though he is a Patriot and you are a Loyalist. Or has that changed?"

Tabitha fought the urge to wiggle under his close perusal. How to answer without openly declaring herself his enemy? "I admit, I hold a greater appreciation for independence now, Mr. Jackson."

"And I would not take that away from you, Tabitha. But one can often find the greatest independence under a strong and benevolent leader."

Tabitha swept her lashes down. "At times, perhaps." He was cleverer than she had anticipated, a master of words—she would give him that. But had not Satan himself founded his arguments on a scrap of truth?

"Now that you know my motivations, my heart, pray, do not

dismiss my suit so quickly only to come to regret it later." He reached for her hand, but when his fingertips brushed the calluses crowning her palm, he could not quite hide his wince. He covered it with an explanation as he withdrew. "As my wife, you would never again be forced to demeaning labor."

What could she say? A response flashed to mind with sudden clarity. "I will...pray on it." That she could do. Pray for God to show her how to outmaneuver Julian Jackson. Now, at least, she was smart enough to know she could not do so on her own.

Julian rose and gave a brief bow. "Then I will take my leave. For the moment." Settling his hat on his head, he strode down her steps with the assurance of one who had hope.

Hope. A dangerous thing. But not as dangerous as rejection. Edmond would want her nowhere near Julian Jackson. And Julian must never learn how she truly felt about Edmond.

CHAPTER TWENTY

Bathed and shaven after his latest scout, Edmond rode
Maximus toward Tabitha's cabin with a light heart.
Banners of late-July sunlight slanting from the west through
primeval trees alive with the songs of exotic birds and winged
insects signaled the coming of evening. The sultry air held the
lemony scent of devil's walkingstick abloom with creamy clusters of small flowers that reminded him of Tabitha's hair. In
deference to the heat, Edmond had opted for a linen waistcoat
over his shirt instead of the heavier hunting shirt he normally
wore. Hopefully, the timing of his arrival would produce an
invitation to supper.

He couldn't wait to see Tabitha. To share the drawing he'd
been working on of an evening by the campfire. But if he were
honest, it was more than that. He'd missed her these past two
weeks. Thought far too many times about the way her slender
waist had felt under his hands, and her hands in his, as he
taught her jig and hornpipe steps to the notes of Alastair's
fiddle. And he was hoping for a peaceful season ahead far more
than a Patriot officer who wanted to lick the lobsterbacks once

and for all should—so he could see Tabitha often as they worked together on her land.

'Twas a dangerous thing to allow this attachment to grow, for despite what he had told her, this need to be near her went far deeper than that of a business partner or friend. But it felt good to be needed...and to finally be able to do something to make a difference. Was it wrong to enjoy that pleasure a little longer?

As he rode into the yard of her cabin, Tabitha came out on the porch. She lifted a hand, her face breaking into a smile, and then ran down the steps.

There was no denying the way his heart leapt at the sight of her.

Cyrus waved from an outdoor fire where he was turning a chicken on a spit.

Edmond waved back and dismounted as Tabitha hurried forward to greet him.

"Edmond! What a nice surprise. You look well." She swept her gaze over him—was that approval in her eyes?—and flushed as he bowed over her hand.

"Thank you. As do you." She wore a light-blue dress he had not seen before, her mob cap concealing most of her hair. Edmond flashed her a teasing grin. "And I *am* well, for there was no evidence of Loyalists on my last scout, and I am here now. With you."

Her fluttering lashes and the way she pulled back, concealing her hand shyly in her skirt, confirmed that yes, he had actually said that aloud.

He hurried to explain. "I have something I want to show you."

"Oh? What?" Curiosity sparked in her brown eyes. Clasping her hands behind her, she resembled a girl anticipating a present.

"Inside. If I am welcome?" Edmond raised his brows.

"You are always welcome. But can it wait until after supper?" Tabitha turned as Cyrus approached.

"Lemme take Maximus to graze," he said.

"If I am not mistaken, Cyrus, the bird is ready for carving."

"Yes, ma'am. I will bring it in soon as I get Maximus here on the picket line."

"Thank you." As Cyrus led the stallion toward the creek, Tabitha gestured to the cabin. "Come in."

Edmond's stomach rumbled at the idea of a home-cooked meal, and he gave her a wink, playing off the literal meaning of her invitation. "Am I invited to supper too?"

"Of course, you are." She swatted his arm, then grabbed it to pull him up the steps. "Silly man."

The affection thickening her voice wreathed his heart with the warmest insulation. Was this what coming home felt like?

"You picked a good evening to visit," she said as she preceded him through the open door. "Dulcie's parents paid us a visit today, and Annabelle brought her famous bread—and buttermilk pie."

Dulcie looked up from slicing a crusty loaf on a platter at the table. "Welcome, Lieutenant. So nice to see you." She gave him a warm smile, then cast a glance at Tabitha that seemed full of meaning he couldn't decipher.

"Yes. Well. I shall set another place." Tabitha hastened to the sideboard, where she fetched a fourth creamware plate and pewter mug and set them beside her own spot.

Edmond frowned at the creamware pitcher from which colorful wildflowers nodded in the center of the table. "I did not remember you having those dishes."

"We did not. Annabelle brought them today. Do they not look nice?" Her voice sounded overly bright.

"Yes, but will she not get in trouble, carting off things that belong at River's Bend?"

"'Twas only our second-best set. She said the Jacksons

shan't mind. Let me fetch the beans from outside and take Cyrus this dish for the chicken." Taking up a creamware platter, Tabitha hurried through the door.

Edmond turned to Dulcie, who set a crock of jam on the table, her lips pressed tight. "I am sure you enjoyed a visit from your parents, but you must share my concern that the Jacksons will disapprove of their coming here—and bringing presents."

"Oh, the presents were why they came. Master Julian sent them."

"'Sent them'?" Edmond's heart bottomed out. "Your parents? Or the presents?"

Before the servant could answer, Tabitha preceded Cyrus back inside, carrying the platter of chicken while he toted a wrought-iron pot with a rag wrapped around the handle. "Edmond? Would you do the honors and carve?" Placing the tray on the table, Tabitha faced him with a brilliant smile.

"'Twould be my pleasure." Though concern now diminished his appetite.

Still, he could not but enjoy the delicious meal, especially after weeks of jerky and hard biscuits on the trail. And maybe he only imagined that Tabitha kept him talking rather than offering her own updates. "You said there was no sign of Loyalists north of the Satilla, but what news do you hear?" she asked as she poured real coffee into a creamware mug before him.

Her touch on his shoulder drew his attention from his buttermilk pie. "No sign, but Lieutenants Robinson and Cannon, who are currently in command at the fort, have received intelligence that local Loyalists have been meeting with envoys from East Florida."

She paused at his side, her face going slack. "Planning an invasion?"

"So they believe." Edmond fixed a firm gaze upon her.

Cyrus sipped his coffee and set the mug back down. "Two

lieutenants, you say? What happened to the captain who was at the fort?"

"Reassigned. And in the absence of senior officers, discipline suffers. The handful of men I commanded as a sergeant are the only ones I can count on to get anything done." Edmond raised his mug and savored the flavorful brew as Tabitha moved away.

"Will they assign someone new?" She placed the pitcher on the hearth and resumed her seat beside him, drawing her own slice of pie close.

He shrugged. "Perhaps. But not one of the McIntoshes." Edmond cut another bite of pie but finished his explanation before forking it. "You may have heard the Council of Safety refused George McIntosh's request for a trail in Georgia. They planned to humiliate him by sending him to Congress under a strong guard. He fled to Darien last month, only to discover that men who said they were acting on the governor's orders had ransacked his plantation."

Cyrus grunted. "We did hear that. Mr. Long told us they seized his slaves so he could not get in his harvest, and they were huntin' Mr. George like a runaway through the swamps."

Chewing and swallowing, Edmond nodded. "That is the last I heard too. I imagine he and Lachlan will have to leave the colony to find any justice. 'Tis a shame for a family that has served Georgia so well to be treated thus. In the meantime, we do all we can to hold things together at Fort Howe. I pray an invasion does not come soon."

After they finished dessert, Dulcie cleared the board while Cyrus went to the porch to light his pipe and Tabitha turned to Edmond with an eager smile. "Will you show me your surprise now?"

Edmond pushed his coffee back. "That I will." He reached into the pocket inside his waistcoat and drew out the folded paper. Opening it, he laid it flat before her and waited in expectation as she leaned close and studied the drawing.

After a moment, she gasped softly. "Why, this is my store."

"I've done a rendering of how it will look from the front as well as a floor plan."

She touched the bottom of the page, then looked up at him, her brown eyes aglow. "Down to all the measurements and elevations. Why, Edmond, this must have taken you quite some time."

He shrugged, though warmth flushed through him. "A good way to pass the long evenings." Leaning forward, he pointed to the layout. "You see 'tis twice the size of a regular single-pen structure, but all under one roof. Thirty-two by forty. That way, we can use the standard length of timbers, and if you approve, I can request planks that same measurement be milled when we deliver your logs. We can join them to timbers running crosswise in the center, with supports beneath, to prevent sagging. That will provide plenty of room to display your merchandise, even larger items."

"That would be perfect." For all its enthusiasm, Tabitha's reply was slightly breathless, and when their fingers bumped over the drawing, she shot him a quick glance and curled her hand. "Is this space in the back for storage?"

"This portion might be used for barrels and crates and such. You can store smaller items upstairs." Edmond pointed to the measurements of the second story, then tapped the majority of the main floor behind the store. "This part would be given to living quarters. Two rooms—a common room and a bedroom."

She sucked in her breath. Raised her head and glanced at him, then at Dulcie, who was wrapping up the remainder of the pie. "I could give Dulcie and Cyrus back their cabin."

The servant shook her turbaned head. "'Tis not our cabin, Miss Tabitha, but yours."

Tabitha seemed not to hear her. "But how could I live alone? That would not be safe."

Edmond met her questing glance. "I do not imagine it would." Awareness grew between them as his meaning settled over Tabitha, and a flush spread across her cheeks.

"Oh."

"'Tis only an option for the future." He found he couldn't look away. The more he helped design Tabitha's future, the more difficult it was not to picture himself in it.

"Seems you have more options than you thought." The low-spoken pronouncement from Dulcie broke the moment.

Edmond glanced at her, then back at Tabitha. "You are considering something other than a store?" Had he done all this planning for naught? What had changed?

"No. This is perfect." Tabitha drew his drawing toward her as if she feared he might scoop it up and dart out the door with it.

"She shan't need living quarters in it, though, if Mr. Julian has anything to say about it." The mulatto woman sashayed past, brows raised, taking the rest of her coffee with her to join her husband on the porch. A timely exit after dropping a cannonball on them.

Tabitha gasped. "Dulcie." But with a swish of petticoats around the corner, Dulcie left them alone. Judging by Tabitha's panicked expression as she turned back to him, this was the subject she had been skirting all evening. "Pay her no heed. Julian Jackson does not influence my decisions."

"Then why are we talking about him? And why is he sending his overseer with gifts?"

She let out a little breath. "A vain attempt to sway me."

"From working with me." Edmond's body went tense. Why had he thought the Jacksons would simply bow out if Tabitha found a means of supporting herself? That they would take no notice of his involvement? Indeed, his very presence in her life had probably doomed her. Julian would never suffer a lesser man to win—especially Edmond.

"I did not listen." Tabitha ventured to touch his arm, but he withdrew.

"And what does he suggest you do instead?" He already knew the answer. And the way she firmed her mouth and blinked confirmed it. "He still wants to court you."

"He claims to approve of my plan for income."

"But he wants to be part of it. Of course, he does."

"He thinks diversifying is better than planting the land in rice. He says he wants to go about things differently." She was doing it again—talking around things rather than responding directly.

Just like Julian with his silver tongue.

Tabitha lifted one shoulder. "Perhaps we worry overmuch and he is not the foe we think him. After all, we know a son can chose a different path from his father."

Edmond's breath hissed in. How dare she compare him to Julian? "He is exactly the foe I think him. Men like him do not change." He slid the sketch toward him and folded it, but Tabitha grabbed his hand before he could return the paper to his waistcoat.

"Stop. Edmond, I want to keep that. Even if he has changed, I would never marry Julian Jackson."

"Did you tell him that?" He speared her with his gaze.

Her slender throat worked over a swallow. She had not. "I told him I valued my independence and that I knew he would understand that...just as you do."

"I do." And for some reason he wanted to run from, it pierced him like a bayonet. How far short of his hopes the reality of this evening now fell. Leaving the plans on the table, Edmond rose and stepped behind the bench. "Send Cyrus with a message when you decide about building."

She scrambled up beside him. "Of course, I want to build. I haven't changed my mind. Why would I? Why are you so angry with me? I did not ask Julian to call." She trailed him into the center of the room.

Edmond whirled to face her. "You really need ask that? After I told you what he and his father did?"

"You think I should have sent him packing." Her brow hardened to the appearance of marble. "But you forget, I still owe him a hundred and fifty pounds. Until I am free and clear of him, I am not safe. Is it not better to know the movements and plans of your enemy? Is that not why you spy and track and scout?"

Hmm. She made a fair point. But Tabitha going up against Julian was like a doe flailing her hoofs at a panther. "There are some foes you never allow into your territory."

Her fingers curled around his arm, and she moved closer, her eyes blazing. "And to do that, you have to have ammunition. You have to have a way to keep him out. I have none. Not yet. But I'm getting it, with your help. The timber, the store, the income they will generate—*that* will be my ammunition. And you, if you will stand beside me." She held herself firm with determination, her touch searing through his shirt, and her mouth trembled, full and inviting.

A quick step forward and Edmond curled his fingers around the back of her neck, tilting her face up to his.

She gasped, her lips parting.

"I am right here." He touched his forehead to hers, their noses bumped, and he closed his eyes, inhaling the sweet citrus scent of her. His body hummed with desire, and her quick breaths betrayed her response to his nearness. But if he kissed her, there would be no turning back. And he couldn't risk his heart to another woman who might tear it out and offer it to his enemy.

He took her by the arms and set her away from him. Confusion, then hurt, struggled over her face. Edmond's fingers tightened on her flesh. 'Twas more important he kept her safe than spare her feelings. "I will help you, Tabitha, but you must stay away from Julian Jackson."

CHAPTER TWENTY-ONE

abitha had done exactly what Edmond bid her not do.
She had not only seen Julian Jackson. She had gone to
Jackson's Bluff on the foolish hope that Julian had persuaded
his father to set things right between them.

Julian's written invitation to help him and his parents *host a
supper for like-minded friends* had arrived several weeks after
Edmond's warning. Edmond had been busy enforcing the
schedule at Fort Howe and making a trip to the lumber mill at
Darien, arranging her shipment. That had been just as well, for
she had yet to vanquish the shame of how he had put her away
just when she had practically begged him to remain in her life.

For a moment, she had thought he might kiss her. Her
whole body had gone weak with longing—quite against her
will. There had never been any point in wishing for that type of
affection—wishing to be with someone she actually desired.
Someone who might care for her pleasure as well. And as it
turned out, whatever desire he felt for her in return he must
have judged of the transient variety, for there had been no kiss,

and he had left her with nothing but an injunction...and a sore heart.

That sore heart had overridden her better judgment where Julian was concerned, especially when he'd revealed that one of the dinner party guests would be a merchant from St. Augustine who could connect her with valuable suppliers for her store. And he'd hinted that to further convince her of his honorable intentions, he'd made strides in persuading his father to forgive her outstanding debt.

Your help in entertaining our guests would be invaluable, he'd written. *Afterwards, we will take of new beginnings. Let us erase the misunderstandings and mistrust and move forward as friends and neighbors.*

In the end, Tabitha had decided to give Julian a chance to make good on his promises. After all, she would be safe enough in company. 'Twas not as if she would be alone with him. And how could she spurn even a chance of ending this malignant showdown with the Jacksons? Nothing they had tried thus far had worked. Would it not be an immeasurable boon to move into her future free of their control? If Hugh would agree to release her from Henry's obligations, perhaps give his agreement in writing, she would find a way to dissuade Julian's interest in her.

Of course, Dulcie and Cyrus had argued as vehemently as they dared. Dulcie had gone to muttering her Scriptures about wounds of a friend being better than the kisses of the enemy and wise counsel being found in the multitude of counselors. But in the end, she had ridden here with Tabitha and dressed her like the fine lady she'd once been in a guest room upstairs.

While Dulcie waited in the detached kitchen, had Tabitha suffered through a multi-course supper, hopefully without betraying to the Jacksons' guests her altered circumstances or political loyalties. The South Carolina planter who sat beside her made no secret of his allegiance to the Crown. The St.

Augustine merchant—if indeed he was a merchant—had been in attendance as well, though he possessed the loquaciousness of a politician and showed no interest whatsoever in Tabitha. Neither did Hugh Jackson. In fact, the only one who took notice of her was Julian, who watched her intently with a gleam in his green eyes.

As the meal ended, the rich food churned in her stomach. Edmond had been right, and she'd been a fool. Would she never learn not to trust men? Clearly, Julian's only goal had been to lure her into his vicinity. His father probably had no idea Tabitha expected to meet with him after dinner. She had to make her escape—and the perfect opportunity arose when the men closeted themselves in the gentlemen's study, while the ladies gathered in the sitting room. She would get Dulcie and ride home before Julian realized she was gone.

Tabitha waited less than a quarter of an hour before making her excuses and slipping out of the fine parlor, but the drone of the men's voices made her pause in the hallway. She had a chance of overhearing the real reason they were here—if no servants came along while she attempted to listen through the study's thick pine door. Wouldn't the risk be worth it if she could take some information back to Fort Howe?

She would only linger a moment.

Tabitha tiptoed down the hallway, then leaned on a glossy walnut table to remove one of her silk-covered shoes that matched her black dress. Should someone happen along, she would say she had twisted her ankle on the way back from the privy. Closing her eyes, she sent up a little prayer. Did God help deceivers if their reason was good enough?

With a glance up and down the empty hall, she edged close to the door.

Hugh's bass voice rumbled on the other side. "We know that Donaldson, the shipwright from Philadelphia, has been building a seventy-four-gun ship and four frigates at Southerland's Bluff." Tabitha knew the location—on Sapelo Island, near Darien. "But our main obstacle would be the six row galleys commanded by Commodore Bowen. While not under sail, they are highly maneuverable in coastal waterways. And each carries multiple swivel guns and an eighteen-pounder in the bow."

"'Twould be imperative that Governor Tonyn deployed ships near Darien and in the Frederica River to support any land invasion." That was Mr. Culpepper, the South Carolina planter. But why was he concerned about what the Florida governor did here in Georgia?

"Governor Tonyn has already illustrated his commitment to subdue Georgia from the south." The Florida merchant-politician spoke sharply. "What of our Loyalist brothers from the north?"

A throat cleared. "With Brown and his Indian allies, the East Florida Rangers, and the British Navy, we would consider—"

A hand touched Tabitha's elbow. She jumped and dropped her shoe as she whirled to face—"Julian!" Her heart raced, and blood rushed through her ears. He had not been in the study, after all, but had come down the stairs behind her, and she had been so engrossed in eavesdropping, she had failed to heed his approach.

His expression hardened into a cold mask. He grabbed her arm and pulled her into the rear of the hall, near the back door that led to the kitchen. "What did you hear?"

"I...nothing! I was only trying to see if you were in there before I knocked."

"I do not believe you. Guilt is all over your face." He pulled her closer, looming over her, his hot breath fanning her cheek. His chest heaved beneath his silk coat and waistcoat.

She pointed to her shoe, still lying in front of the study

door. "I twisted my ankle coming in from the back steps. I planned to beg my leave for the evening."

His glare neutralized the sting of her conscience. "You would leave my mother to entertain the guests alone?"

Tabitha had agreed to play the spinet when the men rejoined the women in the parlor. Julian's mother was such a meek and nervous woman—hardly surprising, given her husband's and son's domineering natures—that it failed to surprise Tabitha that she would quail at speaking or performing before her own guests. Or that Julian might be drawn to Tabitha because of her stronger nature.

And now, she needed to placate him. If he thought she was deserting him, he *would* believe she had overheard something of value. "Perhaps if I just sit down a minute..."

"Indeed, for you *must* stay. Surely, you haven't forgotten our meeting with my father."

His suggestive tone and sidelong glance warned her not to blurt out that she knew the truth, that no such meeting had ever been his intention. "Of course not."

"Good, then." Julian guided her to a settee near the back door and went to fetch her shoe. She had barely settled on the velvet cushion before he returned, but he did not put the slipper in the hand she held out. He took a knee and reached for her foot.

Tabitha gasped as his warm hands moved over the embroidered silk stocking that covered her ankle, firmly but gently kneading the muscles and tendons beneath.

"It seems sound enough." His gaze sought hers while his fingers slid up her calf, as if continuing to probe for injury. But a mirthless smirk upturned the corners of his lips. "Are you lying to me, *Lady* Riley?"

"How dare you?" Tabitha stiffened, drawing her leg back.

"What were they speaking of in the study?"

"I have no idea. Release me, sir." She shoved at his arm, but he was as immovable as a steer in a privet hedge.

He squeezed her knee where a ribbon held her stocking in place. "My guess is that you've learned something you plan to report to your precious lieutenant at Fort Howe."

"He is not my lieutenant. And your actions are highly inappropriate." Finally, she succeeded in pushing him away.

"As are yours." Julian's eyes blazed suddenly, and he shoved her shoe on her foot and jerked down her petticoat. "I admit, I invited you here to see how you would behave. If the wilderness has made you wild. And it seems it has."

"I came, did I not?" Tabitha pushed herself to the edge of the settee, her hands pressed on either side of her. "I acted the part expected at supper. Did that not show where my loyalty lies? So if you will excuse me..." She rose, but he did likewise, standing only inches from her.

He braced her by the arms. "Careful. We wouldn't want you to further injure your ankle."

"I believe I can make it upstairs just fine."

"Why in such a hurry? You were looking for me, were you not?" He brushed her ringlets back over her shoulder. His gaze fell to where her pulse thumped in her throat. "If I'm to take your word that you are not a little spy, there is only one way a man can interpret a woman lingering about in the hall waiting for him, and that is that your desire matches mine." Before she could react, he dove forward and planted his lips on her throat. Then the hollow beside her collarbone.

Tabitha cried out and attempted to shove him back, but he held her fast by the arms. "You *mis*interpret, sir."

He cupped her chin, forcing her face up. "I've wondered for some time what it would be like to have a woman with your spirit." His rough mockery of a kiss nicked the edge of her jaw.

"Let me go!"

The hand at her head moved to her waist, and Julian

crushed her mouth with his, forcing her lips apart, mashing the lower one against the sharp point of her teeth. His exultant moan covered the cry of protest that lodged in her throat. His other hand moved to her breast and squeezed.

Tabitha wrenched free just enough to bring up her hand and slap his cheek.

His eyes shot open wide. When he raised his fingers to his face, she attempted to flee, but he grabbed the front of her bodice. The thin silk fabric ripped. He caught her by the waist again, but she beat him off.

"Edmond was right! You are a snake!" Before he could take hold again, Tabitha stumbled for the back door. Sultry evening air enfolded her as she raced for the kitchen with its golden light burning in the windows.

∾

I n the officers' quarters at Fort Howe, Edmond was cleaning his two dragoon pistols and the fine Kentucky rifle he'd purchased in Savannah when a cry rang from the wall. "Riders at the gate!"

He set aside his oil and rag. He did not expect the return of any patrols, and when he stepped out onto the porch, only a sliver of golden light remained on the horizon. Who would approach at this time of the evening? And the sight of them only increased his astonishment.

Two women rode into the compound. There was no mistaking that slender figure in black silk, even though Tabitha sagged in the saddle as he'd never seen her do before. That and the way her uncovered hair straggled about her shoulders set his legs into motion. He ran to help her down.

She fell against him with what sounded like a small sob, and he held her up while his heart surely pounded through both of them.

"What has happened? Where were you?" Had she gone back to River's Bend for some reason?

Dulcie slid down from her mare. "Jackson's Bluff."

"What?" A bolt of cold fear shot through him. He grasped Tabitha's arms in an effort to move her away enough to glimpse her face, but she sucked in a breath as though he had hurt her and shook him off.

"Please do not hold onto me like that." Chafing her upper arms, she allowed Dulcie to encircle her shoulders. A flap of rouched fabric fell open at Tabitha's bodice, exposing her embroidered stays.

Frozen in horror, Edmond managed to raise his gaze to hers. "What happened?"

"Julian... You were right... I'm sorry, Edmond." When Tabitha's face crumpled and she sagged against Dulcie, Edmond did not hesitate. He stepped forward and wrapped her in his arms.

Dulcie allowed it, moving back. "He attacked her, Lieutenant."

"He what?" Edmond's anguished cry wrought a shudder through Tabitha's limp form. He cradled her against him while he stared over her head at her servant.

Dulcie met his gaze. "She got away, and we rode for the river. Only, the ferryman has gone for the night, and I did not think it wise to attempt to swim the horses across in her present state of mind."

Edmond tightened his arms around Tabitha. Could she feel their shaking? "No. I'm glad you came here."

"I need to tell you...what they are planning." Tabitha lifted her tear-streaked face to his.

"Hush. Wheesht." Edmond fell back on his mother's Scottish term to soothe her, wiping the dampness from her cheek. "Come inside, both of you." Thankfully, the other lieutenants were out, one on a scout and the other supping with some of the men. Edmond led the women into the officers' cabin and settled Tabitha on the chair where he had been sitting.

Dulcie took the other chair at the small table.

Edmond gestured to the clay pitcher there. "Cider?"

Both women shook their heads, and Tabitha whimpered and wiped her eyes.

His heart squeezing, Edmond sank to his knees before her and took her hand. "Tell me everything." At the end of the telling, he might reassemble his guns and ride south. Dulcie said Tabitha had "got away," but her lower lip was swollen, and was that a cut?

Tabitha refused to meet his gaze, keeping her lashes lowered. "The Jacksons have guests, a planter from South Carolina and a man from East Florida who was supposed to be a merchant, but I think he is a politician. Julian had indicated the man could connect me with suppliers for the store."

He couldn't believe his ears. "That was why you went there?" He could have done the same for her in Darien.

"Not all." She darted the briefest of shame-filled glances at him. "He also said he had convinced his father to forgive my loan—well, that is what he implied. They needed my name, background, my assistance in convincing these Loyalists they have support in the area. If I helped them entertain the guests..."

Edmond nodded, squeezing her hand. If she weren't so obviously grieved, if she had not been assaulted, he would be angry at her. As it was, he only wanted to get his hands around Julian Jackson's throat.

"I thought if I went, it would placate him at the least, and maybe, just maybe, all this intrigue with the Jacksons could be laid to rest. It did not take me long to realize that was a foolish wish." She rubbed her eyes and grimaced. "I was on my way out when Julian caught me listening at the study door."

"And did this?" Edmond gestured upward with a bit too much ire.

Tabitha shrank back, tucking in the edge of her torn bodice. "At first, I convinced him I had not heard anything. But then he pretended to misunderstand my reason for being there. To think I had come for...for..."

Edmond stood and grabbed his pistol's ramrod from the table. He jerked his rag down its length before he shoved the metal piece back against the barrel. "I shall call him out for your honor. Silence him as McIntosh did Gwinnett. The ingrate deserves to die."

"No, Edmond." Tabitha shot to her feet and gripped his arm. "He must not know I came away from Jackson's Bluff with any knowledge. And you are needed here, at Fort Howe. And with me."

"With you." He turned back to her, no longer able to hide his need. "In what way, with you?"

Her lips parted as she searched his eyes. Finally, she gave a breathless reply. "Any way you want to be."

Edmond froze. "Do you mean that?"

Not breaking his gaze, Tabitha stepped closer.

Dulcie rose without a word and slipped out onto the porch.

Edmond's heart raced. He inched forward, bent his head toward hers. Inhaled the sweet scent of her hair. His fingers brushed hers, and lightning slid up his arm.

Every so slightly, Tabitha lifted her face toward his. Whispered, "Lieutenant, I know not how better to answer without throwing myself at you again."

Could it be? "But I am so far beneath you."

"We are equal in every way." She raised her other hand for a feather-light stroke of his hair. "Complementary."

"My reputation..."

"An officer. A gentleman. One who, if we are fair, is too young for me." Tabitha's fingers slid into the strands at his nape held in check by a ribbon. She dipped her forehead to his jaw and inhaled a trembling breath, as though *he* affected *her*.

Drawing back an inch, Edmond ran his thumb over the side of her face. "And yet, you would not be who you are without every one of your years, even the hard ones." He could speak the truth now, now that he knew Tabitha would not be charmed into Julian's arms. "The woman I have fallen in love with."

Tabitha sucked in a soft breath and batted back sudden moisture in her eyes. "And I love you."

A scoff of disbelief escaped before Edmond laid his cheek against hers, then pulled back just as quickly to cup her chin. Mindful of her cut, he allowed his lips to whisper over hers until she moaned and pressed her mouth to his. Her arms wrapped around his neck, and he crushed her to him as their lips melded with all the sweetness and fire he'd imagined. They kissed until they were both breathless, then pulled back, gasping and laughing.

"I feared you would not want me," Tabitha whispered, touching his face. Her fingers rasped over the stubble on his jaw.

"Oh, I want you." He pressed his lips to hers again. Then again.

"Ow. Ow!" Tabitha giggled and put a finger to her mouth.

"Sorry." He grimaced. "You started it."

"No, you started it." Her teasing melted into a look of such desire that his knees went weak. "And I never want you to stop."

"Then you best marry me." Edmond smoothed her hair back and kissed her temple. As her husband, he could protect her better. They would make a united front against those who would seek to withhold their right to thrive in this land. "We will make our own way. Our own name."

"Lassiter." She seemed to savor each syllable before she

smiled and gave a firm nod. "I see no need to extend this charade further. Let us make it genuine. Yes. I will marry you."

A little whoop and clap from the front porch drew laughter from both of them.

Tabitha's eyes sparkled. "Dulcie approves."

"I am grateful for the ally." Edmond drew back to kiss her hands, then he peered at her, his heart aflame with more love than he'd ever thought possible after Evangeline. How quickly could he make Tabitha his? "We can have the banns read with my family at the Presbyterian Church in Darien next week."

She nodded. "But do you not want to hear what I learned at Jackson's Bluff?"

"Not really." He pulled her into his arms again, running his hand up and down her back. Could this courageous, spirited, beautiful woman truly be his? "For now, I just want to hold you and thank God for what He has done."

Maybe His Father had not abandoned him, after all.

CHAPTER TWENTY-TWO

Early October, 1777

The Ogeechee limes had ripened by the river, the pignut hickory nuts in the pinewoods, and black-eyed Susans nodded by the Old Post Road when Jack McMullan's crew dragged the first yellow pine to the site Edmond and Cyrus had cleared for the store. Tabitha became accustomed to the daily ring of axes through the trees—the sound of her future taking shape. Edmond joined Cyrus every hour he could spare from the fort, but the men there were in sore need of supervision, as unauthorized leaves and desertions mounted with inactivity.

At the end of the last week of October, Edmond rode out to tell her to expect a houseful of guests. His Grant kin were coming for the raising of their new house and store. Freya and Meg had been delighted when Edmond and Tabitha visited the month prior for the reading of their banns. Their minister had agreed to perform the ceremony at Fort Howe at the end of October, and the women had purchased some golden silk fabric from a local merchant that they were making into Tabitha's wedding dress. Once upon a time, yellow had been her signature color. Now she could wear it again with happiness and hope.

For quite some time, she had feared repercussions for spurning Julian's advances, but she had not seen or heard from him or his father. Perhaps Hugh had learned of his son's inappropriate behavior as well as news of Tabitha's engagement and, in light of the Patriot support in the area, encouraged Julian to relinquish his fantasies. She could only hope that paying Hugh at the end of the year would dispense with her obligation to both men forever.

Focusing on the cabin raising, Tabitha and Dulcie had baked for two solid days—corn pudding, cornbread, mincemeat pies, and apple tansy. The day before, they roasted root vegetables and cracked and smoked nuts. They filled their biggest pot with hasty pudding and diced nuts and figs to sprinkle on top the following day. The Grants arrived and were housed at the cabin and some of the men at the fort. Early the next morning, Cyrus put a pig on the spit in the yard, and the scent of roasting pork made every mouth within a mile water. Around noon, the women set out on the path with the pies to check the building progress and sustain the men.

"Ah, I can almost forget there is a war on." Edmond's mother took a deep breath. While the humidity had fallen with the retreat of summer, the sun still split the yellowing leaves with persistent warmth. "While I am sad the McIntoshes had to go to Virginia to aid George's defense, I am glad they will be fightin' there with General Washington and not here in Georgia. Perhaps we will have peace a while."

"At least long enough for the wedding." And a few weeks after, so that Tabitha might feel rightly married. She flushed at the notion.

"I just do not understand why Edmond's superiors did not take your warning more seriously." Dulcie hefted a large jug of cider onto her other hip.

Tabitha sighed. She could have done without the reminder that the Loyalists were likely planning a massive invasion. "Edmond wrote to Savannah with the information, but apparently, when they checked into the Floridian who was at Jackson's Bluff, no one knew anyone by that name."

"He must have used an alias." Aunt Meg shooed a buzzing pest away from her basket. "But maybe the navy will be alerted, at least."

Tabitha shrugged. "Perhaps. As for Mr. Culpepper, the man from South Carolina, I did not actually hear him commit to any particulars. Any dates or locations they could follow up on."

"But why will headquarters not send more men, at least? Especially with how many have been deserting their post?" Dulcie's face twisted into a frown. They all slept lightly of a night, startling at any unexpected sound.

"It seems the frontier is only important to them when the British are overrunning it." Tabitha grimaced and laced her arm through Freya's, jerking her chin toward the clearing ahead. Shouts and the chopping of axes signaled the men were hard at work. "I hope they are far enough along for you to see the space where you might stay."

"Oh, me dear." Edmond's mother squeezed her hand. "I dinna want to intrude on your newly wedded bliss."

"Nonsense. We want you to come live with us. That is, if you will not get too lonely out here in the country." Tabitha smiled at Margaret. "I know your brother's family has been a great comfort to you."

Margaret smiled back. "You can both come visit anytime ye please. And as often as ye please."

"That we will, though I willna get lonely with me new daughter-in-law at hand—and her dear friend, Dulcie." Freya reached back to touch the servant's sleeve. Her inclusive manner warmed Tabitha's heart. This was what family should be like. Freya turned her attention back to Tabitha. "Have ye heard from yer parents and sister? Will they make it to the weddin'?"

"I have not heard back yet." Tabitha pressed her lips together. She had written to her family to invite them, but would her father even allow her mother to come? Tabitha's marriage to a Patriot lieutenant from the merchant class and their plans to make a life together on the frontier flew in the face of all he had expected from her. But she would not allow his disapproval to dampen her joy. "I can only pray my mother and sister will attend."

"Yes, we will pray." Freya squeezed her arm. During their visit in September, Tabitha had explained about the rift with her father and been met with nothing but understanding. If anyone understood about broken families, Freya Lassiter did. "And perhaps I will join ye here come spring."

Tabitha's murmur of acceptance died in her throat when they stepped into the clearing and she beheld the store. Not only did all four walls rise from the stacked-stone footers, but the interior walls were finished as well. And Edmond and his uncle Ian were hammering the shingles Cyrus and Edmond had cut over the past month onto the roof. Only the milled floorboards remained piled to one side.

"Oh, my goodness." Tabitha laid her hand over her heart. "I did not expect it to go up so fast. And 'tis so big."

Dulcie flashed her a grin. "Grander than River's Bend."

"I could not agree more," Tabitha said. "Because 'tis ours." They planned that Dulcie and Cyrus would help out at the store for extra wages. The income would give all of them a better life. Tabitha barely resisted the urge to caper about in a circle like a gamboling lamb, but when Edmond caught sight of her and waved, she did wave back most heartily. She cupped her mouth and called out, "Be careful!"

The way he swung down from the top of the tall structure made her heart stutter. So did the way his shirt clung to his sweaty chest and back, every line and bulging muscle visible without his waistcoat as he approached. He fairly stole her breath even though he only kissed her cheek.

"Mother." He kissed her forehead as well, then he leaned closer to the small basket Freya bore. "What is in there?" Flicking back the napkin, he made a face. "Apples? Where is that meat we have been smelling all morning?"

"You have to wait for tonight." Tabitha laughed. "But do not worry..."

"Dinna fash." Freya winked at her.

Tabitha grinned back and repeated the unique phrase. "Dinna fash. We brought you mincemeat pies also. But first, how about a tour?" She peered past him toward the building which was quickly draining of hungry men.

Edmond bowed. "Nothing would give me more pleasure. Well...almost nothing." His teasing smirk, hinting of unknown pleasures to come, made her hot from head to toe. Before she could go up in flames, he extended his arm to his mother.

Freya set her basket on the ground and took his elbow, eyes glimmering with anticipation.

Edmond waved before him. "Come, ladies, see your future home."

Tabitha followed them to the log structure with an eagerness she could scarce contain, but as Edmond and his mother disappeared in the shadow of the roof, a cloud blocked the sun, and a breeze blew through the forest. The leaves rustled with a sibilant whisper, as if...as if something warned her. Of what?

She rubbed her arms and shook off the sensation. She was being silly. All of the dreams she'd once given up on were about to come true.

Mid-October 1777

The tinge of wood smoke on the evening air hinted of a cozy winter ahead as Edmond forded the Altamaha on his mount. Water dampened his breeches above his boots, but he urged Maximus through the current. Tabitha would be so excited to learn about the supplier for the store he had located on his trip into Darien.

Only two more weeks, and they would be man and wife. She would need to remain in the dogtrot cabin with Dulcie and Cyrus until Edmond mustered out of the army, but he could visit often, especially during quieter times. And the living quarters at the store would be furnished to the point that they could spend the first few nights after the wedding there.

After he'd lost Evangeline, Edmond had never thought he would find love again. But Tabitha's maturity, strength, and determination had inspired his admiration and trust. With her by his side, all the pain of the past would be canceled out.

As they cleared the south shore and came up the bank shedding water, Edmond sniffed in an attempt to detect the scent of roasting meat. What might Dulcie and Tabitha be cooking tonight? He always anticipated the hearty fare and the fellowship he and Tabitha enjoyed with the other couple. But a glimpse of flames through the trees ahead sliced horror through him. This was no hearth fire he smelled. The store was burning!

He kneed Maximus, and they shot forward—to a scene he could scarce believe. Flames licked up at all four corners of the structure they had just finished chinking before Edmond went to Darien. Instinct urged him to ride for help at the cabin, but a movement caught his eye—a man running across the yard toward a horse tethered at the far tree line.

"Hey!" Edmond rode after him, but the man wasn't looking back or stopping. When Maximus drew near enough, Edmond slid his feet free of the stirrups and launched from the stallion's back onto the man's. With an *umph*, they tumbled in the dirt. After scrambling to his feet, Edmond seized the man by the collar of his fine coat. "Get up!"

The miscreant stumbled and again attempted to flee.

Edmond whirled him around and aimed an undercut at his jaw. The man grunted as his teeth clacked together and his head snapped back. His hat sailed to the ground. "What—" Edmond's demand for an explanation died on his lips as he got a good look at the trespasser's face. "Jackson."

It had been two years since he had seen the man. Two years since he'd come home for his university's autumn break to find Julien calling on Evangeline in his absence and confronted him. The surprise on the dandy's face had been the same then as it was now. And both times, Edmond had frozen in shock as well, learning that an enemy had encroached on what he held sacred.

Evangeline. Tabitha. His future.

"You..." Words failed him.

"Nice to see you again, too, Lassiter." Julian rubbed his jaw and somehow managed to grin. He tipped his head toward the store. "Best get to it. Though 'tis too far from the river to put out a fire, even if you had buckets." Indeed, the increasing crackle of the flames underscored the truth.

Edmond could only whisper one word. "Why?"

"A wedding present...for you and your Patriot hussy." Julian had the gall to turn his back and start walking away.

Oh, no, he did not. Not this time. This was the man to blame for the deaths of his father and fiancée and the shame and ruination of him and his mother. For bullying, then assaulting Tabitha.

With a growl building in his chest, Edmond tackled him. They rolled, a tangle of arms and legs and flying fists. Julian got in a crushing blow to Edmond's ribs and a bruiser to his left jaw, but the white-hot rage that consumed Edmond made a blur of everything. Pain. Shouts. Someone calling his name. The spit and lick of the fire. And the satisfying grunts of his opponent when his blows landed.

Julian's first rammed into Edmond's eye. Lightning bolted through his head, and stars exploded. Julian managed to pull himself halfway upright.

Still reeling, Edmond scrambled up in time to bring his knee up between the man's legs. Julian huffed and doubled over.

"That was for Tabitha." Edmond circled him, blinking hard, his chest heaving. "You thought you would ruin me a second time? You are the one who will be ruined. You will come with me to the fort to be brought up on charges."

"Never." Julian gasped for breath, glancing up from beneath the strands of dark hair that fell over his face. "You know she was coming to see me...the night she died." He wheezed, then chuckled.

"You lie." Edmond's vision narrowed.

A woman's figure silhouetted against the burning building drew closer. "Edmond?"

He couldn't focus past Julian's words. Edmond had never understood why Evangeline had been riding by herself outside Savannah when the accident happened. But she would never do anything so foolish as attempt to ride all the way to Jackson's Bluff alone.

"You left her," Julian said. "She had no choice. But that gave her the courage to do what she had always wanted...come to me." When he grinned, his split lip gave his expression an almost garish quality. "With my child."

Rage flooded Edmond in a red frenzy. He roared and rushed Julian again, pummeling him with his fists.

Lacking a soldier's stamina, Julian staggered and fell under the blows, attempting to cover his head and upper body.

"Edmond! Stop!" Hands pulled at his back and shoulders. "You will kill him."

Tabitha?

The terror in her voice broke the vise grip of hatred from his mind. From his kneeling position, he turned. There wasn't only terror in her voice. It was on her face too. She did not just fear the results of him taking Julian's punishment into his own hands. She was afraid...of *him*.

The shock of that kept him frozen even when a scraping and scrabbling told him Julian was escaping. By the time Edmond broke with Tabitha's stricken gaze to look, Julian was hobbling to his horse.

A hand on his reins, he turned back to them. "You will pay for this. Both of you."

Before Edmond could come to his feet, Julian managed to pull himself onto his stallion. Slumping in the saddle, he turned his mount's head south—away from Fort Howe—and loped down the darkening road.

Shouts signaled the arrival of men from the fort. They had ferried over in the boat, expecting to help put out a fire. Edmond's shoulders sagged. Without horses, the men could not pursue Julian in time. They joined Dulcie and Cyrus with buckets, but the building was engulfed in flames. There was no way they could put the fire out in time. And no way Edmond could erase the expression on Tabitha's face when he attempted to reach for her.

She shrugged away. "You never told me your fiancée had chosen Julian. Was that why you left?"

Edmond still panted for breath. He hung his head. He hurt all over but nowhere as much as his heart. "I knew he had turned her head. I never thought he had gotten in her bed."

"Is that what this has all been about, after all?" She swung her arm out. "Revenge? Showing Julian you could get me instead of him?"

"Tabitha, no." Again, he tried to reach for her, but she slapped his hand back.

"Go. I don't want to see you. And I cannot marry you. I do not even know you." She pivoted and ran toward the crowd, to Dulcie's arms, leaving Edmond to close his eyes to the raging inferno that had devoured his dreams.

CHAPTER TWENTY-THREE

E dmond hunched over the small table in the officers' quarters at Fort Howe a little over a week after Julian set fire to the store and Edmond had almost beat him to death before the man slunk off into the night—to the wilds of Florida, according to Mr. Long. As he'd expected, the rangers' belated attempts to mount and follow had come to naught.

Now, 'twas but a few days until the date set for the wedding. Only, he knew not whether it would happen. Unlikely, considering that each of the three times Edmond had called on Tabitha, she had refused to speak with him. Had she had written to her family to cancel the nuptials? He had not had the heart to do so with his.

The Grants might beset him two days hence only to discover he was without a bride. Which was exactly what he deserved.

Only when he had faced Julian Jackson had he understood the depth of hatred he held for the man. No wonder Tabitha could not bear to look at him. What a monster he must have appeared—pummeling a man to within an inch of his life. Even one such as Julian.

The Testament he had borrowed from Dougal that lay open before him bore repeated admonitions to confess the sin of hatred.

Let all bitterness, and wrath, and anger, and clamour, and evil speaking, be put away from you, with all malice.

Avenge not yourselves, but rather give place unto wrath: for it is written, Vengeance is mine: I will repay, saith the Lord.

The anger against Evangeline burned even stronger.

Why? Edmond tangled his fingers in his hair.

Because her betrayal had been magnified a hundred times by the realization that she had far more than considered Julian's suit. He doubted not what Julian said about her pregnancy. Not only did it explain her taking off across country for Darien, but her sister had told Edmond how ill and listless she had been after he left. He had attributed it to melancholy. Was that why she had pled with Edmond to stay and marry her, even after he explained that after his father's suicide, he had no choice but to sign up, as the militia was his only opportunity for an immediate income?

And yet...she had initially come to him and not to Julian, asking Edmond not to enlist. Had she done so because Julian had forced her? Or at the very least, that she regretted what had happened between them? Either way, Evangeline had been naïve—an easy victim for Julian's calculations. She might not have known how to fight like Tabitha. The possibility that Edmond had blamed his fiancée for unfaithfulness when her innocence might have been stolen made him drop his head into his hands. Whatever happened, he'd abandoned her. The weight of that was crushing. And he might never learn the truth.

Forgive me, Lord.

His fingers stretched open across the page. Mark 11:25 read, *And when ye stand praying, forgive, if ye have ought against any:*

that your Father also which is in heaven may forgive you your trespasses.

Had he not done the best he could under impossible circumstances?

No. He had not stopped to ask what God would have him do. He had run from his grief and anger at the first opportunity.

I'm sorry, Lord.

Forgive, if ye have ought against any.

Edmond slid out of the chair and hit his knees. He had been running from what happened for two years, and it had only caught up with him when he once again had something he cared about losing. He had let the darkness wrought by Julian and Evangeline and his father take up residence inside himself, and now it had cost him everything. Even if it was too late with Tabitha, he had to get it out.

He leaned forward and cupped his hands behind his neck. *God, help me forgive them. Julian for sabotaging me. Father for taking his own life. Evangeline for her betrayal. And now, will You forgive me for running from You?*

He waited.

A weight settled over him—not like that of the burden he had been carrying. A sweet weight, like a blanket on a chilly day. Like the arm of one's beloved about the shoulders. Peace. Edmond exhaled and rested a moment in it. Then...

If it is not too late, will You give me another chance with Tabitha?

In a flash, he could've sworn he pictured God chuckling.

And then came the cry, "Rider at the gate!"

Edmond dropped his hands, listening. Yes, God was omnipotent, but it could not be. Could it? He had jumped up every time that call had rang out for the past week. No, he wouldn't go rushing out again only to have the men give him that pitying look. Only to risk disappointment.

Oh, ye of little faith.

Edmond stayed where he was, determined to finish his prayers, though he did raise up to a kneeling posture. That was how the man who cast the shadow crossing the door caught his eye.

"Oh, Lieu-ten-ant..." The young private's singsong voice hinted there was something outside he might want to see.

"Yes?"

The boy's smile faltered at finding Edmond on his knees. "Are you all right, sir?"

"Never seen a man at his prayers, Private?" Edmond had endured a little too much humbling over the past week. His response came out a bit testy.

"Uh, no, sir. I mean, yes, sir." He snapped off an errant salute. "There is someone here to see you, sir."

"Why did you not say so?" Edmond struggled to his feet, almost upending the lightweight chair in the process. Plopping his hat on his head, he stomped past the private and through the door. And there he stopped.

Walking toward him was Tabitha. When she saw him, she came to a halt and pushed back the edges of the hood of her green wool cloak.

His mouth fell open. God really had answered his prayers that fast.

"Edmond?" His name quavered on her lips, almost as if she were not certain it was him. But with such hope. And *she* had come to *him*.

He wouldn't make her wait another moment without knowing how much he had longed for her. He jogged down the steps and, in a few strides, he had her in his arms. Sliding his hand beneath her hood, he cupped her neck and lowered his mouth to hers. Edmond barely heard the hoots from the sentries on the wall. He arched his lips over hers with all the angst he had endured, that she must have endured—

"Mmpf. Mmm?" Tabitha staggered back a step, disengaging

the kiss. Putting her hand to her mouth. Her brown eyes bulged at him...only, they weren't her eyes.

They looked like hers, but something was wrong.

Something was very wrong.

"You're—you're not..."

With a swipe of the back of her hand across her lips, the woman before him gave an apologetic grimace. "I'm not Tabitha. I am Temperance, her sister." When Edmond could do no more than gape, she added, "Her *twin*." She pulled a pair of spectacles from her pocket and slid them on. "I am forever getting myself in trouble for not wearing these. And...well... there is also this little difference..." She parted her cloak to reveal an unmistakably pregnant shape.

He sucked in perhaps the longest breath of life. And thought he might pass out backward. He had kissed Tabitha's sister? A married woman...the wife of that...that scowling captain from the ball...whose child she was carrying. Oh, God help him.

The fort was the most silent Edmond had ever heard it. Then from the nearest bastion, one of his fellow rangers made a sound like a squeaky door, painfully drawn out.

Heat consumed Edmond's face—his whole body. He managed to meet Temperance's gaze and whisper, "I'm...*so*...sorry."

"'Tis all right. That settled one question, at least." She kept her voice low.

"What question?"

"The extent of your...er...*enthusiasm* for my sister." Now she was blushing, too, as she hurried on. "'Tis partly my fault. I should have remembered how alike my sister and I seem to others, but I had been apart from her for so long, I suppose I had forgotten. And of course, you had no reason to expect me rather than her."

Yes. He'd been so sure. And so elated to think she'd come.

Which she hadn't. His joy leached away, replaced by an emptiness that left him feeling hollower than before. "Why *are* you here?"

Temperance cast a glance at the wall, where the young private who had fetched Edmond was doing his level best to pretend great interest in the river on the other side of the wall. "Perhaps we could go inside?"

"Of course." He held his arm out toward the officers' quarters. Edmond allowed Mrs... He couldn't remember her husband's name. He allowed Temperance to proceed him, but before he followed her inside, he shot a scowl at that peering private. He kept the door open for propriety's sake. He could afford no more transgressions on that score. After he settled her at the table and offered her refreshment, which was refused, Edmond took the seat beside her. "Forgive me..." He stared at her a moment before slapping his hand on his knee. "What should I call you?"

Her shamefully rosy lips—his fault—turned up in a gracious smile. "My name is Mrs. Anderson, but you may call me Temperance, as I shall soon be your sister."

"About that..." Had she come straight here from the coast, and he had missed sighting her horse or conveyance? "The wedding...it..."

"Is to take place in three days." She bobbed her head without her smile faltering. Then she sobered. "Though I suppose that depends on you."

"I'm sorry." This might be the third time Edmond had apologized since Temperance arrived. He scrubbed his hand over his eyes. "I'm not sure you understand."

She put back her hood, adjusting her mob cap and spectacles. "Oh, I know about the fire. About Julian Jackson. In fact, 'tis all I have heard about for the past couple of days, ever since I arrived early expecting to bake and stitch and arrange flowers. And a good thing I did, for Dulcie was beside herself, unable to coax Tabitha from her room. And it made me feel I was still some good as a sister that I probably do understand Tabitha better than anyone. So I am here in her stead. First, I would hear your perspective of what happened last week."

Edmond blew out a breath. Little as he wanted to remember—much less, recount—that terrible night, he told Tabitha's sister about riding upon Julian minutes after he had set the blaze, tackling him, and the ensuing fight. "He baited me with a very painful truth, and in my anger and pride, I fell for it."

Temperance's gaze remained steady. "That your fiancée was expecting his child."

"Yes." Edmond had to avert his. "It reopened old wounds. Had your sister not intervened..." He passed his hand over his mouth. "She was right to recoil from me. Even to refuse to see me after. I had turned just as dark as those who had wronged me, though I did not realize it. Only today did I face the sin I carried inside."

"You faced it?" Temperance sat forward. "How?"

He met her eyes again. "Conviction and repentance, Mrs. Anderson. Temperance. The same way all sinners get rid of sin."

She exhaled a soft breath. "Oh, I am glad to hear you say it. I thought from what Tabitha and Dulcie said of you that you must be a believer."

"I am, though I admit, I also believed the lie that God had abandoned me. But thank God for His grace and that He always gives us a second chance. I am not so certain Tabitha will."

Temperance leaned closer to pat his hand. "Do not despair. I have a plan."

"Oh, please tell me." Edmond sagged against the back of his chair. He would grab hold of any lifeline at this point. "Tabitha thinks I concealed the fact that my fiancée had a relationship with Julian to somehow finagle Tabitha into this engagement with me—to get back at Julian. She couldn't be more wrong. I wanted to protect her, not use her."

A crease tucked in between Temperance's dark brows. "But do you understand why that was so hurtful to her?"

"Is she doubting that I truly love her?" Here he had been thinking Tabitha's reticence to see him stemmed from disgust. Perhaps fear. Instead, she was wrestling with her own hurt?

"I think it is more than that. I think the key is in what you just said." She tapped the table. "She needs to know you did not use her. She has told you of the conditional love of our father? Then her husband. Correct?" She waited until Edmond nodded. "Both used her for their own purposes. When she did not fulfill them, she was cast aside. Deemed worthless. They only loved her for what she could give them."

"Oh no." Edmond flattened his hand on the table and sat up straight. "I must talk to her."

Temperance's mouth pressed into a sneaky smile. "I happen to know she was taking the noontime meal to the workers where they are piling the logs near the river today." Edmond knew the place. "If you hurry, you will catch her there, and she will not find it easy to run away from you in front of them."

Edmond stood up and grabbed his hat. "Then what are we waiting for?"

With a light touch to his arm, Temperance stopped him before he could rush out the door. "Er...um...Edmond?"

He subdued his impatience. "What is it?"

"Perhaps it would be best not to mention your...uh...*greeting* to my sister. Or my husband." Her face went scarlet.

"On that we can agree." He grimaced, imagining the ire of both. "We shall not speak of it. To anyone. Ever." And if he had his way, from here on out, Tabitha would be the only woman he kissed forever.

Tabitha sat on a massive cypress stump about a hundred yards from where Jack McMullan's crew stockpiled the logs they had cut farther inland. She ran her fingers over the rough surface, her forehead puckering. Even though the men had been careful to leave stands of the biggest giants of the forest, now that she had seen some come down, she balked at the idea of more logging. After this season, she would do no more if she could help it. The primeval beauty of this place, its ancientness, was what made it magical. The idea of a store had been ingenuous—Edmond's idea. Tabitha bit her lip.

When she had first arrived, the men had been driving the steers, and it had been fascinating to watch them work. They directed the bulls to drag the timbers into separate piles of cypress and yellow pine at the top of the bluff. There they would be stored out of sight until the water level rose to its mid-December height. Then the logs would be rolled down the bluff one by one and floated with a man atop each to the Darien mill.

She had not watched long, for as soon as the workers noticed the basket of food on her arm, they had congregated around her, eager for salted ham, Johnny cakes, and muscadines. Now they sat eating in little groups on the logs while the cattle grazed nearby.

Tabitha had already tossed away the core of her apple, but she did not mind waiting for them to finish and return the napkins that had wrapped their portions. Temperance had been right to push her out of her room. The autumn sun warmed her spirits as well as her body.

Temperance had also been right that she was focusing on none but herself. At first, she could not see past her assumption that Edmond's rage showed that he was not over Evangeline—

and had played Tabitha as a pawn in his scheme for revenge. But he had never taunted Julian with their relationship. In fact, he had gone to great lengths to conceal it from him. He had warned her to stay away from the man. She had been the one who had not listened.

As for his rage, Temperance had pointed out that it could have been a result of Julian coming after a second woman Edmond loved.

How betrayed Edmond must have felt when he realized Evangeline had not been faithful to him. Not only had Julian's cruel comments insulted Edmond's pride, but they had tarnished his intended's memory. The same way Julian had sought to tarnish Tabitha—a fact which Edmond had not forgotten.

That was for Tabitha.

She had heard him say it. Why had she thought he had not truly chosen her? Why would she not want a man who would focus all his honor and passion and loyalty to protect and defend her?

Tabitha leapt to her feet, no longer caring about her basket or linens. She would go straightaway to Fort Howe and find him. But what if he had called off the wedding with the minister and his kin? Would he even agree to see *her* now? Or had she sent him away too many times, selfish and petulant vixen that she was? What other man could put up with her without ever feeling the need to belittle her? To push her back into her place.

Edmond was exactly the man she needed.

She started running along the river, the quickest way to the fort, dodging yellow-leaved tulip trees, brilliant sweetgums, and swamp tupelos with their ripening blue fruit. Her petticoats skimmed pepperbushes and snagged on palmettos.

And then she stopped, for something was coming toward her. Something huffing and crashing that sounded big.

Tabitha's heart pounded. In her haste, she had forgotten about foraging wild boars and alligators soaking up the last of the season's sun.

But when an arm pushed aside a low-hanging spruce pine branch and a man came into view, she let out her breath, all in a rush.

Edmond stopped about twenty yards upriver and stared at her, his eyes going wide. "Tabitha?"

"Edmond!" She bounded forward. At the last moment, he opened his arms, and she ran straight into them. "I was coming to see you."

"And I you." Oh, thank heavens, he bent over her and wrapped her in his embrace without hesitation, closing the lid on the gaping hole in her heart. "Can you forgive me? I am so ashamed of what you saw." He lifted his head, drawing back to look at her. "But it showed me what was inside, and I have set it straight with God."

Tabitha shook her head. "I cannot imagine the pain the revelations about Evangeline caused you."

"Pain, yes, but more than anything, shame. I did not speak of her because I thought I had been too late to help her, just as I had Father. When I enlisted, I knew I ran the risk of her choosing Julian. I just did not realize she already had." He tucked a strand of Tabitha's hair behind her ear. "But she was not strong like you. And she was not the woman God intended for me. You are. I have to know, am I too late for you as well?"

The timbre of Tabitha's laugh matched the golden sunshine highlighting them on the bank. "You can hardly be too late if I was running toward you rather than away from you. And I can promise, I will never run away from you again. Just as long as you promise I will not be too much for you. I know I can be a lot to handle."

"Never." The word was spoken on a vehement breath as Edmond dipped his forehead to hers. "I love every strength that others have deemed weaknesses. I do not want you for what you can do for me. I do not ask you to be a certain way, only that you be yourself. For that is who I choose...today...and forever."

A whimper rose in her throat, and she framed his face with her hands. "Then can we please still have a wedding?"

"Without a doubt." He lowered his head, and his parted lips slipped over hers and sealed the promise.

CHAPTER TWENTY-FOUR

FOUR MONTHS LATER...
MARCH 10, 1778

The morning she awoke at home knowing for certain she carried her husband's child, Tabitha Lassiter opened her eyes to the pre-dawn light and shivered—with delight. She was free. Her debt to Hugh Jackson had been discharged at Christmas. She was married to the man she loved, and they would soon grow their new family. How best to tell him?

She turned her head to find Edmond already awake and lying on his side, watching her.

"Morning." His unbound hair framed a face wreathed in an amused, slightly smug smile.

"What?" Self-consciously, she rubbed her eyes and smoothed her own hair.

"Did you know you wrinkle your nose in your sleep?" Edmond tweaked the tip.

She wrinkled it again, then laughed. "I was dreaming of coffee. With chocolate."

"Well, let me get right to it, milady." He turned toward his side of the bed and threw his covers off as though he would hasten to the hearth in the next room.

Tabitha caught his arm, pulling him back. Rumors that Congress might authorize a third Florida campaign made her fight the daily desire to cling. "I can wait."

All it took was the murmur of suggestion in her voice and he was drawing her against him, his ginger bristles lightly rasping her tender skin as he rained kisses across her face and neck. When his lips found the hollow at her throat, then her collarbone, she tilted her head back and gave in with a soft moan.

At night, Edmond showed how he cherished her, whether by discussing Scriptures with her, or in quiet moments of contentment doing small chores by the fire, or in the type of blissful lovemaking she had never known existed.

In the mornings, astonishment and immense gratitude overwhelmed her when she woke to find him at her side. Of course, there were stretches he had to remain at the fort. During those times, she returned to her old room at the dogtrot cabin. But those only made the time they shared in their quarters behind their store more poignantly sweet.

That they had this place, with the day's new light just highlighting the edges of the shutters as they entangled in marriage's most intimate embrace, was a miracle in itself. The very day they had reconciled last autumn, Edmond's men from the fort and McMullan's crew had worked together to rebuild their new home. Though only the milled floorboards, which had been piled to one side of the lot, and the stacked stones of the foundation and chimney had remained of the first structure, by the wedding night, they had a roof over their heads. Tabitha had not minded one whit that they had slept before the hearth on aught but a pallet and quilt. They hadn't slept much, anyway.

Birds twittered in the trees by the time Edmond tucked his

shirt into his breeches. "I need to get back to the fort this afternoon," he told her over his shoulder.

"Then you'd best get to it." Tabitha giggled and poked his back. "You still have a storeroom to organize." The day before, the balance of the stock they had ordered from Darien had arrived. They had spent the day hauling a cart and a barrow filled with crates, bags, and barrels from the river after the goods were ferried over. "But first..." She pulled the quilt around her chest and sat up, pushing back her long locks.

"First, what?" He turned to look at her, his brow quirked, as though half expecting her to pounce on him. His gaze swept her, and he blew out a breath. "Egads, woman. Do not look at me that way. I will never get anything of consequence done."

"I think you already have." She could not quite mash down the smile determined to erupt on her lips.

He tipped his head. "I do not take your meaning."

Tabitha cradled her hand over her abdomen. She lowered her lashes as her face flushed, but she could not bring herself to say the words. Saying it made it real, and there were so many risks. Especially given her history. "'Tis early yet, but I cannot keep this from you."

He stood there a moment, one brow hovering low, until she finally met his gaze. Then he must have read the truth in her expression, for his face went slack. "You're—you're not..."

She nodded.

His sudden whoop straightened her back and pulled a giggle from her. "Thank You, God! Oh, thank You, Jesus!" Edmond bounded across the bed to sweep her into his arms and cover her face with kisses.

Until that moment, she never would have guessed how much he wanted a child of his own—and how he must have shared her concern that she might be barren. He had always played off any desire to become a father, saying he was not in a hurry and if it was the Lord's will...

Tabitha batted back tears as she held his head to her shoulder and twined her fingers in his hair. *Please, God, keep our child safe.*

He drew back to cradle her face, wearing a smile that lit his entire countenance. "A child of our own! Tabitha, you have made me so happy."

"As you have made me." She kissed his lips, then gave him a little shove, for if he kept looking at her in such a manner, she would melt into a useless puddle of emotion. "Now let us break our fast so you can organize the storeroom and I can go tell Dulcie. As I figure it, her child will be born a couple months before mine." In this, as in so many other things, Tabitha had no doubt Dulcie would go before her, showing her the way. Not as a servant or an employee, but as the truest friend.

"But you have not been sick in the mornings." Edmond stated his realization as they both finished dressing.

Tabitha glanced up from pinning her short gown closed. "Like my sister's, my unsettled stomach has hit in the evenings. Have you not noticed how I have mainly been eating bread?"

"And I have kept pushing you to eat more meat." He chuckled and came around the bed to place his palm against her abdomen. "Still perfectly flat. You are quite certain?" He searched her eyes.

"Quite certain. I just missed my third monthly course. This is real, Edmond." As the cold grip of fear squeezed her heart, she grabbed his arm. "So do not put yourself in unnecessary danger. I do not think I could..." She swallowed, unable to complete the sentence.

He brushed his finger over her lips. "Do not speak it. If General Howe has his way, the new governor's plan for another invasion will come to naught, and I will be here for the birth of our child."

Comforted by his reassurance, Tabitha went to heat the porridge while Edmond disappeared into the storeroom. He returned a few minutes later with a small square tin. She straightened from the hearth and tipped her head to one side. "What is that?"

"Cocoa." His grin could have made the sun stop in the sky. "For your coffee. If this is not a day to celebrate, I know not when it would be." Setting the canister on the table, he came forward with his hands extended, grabbing hers and capering around her in the steps of a Scottish jig that soon had her laughing, breathless, and clinging to his arms.

A year ago, she never would have guessed that the stoic scout she'd accused of stealing her cattle would fill her life with the love and joy she had not believed she deserved.

Half an hour later, after a parting kiss, Tabitha left Edmond working in the storeroom that smelled of fresh pine and spices. His whistled tune trailed her out the back door. *Young ladies in town, and those that live 'round, wear none but your own country linen.* She took it up, humming and swinging her basket. *Of economy boast, let your pride be the most to show clothes of your own make and spinnin'.*

As Tabitha entered the clearing that surrounded the cabin, her humming of the second verse dried up in her throat. Her feet froze.

Men on horses broke from the forest to the south and spilled into the yard, the early-morning light glinting off rifles, pistols, and swords. One of them rode right toward her, his face set in a familiar sneer beneath his wig. His powerful stallion circled her, snorting.

"Good morning, Mrs. Gage." He lifted his cocked hat and chuckled. "Why so surprised? Did I not promise we would meet again?"

Tabitha fought to keep the terror from her face as she stared up at Burntfoot Thomas Brown.

~

Edmond slid a box of cane sugar onto the shelf he had constructed in the storeroom during the winter and straightened with a huff. Not of exertion. Amazement. He was to be a father. He had not allowed himself to hope—to consider the possibility at all, really. During their betrothal, Tabitha had spoken briefly of her inability to conceive during her first marriage. She had not needed to, of course. Her childlessness spoke on its own. Like Temperance, he had hoped the impediment lay with Lord Riley. But he had not hesitated even if it did not. As he had told Tabitha, there were plenty of children in the orphanage in need of good homes.

Most men wished for issue of their own to carry on their name. For the past two years, Edmond had not cared if his name died with him, even if he was the last of his line. But now, having Tabitha by his side, *Lassiter* could mean something different. Something stronger. They could start a lineage with their own godly heritage.

Not could. *Would.*

He blew out a breath, ran his hand over his face, and went back to whistling as he maneuvered a crock of pickled herring beneath the shelf. His mother would be overjoyed. How long before it would be safe to write her? No, they would tell her in person and fetch her back here to her new home, as they had planned. She would be a help and comfort to Tabitha.

At a thump from the front room, Edmond straightened. "Tabitha?" Had she forgotten something? He had unbolted the front door to carry some empty crates to the porch earlier, but why would she not use the back door again?

No answer, only footsteps. Heavier than a woman's. Sounded like boots. This would not be the first person who had stopped in, looking for supplies before the store was fully stocked. Tabitha planned to open next week, but with the shipment they had just received, Edmond could now serve a potential customer. He rounded the shelf only to halt on the threshold into the store and blink against the light.

Riding boots, yes. A tailored dark-green frock coat, a cocked hat over a smooth queue. Hands on a pair of dragoon pistols. With the morning sun coming in behind the man who stood just inside the entrance, it took Edmond a second to focus on his features.

His heart stuttered.

Julian Jackson. A wicked grin split his enemy's face. "Edmond Lassiter. Just the man I was hoping to see."

At the first twitch of Julian's hand, Edmond reached for his sidearm—but Julian raised his own pistol, aimed, and fired.

~

"What are you going to do?" From her spot on the bench beside Tabitha, Dulcie eyed the men ransacking the food in her cupboard, opening cabinets, and tossing her bedding about in their search for food and valuables. Thumps and crashes filled the air. Somehow, even though their hands were tied and Cyrus had been bound hand and foot to a chair, Dulcie had managed to keep her voice from wavering.

Had Tabitha attempted to speak, she would have had no such success. She could barely look at Thomas Brown as he stood leering over her. How had a morning that began with such joy and hope deteriorated into her worst nightmare?

Brown rocked on his heels. "I assume you mean what shall we do with *you*? Unfortunately, our governor might frown on the murder of civilians. Unless you give us a good cause." One corner of his mouth pulled up, as if that was exactly the outcome he hoped for. "However, we can certainly burn you out—after we take the fort. In the meantime, I shall leave a small guard to ensure you do not sound the alarm."

Tabitha swallowed back a whimper.

She must have made some sound, for Brown looked at her and grinned. "Do not worry, madam. Your friends inside the palisade will suffer the same fate. And posthaste this time. Very soon now, you shall hear the report of our artillery."

Clearly, he expected her to quail, for he frowned when she lifted her chin. He did not know that Edmond was not at the fort.

Had her husband noticed the approach of the Florida Rangers in time to warn his men?

Had he known the cabin was surrounded? *Please God, do not let him come here.* If Edmond did, he would stop at nothing to protect her and the child he now knew she carried. And that could get him killed.

~

J ulian was overtop Edmond the moment after he fell, knocked backward by the force of the lead shot thudding into his chest. The shock of hitting his head on the shelf before he slid to the floor registered before the pain of the wound. He tried to drag his pistol from its holster, but Julian kicked his arm, crouched, and took both of his weapons away. He stuck one in his belt with his own while keeping the other in his hand.

"Lieutenant! We heard a shot."

Someone from the fort had arrived! "Here..." Edmond rasped out the call for help, but Julian straightened and looked over his shoulder.

"I had to shoot him. He was drawing his weapon."

The lieutenant the newcomers sought was Julian, not him. Whoever had come had stopped just inside the front door.

Edmond heaved for breath. His hand came away from his chest red, but the shot had entered closer to his shoulder than his heart.

"No, sir," the soldier said, "you are wanted at the cabin."

"At the cabin?" A hungry smile quirked up one corner of his mouth, and Edmond's stomach bottomed out. *Tabitha.* Julian waved his arm behind him. "Go. I will take care of this." He turned to make sure they obeyed. "I shall be right there."

Edmond lunged for his legs. Julian stumbled backward into a shelf and tumbled over Edmond. The pistol flew from his grasp. Edmond scrambled for it, but darkness ringed his vision, and fire shot up his left arm. A thump and a scrape, and something heavy hit the back of his head. Awareness faded as his hands were grabbed and tied.

Julian said, "Guess I have to wait to burn you out a second time. But this time, I shall make sure you go up in flames with the place."

~

The rangers who had entered the cabin with Brown were leaving. The attack on the fort was going ahead. Commands and the drum of horse hooves carried from the yard.

"Are they gone?" Tabitha glanced at Dulcie with wide eyes.

Cyrus jostled his chair in an attempt to free himself from his bonds. "They said they would leave a guard."

"And here we are."

At the familiar voice, Tabitha's head swiveled. A tall form filled the doorway, and her heartbeat faltered. "Julian!"

"My dear Mrs. Gage." He strolled forward, one brow raised. "I must say, 'tis a disappointment to meet thus, with you trussed up with these Patriot traitors. I held out a final hope that being dispossessed of your livelihood would send you to Savannah."

"Then you have not heard." She pulled her shoulders back. "We rebuilt...and it is Mrs. Lassiter now."

The smug look faltered, but only for a moment. He came and knelt before her as two rangers marched in behind him. "But I have heard, and I was just at your new store. Your determination is even more remarkable than I thought. Unfortunately, I did not get a chance to offer my felicitations to the groom before I was called to your side." He thumbed aside the edge of his wool frock coat to display the handle of a dragoon pistol—one that had been lying on Tabitha's bedside table only an hour before.

A breath whistled between Tabitha's teeth. Edmond! "What have you done to him?" Panic flooded her, and she leveraged the rope on her wrists against the table behind her in an attempt to wrest her hands free.

He chuckled. "Shall we just say that this time, I was not the one left in a bad way?"

What did that mean? Surely, he had not...

Horror unfurled in her chest, but she could not let it overtake her. Not if she wanted to survive.

Boom! The foundation of the cabin shook at the sound of artillery fire. Pottery in the sideboard rattled, and the women gasped.

Julian let out a delighted peal of laughter, then clapped like a child watching a fireworks display. "And here we go!"

Tabitha glared at him. "They will never surrender."

"Oh, I daresay it shall not take long with two artillery pieces and two swivel guns." Standing, he rubbed his hands together. "Not to mention, a hundred rangers. But do not worry. Your beloved shan't be caught in the action. I have my own plan for him."

Tabitha held back a cry. So he wasn't dead. She had to get free of Julian. Go find Edmond. This time, it was she who must not be too late.

"Well. Now that the attack has begun, we're to fire your cabin." Julian gestured the two rangers forward, and for the first time, Tabitha noticed that they carried unlit torches.

"No!" Cyrus planted his feet on the floor and straightened his legs at the same time he whipped sideways. The legs of the chair sliced into the nearest soldier's privates, doubling him over with a sharp cry.

The other ranger swung his torch like an ax right for Cyrus's face.

As Dulcie screamed and Tabitha leapt to her feet, the impact sent Cyrus flying backward. The chair bounced on the floor with Cyrus still tied to it, and he landed on his side with a grunt and the splintering crack of wood. A chair leg skittered across the floor. A bright strip of blood appeared with vivid clarity on Cyrus's dark cheek. He gave his head a rapid shake and squeezed his eyes shut.

"Stop this!" In two steps, Tabitha placed herself between the men and her friend's husband. She turned pleading eyes on Julian. "You said you wanted to be different from your father. You do not need to hurt Cyrus. He has done nothing but defend his home."

A bitter tangle of a laugh rumbled from his chest. "Oh, I learned a long time ago that one does not go against Father. The only choice is to help him expand his empire. And for now, that means quashing the rebels. All of them, including you." His fingers wrapped around her forearm, and he started to move her aside.

"Please, Julian. You are better than this." Surely, she could appeal to some nobler part of him.

He leaned closer. "You think so?" His brow furrowed. His grip tightened.

She bobbed her head. "I do. Why not just leave us be?"

He tilted his head first one way, then the other, appearing to consider the matter. "'Tis true that a word from me could spare your pitiful little world."

"That is right." Tabitha held his gaze, nodding faster. She had already lost almost everything once. This time, they could be left with nothing. What would they do then? "We are no threat to you or your empire. Walk away now and you need never hear from us again."

"Oh, but..." His mouth flattened, and he slowly shook his head. "Then you would be living right under my nose, reminding me every day of what I could not have. A man can only take so many rejections, Tabitha. No. This time, you shall have to earn my mercy." He started for the door, tugging her along with him.

"No!" She fought back, but he wrangled her forward. "You are an officer. A gentleman. You wouldn't dare harm me."

The look he slanted over his shoulder was such a fierce mockery of tenderness, it chilled her blood. "On the contrary, I'll be very gentle."

This could not happen. Not this.

Tabitha locked her legs, but Julian pulled her out of the cabin. At the threshold, she kicked his shin and attempted to stumble back inside.

One of the rangers stepped into her path, his pistol drawn.

Julian jerked her by the ropes that bound her wrist, leading her backward across the dogtrot. When they stopped and she spun partway around, he reached for the door to her room. She could not let him take her in there.

A click resounded from across the yard, and a deep, wonderfully familiar voice commanded, "Let her go." Edmond!

She hadn't time to look, for Julian made a move for his pistol at the same instant he tugged on her bonds, whirling her—

Boom!

Julian wavered and fell to his knees, a hole through his chest.

Tabitha heaved a sob of shock and relief.

Across the yard, Edmond lowered his smoking Kentucky rifle. But the motion revealed the scarlet stain on the breast of his waistcoat. She cried out and would have run to him, but boots pounded from within the cabin.

Edmond started running toward the house, drawing his dragoon pistol.

A flurry of movement from the doorway froze Tabitha in place as a ranger burst from the cabin. A shot from Edmond's pistol exploded, and the man staggered backward, clutching his leg.

The other one, probably not yet twenty, face a mask of terror, ran out onto the porch with his own pistol in hand.

Why was Edmond not drawing his other gun? Tabitha's heart contracted into a painful knot when she remembered that Julian had taken it. And with her hands bound behind her, she could not take it back.

The young ranger's face registered the moment he realized Edmond had no other weapon. His arm leveled as he took aim.

Not only was Edmond not drawing a pistol, he was tottering. Falling to his knees in the dirt. His bloodied hand covered his wound. His gaze went to her, anguished. Seeming to beg her forgiveness.

"*No!*" This time, the word she screamed might as well have ripped out her heart. She could not watch her husband, the father of her unborn child, die before her eyes.

Tabitha flung herself toward her foe.

Stumbling out of the cabin, Cyrus held the broken chair in both hands and swung it against the soldier's head.

CHAPTER TWENTY-FIVE

Edmond's chest still ached though it had been almost a month since Julian had shot him. He could still envision Tabitha's panicked face when Dulcie had been unable to fish out the shot. "He needs a doctor, and fast," she'd said.

Tabitha had called for Cyrus to saddle Maximus. While he did, she and Dulcie packed the wound with herbs and bandaged it. With Cyrus's help, they had somehow gotten Edmond on his stallion—his memories remained a blur of pain and snatches of conversation—before she mounted behind him and set out for Darien. How she had forded the river without drawing the attention of the Loyalists besieging the fort, he could only imagine. He recalled flashes of slumping over the horse's neck, Tabitha's arm around him, her voice going from pleading to ordering, *ordering* him to live.

Even now, he chuckled as he rubbed the raised, puckered flesh beneath his shirt and waistcoat, sitting in the sunshine while watching Uncle Ian pounding out a crowbar at his forge.

"What are you laughing at?" Tabitha's chiding murmur

raised his head even as her hand slid over his shoulder to take the one that had been massaging the wound.

"I was thinking of you." He squinted up at her in the morning light. "The way you hauled my sorry carcass all the way to Darien."

"Well, there was hardly a choice in the matter." She stiffened and handed him the pewter cup she held in her other hand. When he took it, she touched the tiny swell of her abdomen. "I am not raising his child alone."

She had been right to bring him, of course. The shot had lodged so deep, Edmond had passed out again while the doctor probed for it. And he had lost so much blood that it had taken him far longer than he'd have liked to recover. He had spent two weeks under the physician's care before being released to recuperate at his uncle's, where he and Tabitha now slept in the parlor.

Edmond sniffed the contents of the cup. "Ugh." As suspected, 'twas not coffee, but another of Aunt Margaret's ostensibly healing herbal teas.

"Drink up." Tabitha patted his shoulder. "The sooner you regain your strength, the sooner we can go home. But not too quickly." A frown pulled down the edges of her mouth. "I have no desire to see you join another expedition to Florida."

Edmond's good spirits deflated. "I should have gone with Colonel Elbert's men."

"You were not ready." Tabitha's jaw tightened.

He sipped his bitter potion and mumbled, "They are probably at Fort Howe by now."

"What remains of it." Tabitha grimaced. "I am only thankful our home and store were spared."

About a week after the attack, she had received a missive from Mr. Long telling them what had happened after they fled. The Loyalists had taken the fort with the loss of only one man, though the Patriots had seen two killed, four wounded, and twenty-three taken prisoner. They had set fire to the structure but remained in the area several days while planning their next move.

Upon discovering that Julian had been killed and Tabitha and Edmond had fled, Brown had remanded the order to also burn the cabin and store, instead deciding the structures would house the officers. Mr. Long had relayed that not only were Dulcie and Cyrus safe—albeit feeding the occupying enemy while nursing the wounded Patriots—but he'd shared that one of the Patriot wounded was Edmond's good friend, Dougal. With Dulcie's expert ministrations, he was expected to make a full recovery.

Apparently, the Loyalists' scheming had broken down in internal bickering, and they had finally withdrawn.

The loss of Fort Howe and fears the British would mount an invasion north of the Altamaha had finally led General Howe to agree to a third expedition. Earlier this month, five hundred Continentals under Colonel Samuel Elbert had begun to move south. Edmond had received orders to do likewise as soon as he was able and instruct the handful of men they would leave behind to rebuild the fort.

Edmond slumped on his stool. "And yet, thanks to me, a second fort was lost. If I hadn't allowed Julian to take me off guard, I would have had time to warn them."

"No." She knelt before him, taking his hand, pinning his gaze with hers. "Edmond Lassiter, this is not your fault. This was the fault of twisted men bent on revenge...and the outcome of a war. You've done more than your part in this conflict. And you saved me into the bargain."

His frown faded as he looked into her face, and love washed over him. "You're right. But I cannot help wishing I could have done more to help those men in the fort."

Tabitha lifted his knuckles to her lips. "You are a good man, but you must stop taking the weight of the world onto your shoulders."

The sound of horse hooves drumming the dirt road followed by a shaggy-haired youth trotting a winded mount to Uncle Ian's shed brought both of them to their feet.

As the boy led his horse close, Ian stepped away from his forge. "How can I help you, young sir?"

"Name's Charlie Fraser. My horse threw a shoe up the road. Left front side. I'm needin' it replaced but dunno if I can wait." The boy's voice cracked with anxiety and adolescence as Ian removed his gloves and ambled over to lift the blowing horse's leg. "I'm to Fort Howe posthaste."

Edmond stiffened. "Fort Howe? Why?"

Charlie jerked his head Edmond's direction. "We live south of the river from Broughton Island. Father is with the men who went to Fort Howe. Mama sent me to tell the officers there that British ships have been sighted in St. Simons Sound."

Edmond took a step closer. "How many, son?"

When the horse shied, Uncle Ian held his bridle.

"Three. Maybe four. They sailed up the Frederica River."

The Continental force could not leave the coast undefended while they marched into Florida. This could change the focus, the outcome, of the expedition. Edmond shot a glance at Tabitha, who held herself erect, her mouth pressed tight. He was not asking her permission this time. This was his chance to rectify his failures with the army. "I will go."

The boy blinked at him, faltering a step back. "But sir, Mama said…"

"I am Lieutenant Lassiter, assigned to Fort Howe." Edmond touched the boy's shoulder. "You have done well to bring this message, but your horse is tired, and 'tis a long ride yet."

"Yes, sir." Charlie relaxed, letting out a soft breath. With his thin frame and dusting of tawny freckles, he could not be more than eleven or twelve.

Edmond gave Charlie's shoulder a brief squeeze. "There is still a contingent at Fort Darien. While my uncle shoes your horse, you should warn them. Assure them I am alerting Colonel Elbert at Howe."

The young man stood straighter. "With pleasure, sir." He snapped off a salute that drew Edmond's smile.

It faded as he turned to Tabitha.

Her brow furrowed. "'Tis too soon."

"'Tis aught but a lark on Maximus."

"Do you promise you will not go off to fight?"

Edmond reached for her hands. "I have my orders. I will deliver the message and stay at the fort."

"Orders can be changed."

"Colonel Elbert knows of my recuperation. He has plenty of fit soldiers." His grip tightened on hers. "I need to do this, Tabitha."

Her mouth trembled. "I know." She brushed a tear attempting to escape the corner of one eye. "Oh, blast it. I did not used to be such a lily-livered female."

A grin broke out on his face. "Then you fell in love."

She pulled her hands back and swatted his arm. "That will be enough from you, sir."

"Very well." He chuckled. "Your strength will be needed for packing and making Mother ready to travel. With these ships on the coast, you, too, must haste inland. You should leave tomorrow morning, at the latest."

She nodded, her jaw firm. "I will meet you at home."

"Meet you at home." Edmond repeated the phrase before he turned toward the stable. God willing, he would deliver this intelligence in time to keep the home they both loved safe.

~

APRIL 20, 1778

W here was her husband? Uncle Ian's wagon had transported Tabitha and her mother-in-law safely to the Altamaha ferry four days before. They had passed troops on the road, bound south for Darien. While she had not seen Edmond among them, she had no way of knowing if he had been sent to the coast with another company of rangers after their arrival.

In light of the military activity in the area, Tabitha and Freya slept in her old room at the cabin, now emptied of Patriot wounded. As wonderful as it had been to catch up with Dulcie and Cyrus, Tabitha's impatience mounted by the hour. If only Edmond would arrive with the news that it was safe for them to return to their own home and at last open the store. Even though their British visitors had made off with most of the stock, the remaining income from the timber had enabled Tabitha to place another order with their supplier while she had been in Darien.

Five days had passed since Edmond rode for Fort Howe. Why had he not been allowed to come see her? Had Colonel Elbert sent him on another mission, after all? Worry gnawed at her insides as Tabitha mounded dirt for planting the garden she and Dulcie shared. Or maybe that was actual nausea. She sat back on her heels and raised a gloved hand to her mouth.

"My dear, ye shouldna be workin' so hard on yer hands and knees like that." Her mother-in-law's gentle brogue cajoled her from the front porch, where Freya was mending one of Edmond's shirts. "Come sit with me a spell."

"A cup of cool cider might be nice." Already, 'twas growing warm. Tabitha rose, removing her gloves and brushing off her petticoats. She had just started for the porch when approaching horse hooves had her whirling toward the path. As the figure she had longed to see rode into view, she gave a cry and ran to greet him. "Edmond!"

He swung off Maximus and scooped her into his arms, pressing a firm kiss to her lips.

She drew back far enough to check him for signs of injury, then laid her hand over his chest. "Are you well?"

"Yes, I am fine. Are you?"

"We are well." Tabitha smiled and rested her hand on her abdomen. Then she stepped out of the way as Freya scurried up to embrace her son.

"Wherever have ye been?" Her chiding preceded the one Tabitha had been about to give. Freya patted Edmond's cheek. "Here ye drag me off to what is supposed to be me new home, an' then ye dinna show up."

"I know. I am sorry...but glad you are here safely." His chest heaving as he inhaled a deep breath, Edmond broke into a broad smile and reached for Tabitha's hand. "And as it turns out, we *are* safe. I had to stay on site at the fort until we received the all clear. And it came today."

"It did?" Tabitha's eyes rounded. "What does that mean? The British are repelled?"

He nodded. "Colonel Elbert put his men on three row galleys, with artillery in another vessel, and at dawn on the nineteenth, he fired on three British ships anchored off the ruins of Fort Frederica. They attempted to retaliate, but they were outmaneuvered and outgunned. Then they tried to gain an advantage downriver, but their ships were grounded, abandoned, and captured. The waterways are cleared, the British invasion foiled."

"So you warned them in time." Tabitha drew his hand up to her heart, clasping it between hers. Could he see the pride glowing in her eyes?

"Aye." He shrugged, lapsing into a touch of brogue she found adorable in the presence of his mother. "With a wee bit of help from Charlie."

"Well, we all have to play our part." She smirked, then her smile faded. "What of Brown?"

"Retreated to Florida." Edmond swung her hand between them.

"So 'tis truly over? We can go to our new home?" Hope abounded in Freya's query as she took a step closer.

Edmond reached for her hand as well. "We can, as yes, it is over for now. They are saying more troops will muster at Fort Howe, so 'twill be more important than ever that I help with the rebuilding. And that you open the store. Colonel Elbert awaits the arrival of General Howe with his South Carolina Continentals and artillery, as well as General Andrew Williamson with South Carolina militia. 'Twill take time to muster and supply. I daresay they will make another attempt on Florida before full summer is upon us."

Tabitha could not keep her face from crumpling.

Edmond tipped his head toward her. "But I will request the command of whatever contingent is left to guard the fort. I promised you, did I not?"

"That you would be here for the birth of our child? Yes, you did. But do not take on that weight when it is not something you can truly promise." She could not put that on him either. In a time of war, a soldier could be sent wherever his superiors chose. "We must remember that ultimately, there is a greater commander whose will usurps even the most powerful general's."

"You are right." Edmond squeezed her hand. "Before we go home, perhaps we should pray over this new chapter of our lives. For God's protection and blessing."

Tabitha's chest swelled with pride. "That is a fine idea."

Before they could bow their heads, a cry drew their attention.

Dulcie and Cyrus hurried across the yard. Greetings aside, Edmond drew them close and explained their intentions.

Dulcie's face lit with approval, and she and Cyrus moved into their circle. Brown and white hands joined, they came together in prayer.

Tabitha's heart could burst from gratitude and love. Her husband was home. A babe grew in her womb.

This family and this freedom were priceless gifts from God. Their futures were safe in His hands.

Did you enjoy this book? We hope so!
Would you take a quick minute to leave a review where you purchased the book?
It doesn't have to be long. Just a sentence or two telling what you liked about the story!

~

Receive a FREE ebook and get updates when new Wild Heart books release: https://wildheartbooks.org/newsletter

AUTHOR'S NOTE

By the end of May, 1778, the combined Georgia and South Carolina forces of General Robert Howe finally crossed the Altamaha River to launch the third Florida expedition. This move was accompanied by the announcement on June 1 that France had publicly acknowledged the independence of the United States of America, eliciting a thirteen-cannon volley and a full round of grog. But as soon as June sixth, sickness drove about three hundred men back to Darien. The South Carolinians trailed behind, giving Brown's rangers time to burn and abandon their stronghold on the St. Mary's River, Fort Tonyn, thus eliminating one of Howe's primary objectives. After tangling unsuccessfully with the enemy at Alligator Creek, the Americans were out of rice and decimated by disease. They returned to Savannah while the British retired in the direction of the St. Johns River.

On December 19, 1778, British Lieutenant Colonel Archibald Campbell's army outflanked Major General Robert Howe's paltry force to capture Savannah. As illustrated in *A Courageous Betrothal*, fighting across Georgia became so intense, the middle part of the colony was dubbed "the Hornet's Nest." French and American forces laid siege to Savannah in autumn of 1779 without success. The city remained in British control until the Redcoats withdrew in July, 1782.

The idea for this final installment of my Scouts of the Georgia Frontier Series began to take shape after I learned about the location of Fort Barrington (later Fort Howe) on the Altamaha River. And hadn't Tabitha Scott eloped with Lord Riley at the end of *A Conflicted Betrothal* to his plantation on the Altamaha? I kept worrying about what happened to her down there with the snakes and the gators. What did she do when the war came to her doorstep? How did it change her? Did she ever find love? I simply had to move forward in time a decade and put her story to the page. I hope you like the unexpected way her tale unfolded against the wild and somewhat strange landscape of cattle-grazing no-man's land of Colonial South Georgia. Most of all, I hope you found inspiration in her transformation from a spoiled, selfish beauty, to a widow broken by a cruel and empty marriage, to a strong woman of integrity who finally finds a man who appreciates her.

I'd like to thank the team at Wild Heart Books—including my publisher, Misty M. Beller; my editor, Robin Patchen; Sarah Erredge and Sherri Wilson Johnson—for your skill and vision in helping me bring this story to my readers. Also my launch team, especially my beta readers—Gretchen Elm, Catherine Patton, and Jennie Webb. And you, my amazing readers, who love history as much as I do and support me as an author so well.

If you enjoyed *A Calculated Betrothal*, the last book of The Scouts of the Georgia Frontier, your reviews let publishers know my stories are worth continuing to publish. I notice and treasure each one. Please visit me at https://www.deniseweimer books.com, and I'd also love to connect on social media.

Monthly e-mail list: http://eepurl.com/dFfSfn
https://www.facebook.com/denise.weimer1
https://twitter.com/denise_weimer
https://www.bookbub.com/profile/denise-weimer

ABOUT THE AUTHOR

North Georgia native Denise Weimer has authored around twenty traditionally published novels and novellas--historical and contemporary romance, romantic suspense, and time slip. As a freelance editor and Acquisitions & Editorial Liaison for Wild Heart Books, she's helped other authors reach their publishing dreams. The mother of two wonderful young adult daughters, Denise always pauses for coffee, chocolate, and old houses.

You can visit Denise at https://www.deniseweimerbook s.com, and connect with her on social media.

Monthly e-mail list: http://eepurl.com/dFfSfn

If you love historical romance, check out the other Wild Heart books!

A Winter at the White Queen by Denise Weimer

In the world of the wealthy, things are never quite as they appear.

Ellie Hastings is tired of playing social gatekeeper—and poor-relation companion—to her Gibson Girl of a cousin. But her aunt insists Ellie lift her nose out of her detective novel long enough to help gauge the eligibility of bachelors during the winter social season at Florida's Hotel Belleview. She finds plenty that's mysterious about the suave, aloof Philadelphia inventor, Lewis Thornton. Why does he keep sneaking around the hotel? Does he have a secret sweetheart? And what is his connection to the evasive Mr. Gaspachi, slated to perform at Washington's Birthday Ball?

Ellie's comical sleuthing ought to put Lewis out, but the diffident way her family treats her smashes a hole in his normal reserve. When Florence Hastings's diamond necklace goes missing, Ellie's keen mind threatens to uncover not only Lewis's secrets, but give him back hope for love.

~

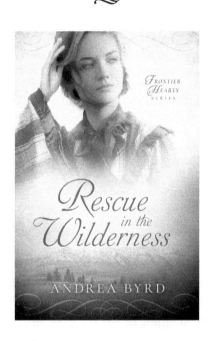

Rescue in the Wilderness by Andrea Byrd

William Cole cannot forget the cruel burden he carries, not with the pock marks that serve as an outward reminder. Riddled with guilt, he assumed the solitary life of a long hunter, traveling into the wilds of Kentucky each year. But his quiet existence is changed in an instant when, sitting in a tavern, he overhears a man offering his daughter—and her virtue—to the winner of the next round of cards. William's integrity and desire for redemption will not allow him to sit idly by while such an injustice occurs.

Lucinda Gillespie has suffered from an inexplicable illness her entire life. Her father, embarrassed by her condition, has subjected her to a lonely existence of abuse and confinement. But faced with the ultimate betrayal on the eve of her eighteenth birthday, Lucinda quickly realizes her trust is better placed in the hands of the mysterious man who appears at her door. Especially when he offers her the one thing she never thought would be within her grasp—freedom.

In the blink of an eye, both lives change as they begin the difficult, danger-fraught journey westward on the Wilderness Trail. But can they overcome their own perceptions of themselves to find love and the life God created them for?

∾

Love's Winding Road by Susan F. Craft

They were forced into this marriage of convenience, but there's more at stake than their hearts on this wagon train through the mountain wilderness.

When Rose Jackson and her Irish immigrant family join a wagon train headed for a new life in South Carolina, the last thing she expects is to fall for the half-Cherokee wagon scout along the way. But their journey takes a life-changing turn when Rose is kidnapped by Indians. Daniel comes to her rescue, but the effects mean their lives will be forever intertwined.

Daniel prides himself on his self-control—inner and outer— but can't seem to get a handle on either when Rose is near. Now his life is bound to hers when the consequences of her rescue force them to marry. Now it's even more critical he maintain that self-control to keep her safe.

When tragedy strikes at the heart of their strained marriage, they leave for Daniel's home in the Blue Ridge Mountains. As they face the perils of the journey, Rose can't help but wonder why her new husband guards his heart so strongly. Why does he resist his obvious attraction for her? And what life awaits them at the end of love's winding road?